White Witch World

KANA'S QUEST

ANTHONY RAY OLHEISER

ISBN: 061588623X
ISBN-13: 9780615886237
LCCN: 2013917030
Anthony Ray Olheiser,
Chandler, AZ

To all the family and friends who believed in me—even when I didn't myself.

Thank you!

Although several characters and events described in this story may be found in the Holy Bible, the tale is not based on scripture. It is made up in its entirety. It is completely fictional. It is a FANTASY!

TABLE OF CONTENTS

FROM THE *TABLETS OF TIME*

PRIOR TO THE DAWNING OF THE THIRD AGE, SATAN'S WEB OF EVIL UPON THE WORLD OF GOD'S CHILDREN WILL BE COMPLETE. KNOWING THIS WORLD WAS VERY SPECIAL TO THE LORD, THE KING OF HELL MADE CONTROLLING THE EARTH HIS MOST FEVERISH OBSESSION. HE CONTINUOUSLY USED HIS VILE CORRUPTION TO DESTROY THE GOODNESS GOD PLACED THERE. ONE DAY, THOUGH, THERE WILL COME A YOUNG WHITE WITCH, KANA BY NAME, WHO SHALL BE MORE POWERFUL THAN ANY WHITE WITCH BEFORE HIM. WITH THE WEAPONS OF GOD AND AN ARMY OF YOUTH RECRUITED FROM THE EARTH, HE WILL DRIVE SATAN FROM THAT WORLD FOREVER!

—Zephrom

PART I

THE GREAT SAHARA

An ageless sea of constantly shifting sand, ancient even in primordial time, the great Sahara Desert's mighty face is constantly changed by the strong forces of nature. Each day, for thousands of years, a prehistoric sun faithfully erupts upon the desert horizon. Long shadows from gigantic dunes stretch across the vast region of sand tinted bronze by the golden sphere in the sky. Steadily climbing, the ball of fire inflames the sandy expanse with relentless heat. Woken by the intense rise in temperature, the wind eagerly began its daily sculpturing, knocking this dune down and building another over there. It was very particular about its work—every little grain of sand had to be just so, from generating great gusts of air for carving, to appointing swirling dust devils to the lighter jobs, to creating small puffs of air for the personal, artistic touches.

By midafternoon, though, the natural artist grew more restless, throwing temper tantrums and destroying creations it had taken great care in making.

The Sahara began to suspect that the day was not going to be the same as usual.

Off in the distance, huge, dark thunderheads were building, streaking the heavens with brilliant flashes of white lightning.

"Finally," the Sahara sighed, welcoming a reprieve from the endless heat.

Ahead of the storm, in its fit of rage, the wind drove a massive brown cloud of sand across the desert floor. Balls of crackling fire similar to hail pelted the sandy surface as the ominous dark mass above covered the late-afternoon sky. Mile after mile, the storm traveled, growing faster, stronger, and angrier. Upon reaching its destination, the black clouds above became a churning mass of confusion in the hurricane-force wind.

Lightning shredded the heavens. Balls of fire bounced across the desert dunes, some colliding with each other and creating explosive bursts of flame in the sand-filled air.

Then, as if preparing for a climax, the wind howled even stronger as one huge ominous cloud darker than all the rest swelled to cover most of the sky. Ripping open, a massive bolt of lightning erupted from the black mass, stretching down to the ground and striking it with a horrendous explosion that shook the area for miles. Then, as if this climatic effort had drained it of all strength, the storm died as suddenly as it had started, leaving a churning globe of sand and electricity on the desert floor in the aftermath.

Inside the sphere, catastrophic forces were at work. Molecular changes were being made. Slowly, as the mighty storm died, the globe began to solidify. When the process was done, the wind covered the sphere with sand, keeping it warm and protecting it from the harshness of the desert, incubating it for thousands of years to come.

The forces of nature, in their unusual dramatic display, spawned an egg.

IT BEGINS

The pungent but pleasantly familiar aroma of Italian seasonings enveloped Mádeohn as he was stepping through the back door of his mom's pizzeria. While striding through the extremely busy kitchen he had grown up in, Mádeohn could feel his phone begin to vibrate. Pulling it out of his pocket, the he began to notice his coworkers snickering at his devil Halloween costume.

With his mom constantly supporting the youth of their small town by employing students from the community college, Mádeohn had the usually—but not always—fun pleasure of working with his classmates. Providing jobs for the students, Mádeohn's mom once told him, "Gives them an opportunity to earn extra spending money while going to school." It was also her way of giving back to the community for so generously supporting a single mother. Over the years, Mrs. Cane's Pizza grew into an icon of the community, the favorite social gathering place of the youth in the small town.

Glancing down at his phone, he could see a new message from Ryon.

Mádeohn's mom swore on several occasions that the two best friends from childhood were inseparable. Working together at the pizzeria for the past several years, both pretty much ran the place for her. Graciously granting them a rare, weekend night off at the same time in order to attend Mitch and Rhonda's party, she sat in her office, overseeing the evening's controlled chaos.

Turning around with a mischievous smile on his face, Mádeohn playfully shouted over the unrelenting kitchen noise, addressing everyone razzing him, "Excuse me! I know you're all extremely jealous of the fact that Ryon and I get to go party while you losers are stuck here. Deal with it! Now get back to work before *I* make your lives a living hell!"

All that did was bring on more laughter, just as he intended.

Smiling at his own joke while turning to enter his mother's office, Mádeohn read the message on his phone, "Be there in five."

Looking up from the mountain of paperwork piled on her desk, Sylvia Cane curiously wondered what all the laughing was about in the kitchen. Recognizing the costume Mádeohn was wearing, she frowned and stopped what she was doing, calmly addressing her son with concern.

"Do you think that's wise?"

Seeing the displeasure written all over his mom's face at his costume, Mádeohn returned his attention to his phone.

"It's Halloween, who's going to notice?" he asked flippantly while texting an answer back to Ryon.

"I can think of one," his mother replied matter-of-factly while leaning back in her chair and crossing her arms beneath her breasts.

Putting the cell phone back in his pocket, Mádeohn openly showed the disgust he felt while quipping sarcastically, "Like he ever notices anything I do!"

"Don't mistake not being bothered the last few years as being forgotten," Sylvia once again calmly responded.

Acknowledging that she was right, Mádeohn softened his own tone while sighing, "I know." He walked around his mother's desk, gave her a kiss on the cheek, and then continued, "Ryon's almost here; thanks for the night off."

"Both of you be careful," Sylvia instructed with concern, watching her only son turn to go and then quickly adding, "love you!"

Wading back out into the wave of taunting in the kitchen, Mádeohn replied over his shoulder, "We will, love you too, Mom!"

Pulling up to the pizzeria just as Mádeohn stepped out the front door, Ryon chuckled to himself as his friend plopped into the passenger seat of his car.

"What?" Mádeohn asked, throwing his hands up questioningly.

"Nice outfit."

"What is it with everyone and my costume?" Mádeohn cried out, annoyed.

"Hm," Ryon put his hand to his chin thoughtfully while examining his friend from head to toe. "Could it be you look gay?"

"Look who's talking," Mádeohn replied, indicating the gladiator uniform Ryon was wearing.

Playfully reaching over to grab the bottom hem of Ryon's costume, Mádeohn smiled mischievously while asking, "Are you wearing anything under that skirt?"

Swiftly blocking Mádeohn's arm, Ryon responded in disbelief, "You did not just try to look under my tunic!"

"Why?" Mádeohn laughed, continuing to try and reach around Ryon's arm. "What do you have hiding under there?"

"Don't make me hurt you!" Ryon jokingly threatened.

Still laughing, Mádeohn stopped wrestling, sat back in his seat, and demanded, "Let's go, Spartacus, we're already late."

Ryon slapped his fist against his chest in a Roman-style salute while mockingly replying, "Yes, Your Evilness!"

As he started to weave the car through the busy parking lot, he continued to tease his friend, asking, "Where's your pitchfork?"

"Back there," Mádeohn responded nonchalantly while pointing behind them.

Perplexed, Ryon quickly glanced over his shoulder. A red devil's pitchfork lay right there on the back seat next to the spear he had brought.

Looking confused, he said, "Seriously! You did not get in the car with that thing. How did you get it in here?"

"Seriously! What have you been smoking? How do you *think* it got there?" Mádeohn charged with a look of disbelief on his face. "Do I need to drive?"

"No, you do not need to drive," Ryon retorted, annoyed. He was positive Mádeohn did not have a pitchfork when he got in the car. "Just sit over there, and stop being a pain in the ass!"

Reaching the road running along the lakeshore, both became mesmerized by the serene vista surrounding them while traveling the last few miles to Mitch's parents' house in silence.

Smiling to himself peacefully, Mádeohn sat watching the reflection of the full moon following along with the car on the dark, calm water. Lightning flashing in the distance, suddenly shattered his tranquil state of mind. Narrowing his eyes in concern, he suspiciously glared at the dark clouds forming over the mountains on the opposite side of the lake.

Noticing Mádeohn intensely watching the brewing storm, Ryon commented, "Your staring at it won't make it go away."

"You would be surprised at what I can do," Mádeohn responded, tearing his attention away from dark clouds in the distance. Something bothered him about the brewing tempest.

"In that case, oh, Master of Disaster," Ryon replied with a grin, "make sure it doesn't come over here and rain on our party."

"I'll get right on that," Mádeohn retorted.

Pulling into the massive circular driveway of Mitch's estate, Ryon began searching for a parking spot. The huge driveway surrounding a well-lit, three-tiered fountain made up of playful cherubim was already packed with vehicles of the other party guests.

No matter how many times he drove out here, the size and luxury of this place would never cease to amaze Ryon. "It must have been torture growing up here," he said sarcastically.

Mitch literally lived in a mansion.

"You say that every time we come out here." Mádeohn rolled his eyes while sighing.

Soaring columns supporting porches across both the front and back of the two-story plantation-style estate offered a majestic view of the lake in the rear. In Ryon's mind, the landscape lighting of the grounds at night had to be the place's all-time coolest feature. The white columns, green shrubs, and massive shade trees were accented by artistically placed floodlights that ranged in color from white, to red, to blue and green.

Finally locating a place to park, Ryon turned to find Mádeohn grabbing the mysteriously appearing pitchfork from the backseat with an irritating grin. Without giving his friend the satisfaction of a response, Ryon retrieved his own spear before exiting the car, and then began weaving his way between cars across the driveway.

Making their way along a tree lined, lit walkway winding around the right side of the house, the sound of party music and people laughing steadily grew louder. The dark trees suddenly gave way to the bright lights of the pool area, where several people were dressed in a vast array of Halloween costumes.

"Hey, soldier, I need IDs and car keys, please," a sweet voice from inside a small booth at the end of the path stopped Ryon.

Turning from observing what was going on at the party, he locked eyes with the most beautiful woman he'd ever seen. She sat there smiling seductively while waiting patiently for him to stop gaping and respond. He stood stunned until the alluring creature began provocatively motioning him with a finger to approach the booth.

Gallantly slapping his fist to his chest, Ryon replied, "As my lady commands!"

Grinning, she took his keys while looking at his driver's license.

"OK, Ryon, hold out your arm."

While doing so, he asked, "Is there anything else you require? I'm at your service!"

Placing a plastic band on his wrist to indicate that he was over twenty-one and free to consume alcohol, the woman slowly began eyeing Ryon from head to toe. Enticingly licking her ruby-red upper lip, she leaned forward and whispered in his ear, "Who knows what act of chivalry a girl may need before the night is over. Now go have fun, and tell your friend to come over here."

Stepping back and slapping his fist to his chest once again, Ryon bowed to the beautiful creature in the booth before turning to Mádeohn.

Standing at the end of the pathway, trying to guess who was who mingling around the pool, Mádeohn had absolutely no idea Ryon wasn't at his side until he felt the spear poking him in the butt.

"You're so going to be sitting on this pitchfork if you try that again!" Mádeohn growled.

Grinning with pleasure, and pointing to the small booth next to them, Ryon informed his devilish friend, "You need to check in."

Turning to the girl in the booth, Mádeohn suddenly locked eyes with a ghost from his past.

"Hello, Mádeohn," she cooed sweetly, taking great pleasure in his surprise.

Silently glaring at the woman, Mádeohn's blood turned icy with contempt.

Taking his arm without asking and placing a wristband on it, she smugly glared back, challenging him to do something in front of all the people at the party.

"Have fun," she chirped, turning his arm loose and smiling sweetly.

Slowly backing away, Mádeohn nudged Ryon, commanding, "Let's go."

"You know her?" Ryon asked curiously as the two began forging their way across the crowded pool deck.

"Forget her," Mádeohn replied sternly.

"You *do* know her," Ryon pressed, grinning. "She certainly was hot!"

"Drop it!" Mádeohn snapped.

"No worries!" Ryon exclaimed, throwing his hands up in surrender.

"I'm sorry." Mádeohn softened his countenance, "Let's have fun and forget past issues for tonight."

His own words rang hollow in his ears.

Why was she here? Why now?

His mother's voice began echoing through his mind, "Don't mistake not being bothered the last few years as being forgotten."

Approaching Connie and Rhonda, Ryon dropped his hands in agreement. Standing by the rock wall overlooking the beach below, he noticed Connie predictably wearing a doctor's lab jacket, scrubs, and a stethoscope. Rhonda, on the other hand, totally rocked a black-and-white 1920s-style fringed flapper dress.

"Hey guys!" Rhonda exclaimed. "Glad you both could make it!"

"Did you really think we would miss your birthday party?" Ryon asked, giving the girl a hug while wishing her a happy birthday.

"Thank you!" Rhonda responded, turning to Mádeohn and giving him a hug too.

"Happy birthday." Mádeohn smiled, returning the embrace.

"Oh my, someone is a little tense tonight," Rhonda observed, rubbing the tight muscles in Mádeohn's neck.

"Excuse me!" came a sharp male voice from behind the two guys.

"Ma'am, what did I warn you about soliciting around here?"

Mitch, Rhonda's boyfriend, stepped into the group wearing a police officer's uniform.

"You're so busted," Ryon grinned.

Turning away from Mádeohn, the birthday girl put her arms around the cop's neck, asking seductively, "Officer, is there any-thing I can do to get myself out of this misunderstanding?"

"Hmm," Mitch replied thoughtfully, running his hands down Rhonda's back and grabbing her butt.

"We might be able to come up with an adequate form of restitution for you."

"Oh, please," Connie whined, rolling her eyes, "get a room, guys!"

"That will be later," Mitch replied.

Rhonda slapped his chest and remarked, "You're pretty presumptuous, aren't you?"

Mitch shrugged his shoulders while taking Rhonda by the arm and announcing, "I have to go check on the cabana down on the beach. You guys want to come with me?"

Agreeing, everyone began following the host, descending a stone stairway zigzagging from the pool deck down to the beach below. Up above on the large pool deck, numerous patio heaters were warding off the chilly lake air. Several degrees cooler down on the beach, Mitch removed the police jacket he was wearing, thoughtfully draping it around Rhonda's bare shoulders. The two girls immediately took off, jetting over to the heat of a large bonfire burning on the beach. Several other people surrounding it were already basking in its warmth.

"Grab us something to drink!" Rhonda shouted back to the guys.

Following their party host to the cabana, Ryon and Mádeohn grabbed a beer for themselves and a glass of wine for each of the girls. Leaving Mitch to check on the cabana's refreshment supplies, they made their way over to the women.

Leaning against his spear and raising his own drink in salute, the Roman gladiator shouted over the crackling firewood, "To the birthday girl!"

Saluting with their own drinks, the various other creatures of the night encircling the giant blaze responded in unison, "To the birthday girl!"

Raising her own glass with a big grin on her face, Rhonda giggled, "Yeah, me!"

As the party wore on, lightning continually illuminated the black clouds moving in across the lake.

"We may have to send everyone inside if that gets any closer," Mitch commented, pointing to the black tempest and observing how frequent the distant claps of thunder were becoming.

Suddenly the sky lit up brightly right over head, and everyone jumped at the deafening boom immediately following the blinding flash. A strong gust of wind swept across the beach, forcing the partygoers to protect their eyes from blowing sand. Sparks haphazardly flew from the bonfire, erratically drifting to a nearby pile of wood and swiftly igniting it.

"Cool, now we have two!" someone drunkenly joked.

"What's that?" Ryon asked, pointing out across the lake.

Everybody turned, looking out to where he was indicating in the dark.

Squinting, Rhonda replied, "I can't see anything."

Lightning flared again, and the dark clouds stretching completely across the sky were illuminated, allowing the group to see what Ryon was pointing at.

A giant water spout was forming over the lake.

"Look at the water line!" Mádeohn shouted over the steadily howling wind.

In shock, they all watched the lake water slowly receding toward the center of the lake and up into the swirling spout.

"That's just messed up!" Rhonda cried in disbelief, recording the cyclone with her cell phone.

"It's sucking all the water up inside itself! How can that be?" Connie asked.

"I don't know!" Mitch had to shout over another crack of thunder before yelling, "Everyone, up to the house—now!"

"Ryon!" Mádeohn stressed while indicating the forest area encompassing the beach with his pitchfork, "There are people in the trees!"

Lightning flashed again, creating a bizarre illusion of a Roman gladiator standing between two pillars of fire, facing off against the devil.

Nodding understandingly, Ryon yelled back over the noise of the wind, "You take that side, I'll take this one!"

Dropping their weapons and sprinting apart, the two disappeared into the tree line surrounding the beach.

All evening, people were sneaking away to enjoy intimate moments together inside the privacy of the forested area. Mádeohn found three such couples already heading for the house. After making certain there wasn't anyone else, he made his own way quickly to the bottom of the stairway, ushering those racing across the beach from Ryon's side up the stone steps.

Anxiously waiting for his friend, Mádeohn looked out at the massive storm over the lake. The entire scene looked so surreal to him. As frightening as it was, in his opinion, the tempest really was quite beautiful. Continuous bolts of lightning arched down from the top of the cyclone, smacking the now empty lake bed and creating small eruptions of mud clumps with each strike. The waterspout itself, seen through the continuous forks of electricity, looked like the trunk of a giant weeping willow, with luminous branches draping down all around it. The whole eerie scene had a purplish hue to it.

Mádeohn saw Ryon burst out of the trees and race across the beach. Just past the two piles of blazing wood, he suddenly stopped dead in his tracks.

"What are you doing?" Mádeohn asked out loud to himself, worrying about how close the lightning and waterspout was getting to the beach.

Following his friend's gaze, he soon saw the reason for Ryon halting. There was someone trapped underneath the remains of the now collapsed cabana. Raising her arm and clearly trying to shout over the howling wind, Mádeohn immediately recognized who she was: the woman from the check-in booth.

"Ryon, no!" Mádeohn pointlessly tried shouting into the wind as he started to run to his best friend's aid.

With an explosion of lightning, a sudden microburst of wind smashed him flat to the ground, trapping him there. Unable to rise, Mádeohn looked out across the blowing sand to see Ryon pinned down also.

The lightning and cyclone of water were getting closer and closer. Mádeohn had to do something to protect his friend from the deadly storm. Straining with great effort, he was able to stretch his arm out in front of him. Accomplishing that difficult feat, he stopped, noticing Ryon amazingly struggling to his knees, every muscle in his friend's body bulging with the strain of pushing against the wind.

Facing the swirling column of death towering over him, the gladiator on the beach painfully began raising one arm into the air.

Watching in disbelief, Mádeohn witnessed a bolt of pure-white energy leap from Ryon's outstretched finger, striking the churning mass of black clouds above with a terrific explosion. He then collapsed to the ground unconscious, as the column of spinning water came crashing back down into the middle of the lake bed, creating a massive tidal wave that raced toward the beach.

No longer pinned down by the wind, Mádeohn leaped up, desperately sprinting to reach his friend before the wave of frothing water struck the beach. Upon arriving at Ryon's still form, someone suddenly slammed into him from behind, tackling him to the ground. Rolling over, Mádeohn recognized the ghost from his past sitting on top of him, not quite as trapped as she had led on to be.

"You're too late!" she cackled wickedly. The strong rush of air being pushed by the approaching wave of water was violently whipping the woman's hair across her face, adding to her already crazed look.

"I promised you!" Mádeohn roared as he doubled up his fist, smashing it across the side of her jaw. The sudden, unexpected blow forcefully spun her head around, instantly snapping the woman's neck.

Tossing the corpse to the side, Mádeohn scrambled up, throwing himself on top of Ryon. Mádeohn erected a force field around them, and the tidal wave came crushing down upon the field of energy protecting the two. After flooding across the beach, crashing against the stairway wall, and then frothing up and spraying the pool deck with a dirtied white foam, the water began receding back into the lake. The two young men lay on the beach unharmed, the night's full moon quietly shining down as if the storm never happened.

Checking to see if Ryon was all right, Mádeohn slowly climbed to his knees, trying to come to grips with the shocking realization of what had just happened. Looking down at his unconscious friend, he whispered, "You're the one he was trying to kill!"

Noticing Mitch and the others appearing up by the pool-deck wall, Mádeohn cried out across the flood-ravaged beach, "Somebody call nine-one-one!"

In the White Witch World of Lysta'cu'mha, Kana adjusted one of his elbow-length gloves while quickly striding down the palace's main hallway leading to his Father's throne room. Wearing the uniform of a White Witch Warrior of his high rank, per protocol, he gave no notice to the royal red carpet hovering a foot above the floor and holding solid under the determined march of his black boots. Swiftly passing by sacred weapons and artwork spanning eons of White Witch history floating upon the glowing walls, the prince focused solely on his task ahead, not the palace's fantastic features.

Racing to the throne room, his upcoming meeting with the counsel dominated his every thought. The prince absolutely believed the news he was bringing to the day's session would turn into the catalyst enabling him to finally move forward with his life. Excitement surged through every fiber of the White Witch prince's body like electricity.

Reaching his destination at the end of the hallway, the huge brass doors to the throne room slowly swung open on their own with a small gush of air. Pulling his hood back and letting his long dark hair fall into the collar of the shimmering cloak swirling in his wake, he continued on, crossing the lavishly decorated room. Stopping, he knelt before the middle-aged man sitting on the throne, reverently kissing the ring on the king's outstretched hand.

"Father, my ward has expressed unusual powers today," Kana proclaimed without hesitation, returning to his feet.

"Yes," the king calmly agreed, also standing, "I take it you think this is a sign?"

Descending from the throne and adjourning to a side table, the prince began pouring them both a glass of wine while confidently answering, "It has to begin somewhere."

Reaching down to the game of Karn already in progress on the table, Kana watched his father carefully to see any sign of agreement while moving a black World. Marcan countered the move with a white piece, one of the spirits, placing it with another of his white pieces in the VOID, or four squares in the center of the game board.

"Yes, I know, but what makes you think it's now?"

Staring at the red liquid in his goblet, the prince replied with what sounded to Marcan like a well-rehearsed speech, "Father, all my life I have been schooled by the best teachers, prophets, and scholars, preparing me for my destiny. So much schooling I can't even remember it all. I feel that I'm wasting all my time learning and not doing. There is a time when preparation must end and action must begin. If you spend all your time preparing for a battle and not fighting it, you cannot win."

"Kana," King Marcan responded gravely to his son's well thought-out dissertation, "a person never knows enough to face his destiny, no matter how great or small it is. You have a very difficult task ahead of you—one that will take more power and courage than any one White Witch ever thought about possessing. You have been taught powers greater than anybody in this world ever thought could exist. What you do not remember will come to you in your time of need, but none of this will do you any good if you do not have the fortitude to use what was given to you wisely!" Continuing with a hint of annoyance in his voice, Marcan sighed, "The council is in session. Some of those ol' farts get very impatient, so let's not keep them waiting."

With that, Kana watched his father turn and enter a door next to the small table. Standing there for a moment and swirling the liquid in his goblet, he thought to himself, "He didn't agree, but he didn't reject it either!"

After flinging the rest of his wine down his throat (that would help him face all those ol' farts), the prince followed his father into the Council Room.

Entering the richly furnished chamber, the prince immediately became aware of thirteen pairs of eyes focusing on him. Sitting at a massive, rectangular table made of black marble, the twelve elders of the council and the king were silently waiting for him to take his seat. The king sat at the head of the table, leaving the chair at the opposite end empty.

"Are you always in the habit of being tardy, Prince Kana?" Cyphis, elder adviser under the high priest asked as Kana took the empty chair.

"My apologies to the council," he replied while adjusting his cloak to a more comfortable position. Carefully concealing his disdain for the sanctimonious little priest, he noticed a slight smirk upon his father's face.

"You better find a way to get along with him," Marcan had told him on several occasions. "Our beloved Zaia will not live forever. Cyphis is next in line to be high priest, and you king. He is the one you will be working with during your reign."

Shaking his head and praying for a miracle, Kana pushed that unpleasant thought to the back of his mind. Biting his tongue, the prince silently sat waiting.

Commanding everyone's attention, King Marcan began, "The prince believes it is time for him to earnestly begin his quest. I wish to hear the council's pros and cons, a report on his schooling, and what the prince himself has to say. Zaia?"

High Priest Zaia thought for a moment before speaking. This was something he always did, and everyone just had to be patient with the Holy One.

"The dark one's grip upon the earth grows tighter every day. If we do not begin at the proper moment, his fist will be closed!" The old man then clenched his own fist for emphasis.

"But if we jump in blindly again," Cyphis sat forward, protesting, "it could end up just like before with the Romans, Greeks, and Vikings.

With a look of annoyance, Zaia countered back, "In those days, the men of earth were but babes. That mistake will not happen again."

"Good, Cyphis," Marcan patiently interrupted, "we do not jump in blindly or go unprepared. You yourself have been instrumental in that portion of the operation."

The councilman bowed his head in acknowledgment, quietly settling back in his chair. Complimenting him, Marcan knew, was one of the best ways to shut Cyphis up.

Continuing, the king turned to the head of the council of teachers, "Master Otton, will you give me your report on the prince's schooling?"

Kana mentally smiled to himself while thinking, "This should go very well!"

"The prince is quick to learn all that we have taught him," Master Otton began. "His reflexes are exceptionally fast. He is emotionally sound, although he likes to be a little more dramatic than is good for him. It is the belief of the all the masters that Kana now knows more of the universal powers than any other White

Witch has known for centuries, although a lot of that knowledge may be buried in his subconscious."

Thanking the master, who bowed his head in acknowledgment, Marcan continued, turning back to the high priest, "Zaia, your opinion on the boy's readiness?"

Kana held his breath, waiting through the usual silence before the high priest spoke. He knew Zaia's opinion carried a lot of weight with his father.

"Since he was but a child, the prince has spent his life learning, praying, and preparing for what he must do," the holy old man spoke slowly. "I have accepted and acknowledged Master Otton's report. For years I have watched the boy grow mentally, physically, and spiritually, learning well everything taught to him. It is the opinion of this old one that there is a time when learning must end and action begin!"

Looking to the prince at the far end of the table, Marcan noticed Kana grinning while keeping his attention deliberately focused on his hands clasped together before him. Well, now he knew from where that phrase from his son's little speech earlier had come.

"Prince Kana, you have an incident to relate to the council?" the king knowingly inquired.

The prince stood up, informing the group of learned men about the dark one's storm upon earth, and the unusual power his ward, Ryon, had demonstrated, destroying it. Finishing, the prince stood waiting anxiously while thirteen pairs of eyes gazed back at him quietly.

"It begins," Zaia said softly, breaking the silence.

"Cyphis," Marcan spoke up, "tell us of your preparations for the prince's entry into the mortal world."

"The prince will be enrolled into the learning institution his ward is attending. That is where he will begin his work. All is in readiness for his induction onto earth."

"Then the council is decided!"

Kana smiled inwardly, with the king's decree echoing through his mind.

THE MYSTIC ARTS CLASS

Pushing his glasses up onto his nose while turning into his classroom, Mr. Wenstrom proceeded to the crowded shelves behind his desk. Carefully placing the book he was carrying into its designated spot, the instructor of the Mystic Arts Class at the small community college sat down at his desk. Glancing around the room, he smiled with satisfaction upon noticing everyone present for a change, including the two new transfers. Where they came from in the middle of all the chaos the last two weeks, he had no idea.

Thankfully, the media circus attracted by the freak storm finally left town a couple days ago, restoring a small sense of normality back to the students' routines. Pictures and videos of the tornado draining the lake immediately went viral on the Internet the next day, precipitating the media invasion. Since the majority of his students were at the lake the night of the storm, a lot of them became the focus of interviews for all the national news groups. The two beach-flood survivors, Mádeohn and Ryon, immediately went into hiding, avoiding all reporters and completely missing all their classes. Although skirting attention was definitely characteristic of Mádeohn, Wenstrom found Ryon shunning the limelight to be very strange. As far as the instructor could discern at this point, no one really knew what happened to the two of them on the beach that night, and they weren't talking.

Looking at his watch, Mr. Wenstrom decided it was time to call the students to their seats, instructing them, "All of you have a report to finish; I suggest you get busy on it."

Ryon stood up, walking with Shilo to the bookshelves behind Wenstrom. Retrieving one of the ancient texts they needed for their report, the two returned to their seats and began working together. Shilo was a new girl Ryon had discovered sitting right next to him the first day he returned to school, and he became immediately mesmerized by her. Asking him to be her partner for this assignment was nothing short of an invitation from angel.

Ryon found Shilo was not the only new transfer. Keeping mostly to himself, the other new addition rarely spoke to anyone. Ryon couldn't even remember the guy's name, and when he asked anyone else, they couldn't recall it either. Rumors that there was something weird about the stranger were already spreading throughout the school.

Toward the end of the class period, Wenstrom suddenly grunted at the book he was reading, attracting everyone's attention. Getting up with it in hand, the instructor began walking to the rear of the room, still reading. Seating himself at a table with a chess game set up on it and referring to the book, he put his fingertips on his temples while closing his eyes. A wave of shock suddenly swept throughout the classroom, followed by absolute silence. One of the bishops on the chessboard began to rise into the air all by itself. After floating about six inches above the board for several seconds, it dropped back to the table before rolling off and onto the floor.

"Amazing!" the instructor exclaimed while exhaling the breath he had been holding. "The simplest form of levitation I've found yet!"

Laughter broke out from the front corner of the class.

"You know nothing about levitation!"

Everyone turned to see the new guy grinning with amusement.

"Oh! And I assume you know more?" Wenstrom asked, a little irritated at the young man's arrogance.

His watch began to chime, signaling the end of the class period. Not one of the students made a move to leave, silently waiting to see what he would do.

Deliberately calming himself a moment by turning the alarm on his watch off, Wenstrom looked up at the smirking pupil, instructing, "I trust tomorrow you will give us a demonstration of your extensive knowledge on this subject."

Watching the young man bow his head, accepting the challenge without hesitation before calmly strolling out of the classroom, Wenstrom's aggravation slowly turned to curiosity.

Watching the stranger leave the room, Mádeohn quietly sat in his chair, perplexed. The whole incident that just took place was spawning major warning alarms in his mind. Apprehension created by Ryon's actions at the storm fueled the nauseating dread already churning inside him. He feared that the peace in his life the last few years was about to turn into chaos.

Sitting at his desk the next day, completely disappointed in himself, Wenstrom once again went over the events of yesterday. Staring out the glass wall making up one side of his classroom, the instructor continued to berate himself for losing his temper in front of the students. Not once in his career, whether in a class or out in the field, had he ever vilified a pupil for challenging something he said. On the contrary, he always found it encouraging when students questioned him; it was a sign they were listening, which meant they were learning.

"Why was this young man yesterday so different?" he wondered.

For some unknown reason, he could never remember this particular young man's name without looking it up.

That bothered him also. Wenstrom always took pride in being able to call each of his students by name from memory.

Gazing outside brought back pleasant memories of the first time he saw this room and the all-glass wall each classroom on this side of the building shared. Enjoying the view overlooking one of the campus parking lots and the small town spread out beyond brought a momentarily reprieve to his self-pity party. With the sun shining through the glass on the cool autumn day, creating a warm, lazy feeling, his students slowly began to file in.

Turning his attention again to the empty seat where the young man (whose name he could not remember) had sat, Wenstrom sighed.

"I hope he isn't dropping the class because of my selfish ego!" he thought.

With that new thought haunting his mind, Mr. Wenstrom brought his class to order, instructing them, "We were to have a demonstration today, but our demonstrator isn't here, so continue working on your reports. They need to be finished and on my desk by the end of class tomorrow."

Twenty minutes into the period, Wenstrom caught himself staring blankly at his laptop again. While attempting to read an article about a new village unearthed on a Mediterranean island, his mind kept wandering. He just couldn't stay focused on the article, even though he really wanted to read about what had been discovered.

Closing the laptop, he set his glasses down on the desk before leaning back in his chair, sighing in defeat. Relaxing, the instructor began rubbing the bridge of his nose, looking out at the class over the back of his hand.

Obviously he wasn't the only one having trouble concentrating. It appeared that the sun's warmth from the east wall was having the same effect on all of them, lulling the entire room into their own little worlds of happy daydreaming. Perfectly content to drift off into his own random musings, the idea of the class wasting time and not working didn't bother Wenstrom the least bit.

Then suddenly the room went dark as if someone had flicked off a light switch.

Connie screamed at the sudden change, bringing the whole class back to reality.

Or was it reality?

Where clear glass should have been looking out over the town, there was now a solid wall of moving colors. Browns, crimsons, greens, and violets, churning and swirling like liquid.

"What's going on?" Ryon whispered, watching the flowing colors on the glass wall.

The same murmurs of confusion swept throughout the entire room. Even Wenstrom sat confounded by what they were all seeing.

Suddenly, a voice began to speak out of nowhere, yet seemingly coming from everywhere.

"Welcome to the world of the White Witches, where what isn't real can be. Where the impossible is possible, and where the unnatural thrives. It is a world with a kaleidoscope of colors beyond your wildest dreams! Mr. Wenstrom, yesterday you asked me to demonstrate what I know about levitation."

A sudden flash of energy exploded under the instructor's desk and chair. Slapping his hands down upon the desktop in terror, as if trying to balance himself, Mr. Wenstrom and the furniture began to slowly rise off the floor.

"Levitation," the voice continued, "is actually relatively simple, especially when you compare it with the rest of the vast knowledge of the universe."

Out of the rear right corner of the ceiling, a three-inch, light-blue beam of energy suddenly shot to the right front corner. Then it continued streaking across to the left front corner before rocketing to the left rear side of the room. Zipping to the center of the back of the room, the light beam abruptly turned and started racing back toward the front again.

Following the beam of light shooting around the classroom left each of the humans sitting in a state of open-mouthed disbelief.

Halfway back to the front of the room, the beam's flight abruptly stopped with an explosion of sparks. Everyone except

Shilo began scrambling away from the glittering shower to stand by the classroom walls. In the center of the ceiling, a slowly spinning, sparkling ball of energy was all that remained of the strange light show.

"You see," the enigmatic voice continued, "levitation is merely taking hold of the fabric of gravity and stretching it to the thinness you desire."

Standing safely around the edge of the room, everyone continued watching as small streaks of light began shooting out of the sphere, only to retract back. Each beam of light would lash out again even farther, fluctuating back and forth, like little children gaining a bit more courage each time to venture farther away from the safety of their mother's arms. Soon the light beams spread to the far reaches of the classroom.

With the shafts of energy pulsing across the ceiling, the mysterious voice went on, explaining, "What you mortals consider astonishing feats of mystical power is...mere child's play to me."

A shimmering light began to gently fall from the spinning ball, spreading out to about four feet in diameter across the floor. Then, in the center of the light, a person appearing to turn through a doorway became an angelic figure standing in the center of the room. As mysteriously as they came, the dazzling lights across the ceiling slowly faded away, leaving only the wall of flowing colors and the beautiful creature standing silently in the middle of the room. He appeared to have a glow around him.

Staring at the gorgeous figure in the center of the class, Connie tried unsuccessfully to exhale. Quietly standing there in what appeared to be a uniform and cape, he was so breathtakingly beautiful! So fit! So...

"He's so hot!" Rhonda whispered next to Connie, finishing her thought.

Standing on the other side from Connie, Mitch gave Rhonda's hand a painful I-heard-that squeeze. Swiftly retaliating, she sharply elbowed her boyfriend in the ribs, invoking a satisfying, "Oomph!" from him.

Staring into the most beautiful pair of eyes he had ever seen, Kana slowly began crossing the room to where Connie stood. Noticing her try to press herself closer to the wall, a little frightened at his bold advancement, the prince raised his arms in a non-threatening gesture. With a reassuring smile, he stopped a couple of steps from the confused woman, reaching out invitingly with his right hand. A rose made of red light suddenly appeared in his palm.

Shifting her gaze from the neon flower up to the stranger's smiling face, Connie noticed him nod reassuringly at her to accept his gift. Hesitatingly taking the rose from him, she smiled with pleasure while curiously watching it slowly became a real flower right in her hand.

Unable to contain herself any longer, Shilo exploded out of her chair, shattering the tense silence in the room, shouting, "Kana, does Father know you're here?"

Reluctantly pulling himself out of the depths of Connie's eyes, the White Witch turned to her, calmly replying, "My dear sister, more importantly, does he know *you* are here?"

With her face turning red from anger and embarrassment, Shilo defiantly glared at her brother and his arrogant grin. He always did this to her. Turning away and facing the wall of flowing colors, the princess swore she would make him pay.

Still floating four feet off the floor, Wenstrom tried to clear the large lump in his throat, hoarsely asking, "Who are you?"

"Mr. Wenstrom, pardon me for forgetting you!" Kana apologized while lowering the instructor, showing no effort in doing so.

"I am Kana, prince of the White Witches, and the Princess Shilo is my sister."

"Princess!" Ryon exclaimed, his infatuation with Shilo rocketing off the charts.

As soon as the desk and chair settled back on the floor, Wenstrom immediately jumped away from them. For a moment, he just stood there, watching to make sure the furniture didn't start to rise up again, at least not with him in it.

"What are W-white W-witches?" the instructor stammered, shifting his gaze away from the desk and looking questioningly at the prince.

With a nonchalant wave of his hand, Kana made the classroom chairs miraculously rearrange themselves into a circle.

"Please sit," the prince invited everyone.

Each student looked hesitantly at the desks that had just shuffled around the room all by themselves.

"Please," Kana bid again.

Rolling her eyes, the White Witch princess took the lead, sitting down. Ryon followed, taking the seat next to her, and the rest of the class slowly did the same.

"All of you listen closely as I explain," Kana began his first lesson. "In the beginning, there was just God. God always was, always is, and always will be. His throne sits in the Kingdom of Heaven, which, back then, occupied the far end of the VOID. The VOID was all that was not Heaven. Lonely, God decided to create spiritual creatures He called angels to live in Heaven with Him.

"One of the angels, an important one, named Lucifer, was the most beautiful of all God's creations. Because of this, Lucifer grew steadily vain about himself. He slowly began to corrupt the other angels about little things. He convinced them that his work was just as good, or even better, than God's work. Over time, his corruption and following grew steadily larger."

The tale the prince began reciting came to life in the center of the room, right before the class's eyes.

LUCIFER'S FALL

Lucifer closed his eyes, taking a few moments to clear his mind of the multitude of plans he currently had set in motion. Relaxing, he momentarily indulged in the exhilarating feeling of wind passing around his massive wings and his long silky hair whipping down his bare, muscular back. Gliding high over Sagun, the first of the seven realms of Heaven, the archangel's bright white light made him appear to be a shooting star traveling across the realm's sky of perpetual twilight.

Noticing all the angelic beings below bowing and averting their eyes as a high member of the seraphim passed above, Lucifer smugly thought to himself, "As it should be."

Stopping for a moment and hovering at the edge of Sagun, he gazed out at the nothingness beyond that was not Heaven, appropriately referred to as the VOID. Visions of beautifully diverse worlds created by him in that vast emptiness passed before the archangel's eyes. Imagining all the inhabitants of those worlds worshipping him as their creator brought a smile to his beautiful face.

First things first, though: obtaining sole supremacy over all angels in Heaven, without submitting himself any more to the authority of the Lord, had to be accomplished before expanding out into the VOID. For right now, conquering Heaven and making his own splendor greater than the glory of God was the archangel's only priority.

"I *will be* the most high!" he whispered confidently.

Turning to look down at the large rebel force gathering below in this realm, Lucifer knew he was on his way to realizing his dream. The effort he put in over an extremely long period of time, subverting and recruiting that army, was about to pay off. The hour for his legion of servants to invade each of the realms of Heaven was finally at hand.

The archangel knew conquering Heaven's seven kingdoms in one swift, surgically executed invasion was an audacious vision, but achievable. The combination of God's current, undeniable apathy for anything outside His crystal palace, combined with his own inexorable ambition, pretty much assured his ascension to the throne of Heaven.

Subconsciously churning through the outline of his plans for the millionth time, Lucifer was quite confident in his army's ability to invade and conquer each of Heaven's kingdoms flawlessly.

The seven realms were uniquely different from each other, presenting the need for individual strategies in each. The outermost, Sagun, bordered the VOID. The desolate realm was nothing more than a vast expanse of black rock, riddled in every direction by rivers and lakes of liquid fire. The main body of his imposing force spread out on Sagun's dark surface below, poised and ready to strike, only waiting on the order from him, their master, to launch. Smiling while admiring the flurry of activity beneath him, Lucifer congratulated himself that Sagun, quite literally, was already his.

God appointed the two archangels Aanahel and Azrael to govern over Sagun. Lucifer never got around to asking his Father why this desolate realm needed two governors.

"For that matter," the archangel thought to himself while shaking his head in dismay, "Why even create such a forsaken wasteland?" A perfect example of why there needed to be a change in Heaven's reign.

Lucifer acquired Aanahel and Azrael's loyalty by promising them the highest-ranking positions in his army. Currently the two were devoutly administering the final preparations of the massive rebel army.

Raquia, the second realm bordering Sagun on the opposite side from the VOID, was another bleak realm the archangel saw no point in God creating. It was nothing but a large expanse of dry desert, its sandy surface constantly being pelted with lightning storms. A vast, jagged range of lofty mountains with cold windswept peaks known as The Teeth towered up between the two kingdoms and separated Sagun from the storm-riddled desert.

Looking down at the base of the mountains, Lucifer took the time to observe his own legion of archangels. The elite angelic warriors were monitoring the army's preparations under Aanahel and Azrael's ironfisted supervision. The vast majority of the rebel force spread out across Sagun's black surface and consisted of common lower angels. Soldiers and laborers diligently prepared weapons and engaged in combat drills. After relishing the clashing of metal upon metal and the roar of battle cries surging up from the dark valley floor for a moment, Lucifer left the edge of the VOID behind to meet with his generals.

Archangels Aanahel and Azrael stood warming themselves next to a fire near the summit of one of the Teeth's craggy peaks while observing the last-minute preparations of their massive rebel army. Congregated on the black rock of the valley floor, the ominous invasion force stood poised, tense as a serpent, and ready to strike.

All activity stopped when Lucifer's radiance streaked like a white comet across the dark sky. Alighting on the mountain peak, where he had instructed Aanahel and Azrael to meet him, Lucifer blessed the two prostrate archangels before turning to those kneeling in adoration to him in the valley below.

Raising his arms while extending his wings fully, he lifted his voice, proclaiming, "Rise, my brothers! Rise and continue to prepare for our victory!"

The response from the throng below, rolled up the mountainside like a wave of thunder.

"Lu-ci-fer! Lu-ci-fer!"

Stepping up to his master's side, Aanahel commented on the chants rising from the valley floor, "You are much loved."

Raising his eyes and looking out into the emptiness of the VOID, Lucifer responded, "Yes, I am."

Narrowing his emerald-green eyes while continuing to stare out beyond the edge of the realm, he asked, "What do you see out there?"

Aanahel looked up quizzically, replying, "Nothing."

"That is because you have no vision beyond what you see down there," Lucifer gestured toward the massive military force below.

"Fortunately for us," he went on, smiling with pleasure, "that vision has been immeasurable."

"Damn it!"

Turning, the two curiously watched Azrael beating the smoldering tips of his wings upon the frozen ground.

Looking up and noticing his two brothers staring at him, the archangel snarled, "I'm cold! I got too close to the fire!"

Glancing back at Aanahel, Lucifer charged, "Be ready to move when I get back. My blessings are upon you."

While watching Azrael intimately examine his singed feathers, Aanahel nodded affirmatively and replied with a sigh, "I think I'm going to need them."

Launching himself off the cold mountain peak and crossing into Raquia, Lucifer began his journey home, leaving Sagun and his army behind. In spite of his opinion about this barren wasteland, he did find a certain amount of pleasure flying across the desolate realm. Not only was navigating the violent air currents intensely thrilling for him but sensing and dodging the unpredictable bolts of lightning also made traversing the region extraordinarily exhilarating. For obvious reasons, very few of Heaven's residents occupied Raquia, including its governor, Raphael, one of God's most loyal archangels. There would be very little resistance, if any, when overtaking this realm.

A calming in the atmosphere suddenly marked Lucifer's crossing into the third kingdom, Shamayim. Tranquilly riding the air currents, he took a short respite to enjoy the view below after the adrenaline rush of crossing Raquia. The favorite recreational getaway for all of Heaven's inhabitants, Shamayim boast lush, tropical gardens and beaches of white sand bordering deep-blue seas. Right here is where he expected his army to meet its first resistance. Governing over Shamayim was one of the highest in command of all archangels, Gabriel. Lucifer knew his brother would never give up his beautiful region easily.

After peacefully gliding across the third kingdom of Heaven, he passed into the fourth realm, Machanon, home to the golden city of Heaven and a vast metropolis inhabited by those who were not seraphim, cherubim, or archangels. Encircling the City of Gold were four rivers, twelve walls, and twelve impenetrable gates. Fiercely guarded by Archangel Michael and his army, Lucifer knew taking Machanon could be the making or breaking point of the whole campaign. Strategically placing secret forces throughout the vast city to rupture it from the inside while it defended itself from his outside invasion gave him confidence the city would crumble in bloody defeat.

Lucifer's trek next took him through the fifth realm, Zebul, home to the Angelic Institute of Learning. Everyone in Heaven had the freedom to attend university to further his or her education on any subject God deemed suitable, which actually amounted to a vast amount of knowledge. From the reports he continuously received, archangel Zachiel, governor of Zebul, was seldom ever here. The archangel spent most of his time in Mathey, the sixth realm, studying to be one of the cherubim, God's record keepers and guardians of harmony and wisdom. That pretty much left

Gadreel, the institute's headmaster, in charge of Zebul. The academic administrator was more interested in teaching than politics, which translated into Gadreel being a pacifist. Taking control of the fifth realm would be just a matter of occupation, with little or no resistance.

Crossing into Mathey, the sixth kingdom, Lucifer began anticipating the luxury of relaxing in his own private spa. At the moment, nothing sounded more pleasing than surrendering to his wife sensually scrubbing away the filth from his little foray across the kingdoms of Heaven.

Home to all seraphim, cherubim, and archangels, he fully expected the battle here to be more fierce and bloody than the one in Machanon. Taking this into account early, he began subverting certain prominent citizens of the realm to pledging themselves to him. Together with his wife expertly seducing others to do the same, the conquest of Mathey was already well underway.

That only left Araboth, the seventh kingdom of Heaven. Araboth was not only the location of God's throne room but also the great crystal estate the Lord called home. After completely securing the other six kingdoms, conquering and destroying his Father would only be a matter of time. Then he would claim Heaven's throne for himself. Visions of sitting on that majestic chair and gazing out at all of His creations singing praises and giving exaltations of glory to their new lord brought another smile to the archangel's beautiful countenance.

Taking a much needed break, Gadreel, administrator for the Angelic Institute of Learning in Zebul, stepped out onto his office balcony. From high atop the administrative tower, he enjoyed gazing down at the lush gardens and flowing fountains of the courtyard below. He found watching the constant ebb and flow of angelic beings going about their business brought a welcome reprieve from his never ending responsibilities. His close friend Zephrom—profit, visionary, and interpreter of the past, present, and future—stood quietly contemplating at the administrator's side. After a short time of peaceful mind wandering, Buer—instructor of philosophy, logic, and ethics—quietly joined the two.

Lucifer's light suddenly interrupted Zebul's quiet reflections. As Lucifer silently glided across the campus sky, all activity below immediately stopped, with everyone bowing in reverence to the archangel.

Zephrom slowly looked up while despondently watching Lucifer's light fade in the distance, solemnly stating to his colleagues, "The storm is almost upon us."

"I don't understand it!" Buer exclaimed. "Surely the Almighty Father knows what His upstart is planning; everyone else in Heaven certainly does. Why doesn't He put a stop to it before it begins? It makes absolutely no sense!"

"God's logic and counsel are his own," Gadreel emphasized while suddenly turning to return to his office. Unfurling his wings and shaking out the sudden buildup of tension in his shoulders, the administrator continued instructing, "See to it that the preparations for all those who want to weather Zephrom's storm out here with us are complete."

Wrapping her fluffy white wings around her naked, angelic form, Lilith sensuously sauntered through her bed chamber's open, marble archway. Stepping into a swirling mist enveloping the balcony outside, she continued relishing the feel of her soft, freshly bathed feathers gently caressing her bare skin. It made her tingle all over and yearn for the tantalizing stroke of her husband's powerful wings.

With the thought of Lucifer returning home shortly, a shiver of anticipation ran up the female angel's spine.

Confident that everything inside was perfectly prepared for his arrival, out of habit, Lilith quickly ran through a mental checklist just to be sure. She knew her husband would tolerate nothing less than perfection and intimately reward her for his satisfaction.

The angelic couple's lavish suite crowned the tallest spire towering above the seraphim citadel. As head of the seraphim, her husband was richly endowed with many special privileges, including living in the most luxurious home in all of Heaven, with the exception, of course, of God's crystal palace. Even that would change when Lucifer's plans were complete.

Standing alone in the churning fog, a smile lit up Lilith's angelic face at the thought of living in the Heavenly Father's magnificently luscious mansion.

With a flourish of her wings, Lilith parted the mist hovering around the crown of the tower, allowing the brilliance of Heaven's light to flood across the terrace. Locking her fingers together above her head, the female angel fully extended her wings while sensuously stretching feline-like up onto her tiptoes. Beaming with pleasure while soaking in the comforting warmth of the heavenly light, she couldn't help but admire the luxurious life given to her.

The grandeur of her terrace itself transcended that of most homes throughout all the realms.

Gazing to her left, Lilith became momentarily mesmerized as she watched crystal-clear water gently flowing down over moss-covered rocks and into a dark-blue pond. A glowing blue orb placed behind the water feature by Lucifer himself lit up the beautiful waterfall. Surrounding the inviting pool of water grew rich, green, perfectly manicured lawns. Completing the landscaping of that side of the terrace were deep-green tropical plants and richly colorful flowers of her choosing, along with ornately carved benches for lounging. Several visions of past intimate moments with her husband in or by that pond swept through the female angel's mind.

To her right rose the monolithic marble columns of a gazebo with white silk curtains currently tied back to each pillar and stone benches covered with matching, plush cushions. Many a party or celebration Lucifer's alluring and supportive wife had hosted out here on this beautiful terrace—gatherings she had designed to seduce several of her husband's now staunchest supporters. Earlier, after Lucifer departed to check on the progress of his army in Sagun, Lilith met with each of those allies to make sure they all were completely prepared for when the insurrection began. She knew her report of everyone's readiness would please her husband, sending a thrill of anticipation through her body for the reward he would bestow upon her.

Combing her fingers through the long, semi damp locks of her dark auburn hair, Lilith smiled to herself while thinking about how being the wife of the most powerful of all the seraphim had its perks. Sauntering over to the edge of the balcony, she curled her toes over the lip, gazing out across the marble city sprawled out below. There was no retaining wall around the balcony, and the female angel held no fear of falling off the high tower. If she did, she would simply spread her wings and fly right back up onto the terrace.

The sweet melody of an angelic choir drifting up from below and bells off in the distance chiming in perfect harmony with the choir only added to the serenity of the ethereal view spread out before her. She stood poised like a work of art as she watched angels, seraphim, cherubim, and archangels soar through the air, each attending to some personal task.

Out of the corner of her eye, off in the distant sky, Lilith caught the distinct light of Lucifer returning home. The thought of the bliss she was about to enjoy sent a wave of vertigo through her entire body. Using her wings for support until she was able to will her legs to function again, the wife of the highest-ranking seraphim half ran, half flew back inside to wait for her husband.

The two lovers lounged upon one of the many cushioned benches in the gigantic marble gazebo, a slight breeze ruffling the silk drapes. Completely content after the intimate pleasure she just experienced with her husband, Lilith ran a comb through her spouse's long, silky, blond hair. Obviously very pleased with his wife's success, the euphoria of his reward brought her to new heights of ecstasy that she never knew existed.

Freshly bathed and dressed by his wife, the head of the seraphim prepared to attend God in His throne room, leading the angelic choir in singing praises to the Lord. Regally raising himself from his wife's grooming, the archangel strode across the terrace, perching himself on its edge.

Already missing the warmth of her husband's body against her bare skin, Lilith wrapped her own wings gently around herself, affectionately purring, "You shine so brightly, none will be able to look upon you without covering their eyes!"

"As it should be," Lucifer replied, spreading his massive, white wings and launching himself out into the bright, clear Mathey sky.

Upon reaching his destination in the seventh realm, Lucifer banked left, circling what would soon become the seat of his own kingdom after conquering Heaven and destroying his Father.

God's throne room...Lucifer smiled while admiring the oval-shaped, coliseum-style arena with its constant flow of angelic inhabitants flying in and out of the seven levels of sky archways. Upon seeing him approach, each stopped, reverently bowing to the archangel.

Towering up out of the side of the tallest mountain peak in Araboth, the gigantic, crystal complex glistened brightly in Heaven's perpetual light. The monolithic structure majestically served as the central hub of all activity throughout the seven realms.

"Soon," the rebel archangel thought to himself while smoothly gliding through one of the upper level archways, "I will be the one orchestrating all activity!"

Once inside, he hovered brightly for a few moments near the domed ceiling, treasuring the aerial view of the seat of Heaven below and making sure everyone inside noticed his arrival. He dearly cherished this building.

"This will be the one thing that I will not change after acquiring the throne!" he told himself.

Seven massive crystal pillars rose up from deep in the mountain, supporting seven levels of balconies, along with the enormous, domed ceiling. Each balcony was tiered, producing an unobstructed view of the throne-room floor, with the sky archways providing aerial access in and out.

Lucifer leisurely descended toward the throne-room floor, slowly gliding in a spiral pattern. He took great pleasure in watching the hushed heavenly host congregating in the balconies, reverently bowing to him, the head of the seraphim, as he regally passed by.

Resonating up throughout the holy cathedral was the heavenly sound of the seraphim choir performing for the Lord. Sitting in his ornately carved throne chair majestically rising out of a water-washed dais, the Almighty Father tranquilly listened to the angelic choir praising him in song.

Two crystal-clear springs flowed out of the rock wall on opposite sides of the natural amphitheater built behind the throne for the choir's performances. Lucifer loved the sound of moving water. To him, it was very soothing. Watching it flow also had a therapeutic effect, momentarily taking him away from the complex planning of the upcoming revolution. From his aerial vantage point, his mind slowly cleared of all thoughts while watching the water make its journey through the throne room.

After flowing around the natural stage, the two streams washed across the raised dais of God's throne to be blessed by the Lord's holy presence. Lazily rolling down seven steps to the throne-room floor, the holy water once again divided into two gently flowing brooks meandering through well-groomed gardens. These tranquil park areas of rich green tropical plants, colorful flowers, and manicured lawns encircled the remainder of the arena floor under the lowest balcony. Converging once again at the opposite end of the crystal building, the two tributaries continued their natural odyssey by flowing out of the massive structure. Cascading down a sheer cliff with a thunderous roar, the holy water then plunged into a deep-blue lake at the base of the mountain.

Passing the bottom balcony level, Lucifer brought his mind back to his current obligation. Alighting before God, the archangel spread his wings, genuflecting before the Lord.

"My morning star," God smiled. "You bring light and inspiration to all who are in your presence."

"Thank you, Father," Lucifer replied, rising. With a flip of his wings, he glided to the amphitheater behind the crystal throne, taking his place at the head of the choir.

Seraphiel, Lucifer's second in rank, led the choir to a thundering encore of the canon they were currently performing. As the angelic host filling the balconies exploded into applause, the choir bowed to the Lord and then to those in the arena showing their appreciation. Turning to Lucifer, Seraphiel acknowledged his replacement by the leader of the seraphim, stepping down from the amphitheater.

God's morning star began a new hymn, his mesmerizing voice hauntingly floating up through the throne room, "Holy, Holy, Holy!"

The baritones suddenly proclaimed, "Lord God Almighty!"

Then came the alto voices, responding, "Hosanna in the Highest!"

The entire choir joined in the refrain, chanting, "Hallelujah! Hallelujah!"

Standing with his two generals in their usual meeting place at the top of The Teeth, Lucifer relaxed, silently enjoying the wind whipping through his long, blond hair. Gazing out at the desert realm of Raquia, the three rebel leaders awaited the warrior party Aanahel had sent out to scout the desolate region and report back.

"My Lord," Aanahel turned to Lucifer, proclaiming, "your report you have been waiting for."

The image of a scout bowing down on knee appeared between the three archangels, reporting, "My Lords, it is as you suspected. The entire realm is deserted. Raphael isn't even here. We will be able to pass through freely without anyone knowing about it. I sent the others into Shamayim to begin gathering information there. They should be reporting back by the time you reach the border."

Aanahel looked at Lucifer, who nodded his acknowledgment of the report.

"Very good," Aanahel responded. "Be ready to report when we arrive."

"As you order!" the soldier replied, his image disappearing from the mountain ledge.

Off in the distance, Lucifer noticed one of the desert's lightning storms approaching off to their left. Turning to his brothers, the lord of the rebel force ordered, "Let's move, before that storm gets here!"

"Yes!" Azrael shouted while turning to obey.

As the rebel leaders spread their wings and leaped out as one over Sagun, the army below burst out in a thunderous battle cry. After training for so long in this dreary realm, the anticipation of seeing Heaven's light again ran high throughout the entire rebel force, which feverishly awaited the sign from their leaders, signaling the time to begin the invasion.

Banking in opposite directions, the two archangels swung a wide arc over the cheering army before gliding back toward the mountain range. Surging into motion, the rebel force began rising up off Sagun's black valley floor. Lucifer spread his wings, launching himself out into the open air. At long last, while leading his legions out into Raquia's desert sky, the most powerful member of the seraphim began his conquest of Heaven.

Masterfully navigating across Raquia, avoiding the lighting storms plaguing the barren region, Lucifer safely escorted his invasion force to the border of Shamayim. Flourishing with dense, colorful jungles and cool, clear lakes, Heaven's third realm was an extreme contrast to Raquia's desert.

A sudden twinge of concern crossed Lucifer's mind after hearing Aanahel's scout's report that Gabriel was currently not in Shamayim. In fact, according to their report, only a few of Heaven's inhabitants were presently enjoying a peaceful respite in the tropical realm.

"Gabriel being gone is not that unusual!" Lucifer justified the small, nagging concern.

Deciding to take advantage of the archangel's absence after reassuring himself, Lucifer turned to Azrael, placing a hand on the general's shoulder for attention.

"Take a detachment in," he ordered. "Swiftly and quietly destroy all who are there, before someone can escape to the Golden City and warn them we are coming."

A look of euphoria suddenly burst across the archangel's face at the prospect of finally being able to kill somebody. Azrael nodded, turning to go as instructed. Lucifer tightened his grip on the subordinate's shoulder.

Turning back puzzled, Lucifer emphasized to him, "Quietly!"

The list of things Azrael actually feared was very short. Lucifer was at the very top of that list. After reassuring the rebel leader that he completely understood, Lucifer released him to go execute his orders.

Flying in low and swift, Azrael and his squad did exactly as their master instructed. With stealth, the insurgents quickly swept the region while silently slaughtering anyone they encountered.

Troubled, Lucifer stood silently looking across the four rivers encircling the Golden City of Heaven.

"Michael is not there!"

Like a warning alarm, those four words kept resonating over and over in his mind.

The scout report confirming his assassins were already silently striking down army leaders throughout the twelve walls, weakening the chain of command on the outer barriers, awaited his arrival in Machanon. With his embedded forces attacking inside, diverting attention inward, and finding his brother absent, the Golden City couldn't be more vulnerable to a full invasion.

Michael, the city's guardian and protector, missing? That just kept bothering Lucifer.

With three kingdoms already under his control, obviously there was no choice but to move forward. Fully committed to conquering all of Heaven, he was not about to settle for what he already possessed.

Pushing his foreboding concerns about Michael's absence aside, Lucifer gave the command, instructing Aanahel, "Launch the invasion, just watch for anything strange or unusual."

Smiling mischievously, Aanahel immediately pointed to Azrael.

With a sharp glare and not a word, Lucifer quietly let his commanding general know he wasn't amused by the joke.

Silently nodding his apology, Aanahel immediately spread his wings, launching himself in the air above the rebel army.

Strategically perching himself on an outcropping of red rocks with an unobstructed view of the city's gold walls glinting in Heaven's perpetual light, Lucifer raised his arms palms up. Spreading his wings to full width, his brilliant, white light erupted across the fertile river valley. In a dreadfully stark contrast to their illuminated leader, the mighty rebel army took to the air behind him, spreading across the sky like the dark wings of an ominous demon.

When the invading force was within range, archers from the first wall sent out a volley of arrows so massive that it blackened the remaining sky over the rivers. Undaunted by the approaching hailstorm of deadly projectiles, the dark cloud of the enemy continued swarming ever closer. The rebel archangels effortlessly erected a barrier of energy in front of the invasion force. Watching in despair, the city defenders witnessed their first volley of arrows uselessly striking the energy barrier. With a pinging ring, like metal striking metal, the death-dealing shafts did nothing but bounce and rain harmlessly down to the valley floor below.

Sweeping over the first wall with the fury of a Raquia storm and savagely slaughtering all defenders within moments, the massive wave of marauders continued surging forward. Invincible behind their energy barrier, the invading army viciously slaughtered every angelic soldier defending the walls, effortlessly taking control of all twelve.

Lucifer and Aanahel stood on the last wall and looked over the battle-ravaged Golden City, silently watching Azrael rapturously butchering city soldiers on the street below.

"What is wrong with this picture?" Lucifer asked while curiously rolling the dead body at his feet over with his greave covered boot. The corpse of an archer lay staring blankly up at dark smoke blackening the sky from several out-of-control fires raging across the devastated city.

"Wrong? We are annihilating them!" Aanahel answered, confused by the question. "Thanks to our insurgents inside, we have had very little true resistance. We're easily crushing what is left. The city is ours!"

"Have you seen any archangels?" Lucifer calmly asked.

Aanahel looked around the battle-torn area before admitting, "Except for ours, no, I haven't."

"Exactly," Lucifer continued. "Why would that be? Raphael not being in Raquia is common. Gabriel not being in Shamayim very well could have been good luck. Michael's absence while his beloved city is under siege...I'm sorry, that is not a coincidence! The archangels are not here for a reason. That means God is fully aware we are attacking. The absence of the Archangel Army is a premeditated move by the Almighty Father, but why hold them back and just let the city fall?"

Both stood quiet, trying to fathom the answer to that question while watching Azrael and his troops continue their annihilation of the remaining pockets of resistance in the streets below.

"How many of our assets did you have to commit to the siege?" Lucifer finally broke the silence.

Pointing back in the direction they had come from, Aanahel responded, "A full two-thirds of our army is still outside the first wall."

"Leave what we have inside to help the inner forces finish here; we are moving on with the rest."

"As you order!"

The rebel army rose into the air over the four rivers, further darkening the hazy Machanon sky. Watching the invading horde moving off in the direction of Zebul brought a small measure of hope to those still faithfully fighting to defend their precious city.

With tears flowing freely down his face, Michael stood painfully watching the bloody massacre taking place in his beloved Golden City. Flanked by his brothers Raphael and Gabriel the three impatiently stood waiting before the Lord in His crystal throne room.

Turning to face God, Gabriel once again implored, "Father, you let them slaughter Innocent Ones in Raquia, now the Golden City is falling! Please! Let us launch the archangel army waiting outside Your throne room. Let us stop this wave of death!"

"Wait!" the Lord commanded, holding up his hand. "Let it play out a little longer. Let us see who faithfully stands with Me, and who commits to defy their Lord, God!"

Eerily silent observers filled campus, quietly watching the rebel force ominously passing over the Angelic Institute of Learning in the fifth realm, Zebul.

Azrael began descending, intent on slaughtering them all for not dropping to their knees in Lucifer's presence. None deserved to live for their spineless lack of commitment, choosing not to unite with either side of the battle.

Stopping him, Lucifer commanded, "Save your strength! You can deal with them later. For right now, we must move forward with caution. It has been too easy so far. We have yet to encounter the full strength of the archangels!"

As Lucifer's army disappeared into the distance, the silence encompassing the campus was suddenly broken by an agonizing cry from Zephrom.

Racing over to where Buer stood next to the holy prophet, Gadreel looked questioningly at the ethics instructor, who stood there, looking confused.

The holy prophet was on his knees, sobbing uncontrollably into his hands.

Bending down, the headmaster of the institute put a concerned hand on his friend's shoulder, asking, "Zephrom, what is it? What is wrong?"

"The light of Heaven!" the prophet choked out between sobs.

Once again, Gadreel looked up to Buer to get some form of a clarification, but all the teacher of logic could do was shrug his shoulders in confusion.

"Zephrom, you are making no sense! What about the light of Heaven?"

"I can't see it anymore!" Zephrom shouted, dropping his hands and staring up into the sky. "It is gone!"

Falling over backward in shock, a look of pure horror transfixed Gadreel's face. Looking up to Buer, the instructor of logic and ethics held his hand over his mouth, obviously just as terrified by the prophet's revelation.

A future without the light of Heaven.

God's voice suddenly reverberated throughout the crystal chamber, commanding the archangels. "It is time! Go now! Stop the insurrection before it reaches my throne!"

Gabriel, Michael, and Raphael immediately spread their wings in unison, launching up and flying out of the arena through the sky arches.

Outside, the Archangel Army waiting in the valley at the base of the mountain immediately rose into motion at the sight of their three leaders soaring in the direction of Mathey. Knowing they were about to engage in a battle against their angelic brothers, Heaven's mighty defending force solemnly took to the sky.

Kneeling submissively at the edge of the balcony, Lilith's heart beat wildly while waiting for Lucifer's image to dissipate from the air above. Hiding behind the dark locks of hair draping from her bowed head, her angelic face lit up with euphoria. Her husband's complete domination of Heaven was about to reach its climax. Slowly rising up on bare feet, Lilith stood gazing out across the all-too-familiar view of the busy city below.

"Everything is about to change!"

With the new sense of rapture, Lilith slowly turned away from the city, solemnly stepping to the edge of their balcony's pond. Spreading both her arms and wings for balance, a little trick Lucifer had taught her, she carefully began wading across the surface of the pool. Reaching into the waterfall cascading at the far end, she delicately extracted the blue light mounted there.

With a light thrust of her wings while still cupping the glowing orb tenderly in both hands, Lilith began rising up into the air high above the penthouse. After gently releasing the shimmering ball, she slowly descended back to the balcony on outstretched wings. Perching once again upon its edge with growing anticipation, the female angel silently watched the blue orb hovering over the angelic city. Signaling her network of revolutionists to launch their coup, the floating ball of light suddenly exploded into a brilliant flash that radiated out across the sky.

Lilith began jumping up and down, hysterically cheering with triumph. All her hard work, the deceit and seductions, was set into motion below, ensuring Lucifer's victory and her at his side as queen of Heaven.

The pulse of light slowly dissipated into shimmering dust, falling gently down upon curious bystanders in the streets. Crippling assaults on strategic targets inside the city quickly transformed that sense of wonder into panic and screams of pure terror.

Darkening the Mathey sky like two churning thunderclouds, the massive opposing armies violently met head on, clashing in a tempest of vicious combat. Deadly bolts of energy striking force fields or exploding through the bodies of unprotected warriors lit up the heavens, similar to lightning in a Raquia storm.

The brutal battle instantly filled the air with the deafening sounds of metal crashing against metal and ear-piercing screams of combatants receiving mortal wounds or death blows. Blood, severed appendages, and dead or fatally wounded bodies raining down from the aerial mayhem began turning the white marble of the buildings beneath the battle to a grisly crimson.

Sitting in His ghostly quiet throne room with a tear slowly trickling down His cheek, the Almighty Father's heart tore with pain as He watched His children brutally slaying each other.

Quietly perched on the edge of his balcony, mentally monitoring the multitude of events unfolding in the war around him, Lucifer smiled to himself. While masterfully orchestrating his troop's movements along the ever-changing tides and eddies of the brutally bloody battle, anticipation coursed through every fiber of the rebel leader's being.

Victory was so close that he could almost taste it. Pausing for a moment, he calmly asked, "Have you come to join me, Brother?"

In spite of the fact that he had the tower heavily guarded in every direction, Michael stood quietly on the terrace behind him. Lucifer smiled to himself once again, expecting no less from an archangel. "The truth be known," Michael replied, gazing out at the movements of the conflict in the sky, "I have come to kill you for the unforgivable massacre you have committed, but Father has forbade it. Instead, I have been commanded to take you to Him."

"Aw, our merciful Father," Lucifer cooed, turning to face his sibling. "And you blindly comply without hesitation."

"Do you demand any less from those who follow you?" Michael quipped.

"True," Lucifer responded. "You got me there!"

"But you will not comply, will you?"

"You know me well, don't you, Brother?" Lucifer grinned sarcastically.

"I had hoped not," Michael replied. He smiled before calmly stating, "If you wish to keep that pretty head upon your shoulders, I suggest you turn around and go back inside, little one."

Peering around his brother's huge bulk, Lucifer could see Lilith stopping in midstep, her short sword in hand, trying to sneak up behind the archangel. Nodding for his wife to return to their suite, she turned without hesitation, running quickly to do as he bid.

"And I don't suppose you just flying away would be an option either?" he asked.

"You too know me well, Brother," Michael responded, drawing his broad sword.

With a sound like a clap of thunder and a shower of sparks from metal striking metal, the two archangels unfurled their wings, engaging each other in a merciless flurry of deadly sword-play. From her hiding place inside, Lilith held her breath in awe, watching the two combatants gracefully flowing through the well-rehearsed moves in their grim dance of death.

So engaged in his efforts to break through Michael's defensive moves, Lucifer did not see the shiny metal of a greave covered boot attacking from above until it was way too late. Striking him full in the face, the blow sent the rebel archangel tumbling uncontrollably across the balcony. With a massive shower of water, he came to rest on his hands and knees in the shallow pond.

He could think of only one archangel capable of sneaking up on him like that.

Shedding water while slowly standing up, his assumption was confirmed by Gabriel alighting on the terrace next to their brother. Streaks of Heaven's light filtering down through the canopy of angels battling in clouds of smoke rising from the burning city were dancing brightly across his mirror like, full-body, battle armor.

Turning to Michael, Gabriel bitterly growled, "Stop playing around!"

Michael gave his sibling an incredulous look, as if asking, "Who is playing around?"

"It appears to me," Lucifer commented while casually retrieving his sword from the bottom of the pond where he had dropped it, "I am going to have to do some serious reprimanding of the soldiers I left guarding this tower. That's two of you they have let through!"

"You don't have to worry about that, Brother," Gabriel replied, smirking facetiously. "I have taken care of it for you already."

Nodding his head, Lucifer acknowledged he understood there was no one left alive for him to punish.

"In that case, Brothers," the rebel leader responded, returning Gabriel's smile while producing a second sword in his free hand, "Let's continue to play!"

Spreading his wings, Lucifer launched himself out of the pond, raining water down upon his two brothers. Tucking his wings back close to his body and crossing his arms in front of him, the insurrectionist made a 180-degree spin in midair, enabling him to land behind his two opponents and facing them.

Together, Michael and Gabriel created a dome of energy over their heads to protect their eyes from the spray of water while twisting around and swinging their swords to face where their brother would land.

Lucifer unfurled his wings, suspending his descent, and his brothers' weapons passed harmlessly beneath his feet. Then, laying his wings back to back, he continued his descent to the terrace, unfolding his arms and thrusting his swords at both opponents. Michael used the metal gauntlet of his free arm to swat the flat of the sword away and thrust his own weapon at his brother. Nimbly avoiding the second blade's sharp tip striking at him, Gabriel quickly threw a blast of energy at Lucifer, harmlessly bouncing it off the rebel leader's protection shield. Quickly following suit, Michael flung a second, almost ineffective blast that glanced off the shield.

Noticing their brother yielding a step to the crushing pressure behind the two bursts of energy, both archangels began pummeling him with a rapid salvo of the deadly blasts. Anxiously watching Lucifer retreating one painful step at a time under their merciless bombardment, the two suddenly changed tactics when he finally stepped under the massive gazebo. Switching to the outdoor pavilion's marble pillars, the two began throwing concentrated pulses of energy at the huge columns, shattering each one in an explosion of stone shards that rocked the entire tower all the way down to its foundations. The pavilion's marble roof came crashing down upon

Lucifer with the roaring sound of thunder and a billowing cloud of fine, white dust.

Lilith couldn't breathe. She could feel the entire weight of the marble gazebo pressing down upon her own chest while watching her husband disappear under the crushing mountain of white stone.

She couldn't even scream. Her beloved, he couldn't be gone. It wasn't done. They still needed to take the Crystal Palace.

Collapsing on the floor in the middle of the penthouse with her wings wrapped tightly against her body, she began sobbing hysterically, spastically rocking back and forth in pain.

Outside on the deck, suspiciously watching for any sign of movement in the pile of rubble as the cloud of marble dust began to slowly drift away, neither of the two archangels could believe it was over.

Shaking his head, rejecting the notion that Lucifer could be dead, Michael emphatically exclaimed, "No way! Not this easily, not with him!"

"Quiet!" Gabriel commanded, raising his hand for silence.

Listening intently, Michael could hear a faint rumbling coming from the former outdoor pavilion.

He knew it. There was no way Lucifer could be defeated that easily.

The sound from the collapsed pile of marble grew in intensity, becoming a loud roar. Cautiously waiting, both archangels stood preparing for whatever their brother was about to do.

They didn't have long to wait. With the clap of thunder, a large portion of one of the broken marble columns came exploding off the mountain of stone, hurtling directly at them. Mentally grabbing the massive section of pillar in unison and using its own momentum, they safely guided the deadly projectile over their heads. Shaking the entire tower, the huge chunk of stone came bouncing to rest at the far end of the pond, crashing up against the rock fountain.

Erupting out from under the gazebo's debris, Lucifer landed on the balcony between his brothers and his would-be stone grave. Crouching in a three-point stance, he glared venomously at Michael and Gabriel while quietly leaning against his own down-pointed sword. Slowly pressing the fingertips of his free hand into balcony floor, it began cracking loudly like ice, quickly spreading out toward his brothers in the shape of a V.

Anticipating the marble deck falling out from under their feet, both archangels reflexively spread their wings.

Completely buried in the marble floor, Lucifer quickly jerked back his hand, grinning triumphantly. As if tugging a rug out from under his brother's feet, erupting upward instead of collapsing, the cracking wedge area of the deck became deadly stone shrapnel, taking both archangels by surprise. Flinging Michael completely off the balcony and out into open air, the blast sent Gabriel crashing through penthouse.

Tumbling uncontrollably past her, Lilith swiftly ducked under one of his outstretched wings, fearfully scrambling to get out of the giant archangel's way. Witnessing Gabriel's huge bulk slamming up against the far wall, she couldn't believe he hit with such force, that the white marble cracked behind him. What was even more shocking was seeing him stand up as if nothing had happened. Shaking the debris out of his wings, she watched him swiftly stride right back outside while growling to himself.

Thus, with the angelic war raging in the background, the three archangels' epic battle continued, with energy bolts bouncing off force fields and lighting up the top of the half-destroyed tower like a flashing beacon high over the war-torn city.

VIETORIST I

Unable to tolerate his children's senseless violence anymore, God finally commanded, "STOP!"

Out of sheer habit, the sound of the Lord's demand booming throughout the realms of Heaven brought all battling to an abrupt halt.

Satisfied with everyone's immediate response, God continued, ordering, "Lucifer, attend Me!"

Leaving his two brothers behind on the demolished terrace, Lucifer spread his wings and launched himself skyward. Boldly hovering before the rebel army, his battle armor blazed brilliantly from streaks of angelic light filtering through the smoke-patched sky.

Shouting loud and clear for all to hear the unmistakable defiance in his voice, Lucifer replied, "I will no longer obey Your commands!"

In the blink of an eye, the rebel leader suddenly found himself kneeling unwillingly before the throne of his Father, the Almighty King of Heaven! Feeling the sharp edges of Michael and Gabriel's swords crossed precariously beneath his throat, he instinctively began searching his surroundings for an advantage to exploit in an attempt to escape. Glaring down at him with disappointment clearly reflected in his ancient eyes, God sat upon the crystal throne Lucifer had fought so hard to possess. Packing all seven balconies of the Crystal Palace, murmuring spectators mulled about, gawking down at him and his two brothers.

"If I were you, I wouldn't move," Gabriel growled, applying the slightest amount of new pressure on Lucifer's throat with his razor-sharp weapon for added emphasis.

"No, do move!" Michael countered, smiling eagerly.

"Enough!" God commanded, nodding at the two archangels standing next to their prostrate brother. Reluctantly removing their swords from their captive's throat, Michael and Gabriel slowly withdrew from the throne room, leaving Lucifer kneeling by himself before his Father.

"My shining star," the Lord finally asked, "why have you defied me and given rise to this insurrection? You and your followers have brought death and destruction throughout the realms of Heaven!"

"Because," Lucifer hissed, boldly speaking freely to the Lord, "like a phoenix burning brightly out of the ashes of its own destruction, I will rebuild the heavens with the illumination of my own light! Then all will pay homage to me while gazing upon the beauty and splendor of what I create!"

"My child," God patiently began reprimanding his archangel, "do you not know that your light and all life, in fact, all of creation, come from Me, your Lord and God—from Me alone!"

"You have the power and ability to fill the VOID with all the same wondrous beauty you created here in Heaven," Lucifer countered, "but instead, You apathetically sit here and do nothing but listen to constant praising about how almighty and wonderful you are. As ruler of Heaven, I will not be so lethargic, instead, I will bring the VOID to life!"

"Your ambition exceeds your abilities." The annoyance in God's voice was unmistakably growing clearer as He continued, "My patience is growing thin with your insolence!"

"If You are so almighty and knowing," the rebel leader retorted, "then why didn't you see this coming and stop it before it started?"

"Your arrogance is the seed of your downfall," the Lord snapped. "You presume that I didn't know."

Completely caught off guard by the Lord's revelation, Lucifer stood there, gaping at his Father in silence. "You knew and did not stop it? All Your children who love and worship You, who blindly fought and died in battle for You...You just coldly allowed to do so, when You could have prevented this war from the start? What kind of merciless God are You?"

"The kind of God who wants all to see the wrath I will bestow upon any who choose to stand against Me!"

The anger in the Lord's voice was now unmistakable. "Behold the power of your Almighty Creator!"

Booming like thunder, God's voice rang throughout all seven realms.

Seething with anger, Lucifer jealously watched God mercifully begin healing every injured angel from both sides of the battle. Then, adding insult to injury, the Lord brought the entire heavenly host to its knees in adoration by breathing life back into all the dead.

"I, and I alone, give life!" the Lord God Almighty continued to admonish harshly. "And I alone will decide when it is taken!"

The smoldering flame of Lucifer's rage grew to an inferno while watching God effortlessly recreate his army's destruction, returning everything to its former splendor. By using a similar display of his own power after eliminating the Lord for good, demonstrating to all his own might and glory, all of Heaven would be bowing to him right now.

With the fire of his jealousy welling up inside of him, the intensity of the rebel archangel's white light slowly began to increase.

"You, along with all those you deceived into sharing your desire to occupy my throne room," the anger in God's voice continued to escalate, "I now grant you your wish!"

The entire rebel force suddenly found themselves standing before the Lord, next to their prostate leader.

"You will all, along with the rest of Heaven," the Almighty continued, "learn the price each will pay for the crimes committed against Me and all of your brethren!"

Turning to his generals, Aanahel and Azrael, Lucifer cried out with rage, "Destroy Him!"

"We are unable to move," Azrael hissed, trying unsuccessfully to avert his eyes from the ever-increasing brilliance of Lucifer's light.

Redoubling his efforts to burn God out of existence, the rebel archangel continued increasing his own intense radiance. Scalding steam began rising off the water flowing through the throne room from the extreme heat. The brilliance of Lucifer's luminous power soon became too overpowering to be near. With the air temperature in the throne room rising beyond tolerance, all the angelic spectators in the balconies began fleeing to safety through the sky arches. Circling the skies in mass confusion outside the crystal arena, the denizens of Heaven shrank back in fear as white-hot light came exploding out of the archway openings.

Looking down, the frenzied flock could see the spectacular image of the crystal arena walls glowing brilliantly, reflecting off the deep-blue water at the foot of the mountain.

Fiery tentacles of concentrated liquid light erupting from Lucifer's blazing form whipped haphazardly back and forth throughout the throne room. Writhing with excruciating pain, his entire army stood helpless, irreparably branded by the violently lashing strands of fire. Unable to escape the scorching brilliance of their leader's powerful attack, it was not long before all the beauty God originally endowed each angelic being with was seared completely away. A pitiful mass of ugly, black charred creatures was left. Nothing more than a reflection of their individual selfishness and greed was all that remained of the once powerful invasion force.

Looking up to see God emerging out of the scorching steam in full glory, passing through his searing strings of liquid light as if they weren't there, Lucifer angrily shook in disbelief. "There was no way his Father could be completely unaffected by his light at this intensity!" he told himself.

"Look around you!" the Lord commanded. "I created you to be the greatest and brightest of all your brethren in Heaven! However, you poison the good I gave you for your own selfish splendor! You use your brilliance to attract and corrupt other rebel angels. Look now upon what your deceit, lies, and treachery have created!"

Looking at the horrifying sight of the grotesque horde surrounding him, Lucifer suddenly realized his attack on his Father had only resulted in incinerating his own rebel force.

"Insolent child! All that you are, I gave to you!" God angrily continued admonishing. "And now I take it away!"

Reaching out, the Lord pulled all the brilliant light inside of Lucifer away, crushing it in his hand. The burning radiance and the tentacles of liquid fire permeating throughout the Crystal Palace suddenly dissipated. Collapsing to the floor, Lucifer lay with exhaustion for a moment, completely drained from his failed effort to destroy his Father.

Lying there in a haze, the defeated archangel slowly began to examine himself. The bone-chilling realization of the repulsive creature he had become without his precious white light spread its icy grip throughout his limp body. The repulsive sight of his skin and the feathers of his wings—a hideous, jet-black color—brought burning, acidic bile to his throat. Releasing a long, pitiful moan echoing throughout the Crystal Chamber, Lucifer also realized his long, silky mane of white hair was gone. Slowly turning with eyes burning white fire and looking up to the Lord, he could not believe his Father would leave him as this hairless, disfigured creature.

"You will no longer be known as Lucifer, my shining star," God vehemently continued, glaring down at the crumpled form by His feet. "From now on, I will call you by your true name, Satan, the deceiver!"

Then raising His voice so that all of Heaven would hear His wrath, the Almighty Father proclaimed, "Behold the punishment for all who chose to oppose and disobey the Lord, your God!"

In a mighty display of His awesome power, God took hold of Sagun, the first realm of Heaven, forcefully tearing it away from the other realms. He then threw it to the farthest part of the VOID away from Heaven's light.

"There now lies the kingdom you so coveted!" He said to Satan. "I now exile you to that realm, always apart from the light of Heaven!"

After spitting the fire of His anger into Sagun and renaming the dark realm, Hell, He flung Satan, along with all of his evil army, down into the fiery kingdom.

Some, however, began crying out for mercy while hurtling across the expanse of the VOID and down toward the dark pit of Hell. Having compassion for those few, the Almighty Father brought them back to His throne room again.

Looking at each one groveling on the floor before Him, seeing their genuine repentance, God took pity, proclaiming, "You I sentence to watch over the souls of those I will create—souls which are not clean enough to enter Heaven but not corrupted enough for Satan to claim. Like those souls, you will one day see the light of your heavenly home again."

Exiling them to the desolate, storm-swept region of Raquia, the second realm of Heaven, God continued with his trial. Gadreel, Zephrom, and all of those who stood by and did nothing to resist the rebel army in the defense of Heaven found themselves before the Lord in his throne room.

"When the army of evil rose to destroy your Creator, you did nothing to defend Me! Instead, you cringed in your ivory towers, waiting to see who would be the victor. For your lack of faith in Me, your Lord, I sentence you to mortal bodies, stripped of your angelic spirit. You will be the first line of defense against Satan and his evil in the universes I will create. At the end of time, you too will see the light of Heaven and once again regain your angelic stature."

After removing the heavenly spirit from each, creating mortal bodies for them, God placed the group of former angels in Shamayim, the third realm of Heaven.

With all of Heaven bowing in awe and all those in Hell cringing in fear, the Lord Almighty began filling the VOID with a multitude of universes and a diverse assortment of life. Taking a section of what He had created and placing Raquia there, he renamed the realm purgatory and then renamed Shamayim as Lysta'cu'mha, setting it next to purgatory. After creating other universes special to Him in the same area, God named the whole section, Myshunar, meaning "Blessed Worlds," and decreeing, "Satan and his followers are banned from entering the universes I have placed in Myshunar!"

Staring up at all the wondrous universes God was creating in the VOID, Satan stood transfixed, systematically assessing each one through the burning white slits of his eyes. Contemplating what he would have done different, Hell's new master was completely oblivious to the throng of fallen angels silently waiting to see what their leader would do. Slowly emerging from his private revelations, Satan quickly became aware of the hushed mass intently gazing at him.

"Prostrate yourself before your king!" he commanded, watching the ugly horde obey at once.

Satisfied with their immediate response, the new ruler of Hell went on, decreeing, "All of you, and this entire realm, now belong to me!"

Noticing a pile of black feathers at his feet, the dark lord began examining his wings. It appeared he had been molting for quite some time. All that remained of his beautiful white-down appendages were two black, leather-covered membranes.

Stepping past Aanahel, Satan entered one of the many caves that pocked the face of The Teeth, announcing as he disappeared into the cavern's darkness, "I need time to think!"

Back in Araboth, after observing the work He had just finished, God declared, "It is good!"

Seraphiel, now officially head of the seraphim, began leading the angelic choir in praise of the Lord. Sitting back on His crystal throne, a smile of satisfaction brightened His ancient face, and the Lord relaxed to the choir's lively melody.

Holy, holy, holy, Lord God Almighty,
Heaven's filled with Your glory,
Hosanna in the Highest!

Silently staring at the images of Kana's tale slowly fading from the center of the room, everyone in the Mystic Arts Class sat wondering the same thing: "How do you respond to something like that?"

After giving them all a few moments to absorb what they had just seen, the prince continued, explaining, "What you just witnessed is written in an ancient book known as the *Tablets of Time*. They are the recordings of what took place in Heaven by one of the original White Witches, a great prophet known as Zephrom."

Connie broke the class's silence, asking, "The Zephrom we saw in Heaven?"

"Yes," Kana replied while indicating himself and Shilo, "White Witches are decedents of the angels who stood neutral during the war in Heaven. Their exile is the future you heard Zephrom envisioning, a future without Heaven's light.

"In the story, you heard God charging the White Witches with the task of protecting the universes from Satan and his fallen angels, who became known in the *Tablets of Time* as the Black Witches.

"Then there is the group of fallen angels who were sentenced to purgatory. These very obscure beings are referenced in the *Tablets of Time* as the Gray Witches. The *Tablets of Time* also refer to the trial God held in Heaven, sentencing all of those who did not show their allegiance to the Him, as Vietorist I.

"Everything you have just seen and heard happened in what is called the First Age. The beginning of the Second Age is marked by the creation of God's children. Placing them on earth, in a garden named Eden, and naming them man, the Lord promised His children they could live forever in the beautiful garden if they would always obey Him. But Lucifer also heard of the coming of man from his dark spies. He set long prepared plans into motion, knowing that these children were very special in God's heart. The dark one succeeded in touching man's soul, which brought such anger to God that it was heard throughout the universes!

"The Lord took Eden away from earth, placing it in Myshunar and commanding the White Witches to concentrate solely on guarding man against Satan. That is when the White Witches became your guardian angels. In the early days, they were freer about exposing themselves to man on earth. During that time, the children of God stood in awe of our mystical powers, mistaking White Witches for gods. Whether Egyptian, Aztec, Greek, Roman, Viking, or other, we were the origins of the myths, legends, and religions shaping each of those cultures. Satan's carefully orchestrated dark web of lies naturally had a hand in turning man toward this falsehood.

"After that," the prince brought his tale to a conclusion, "White Witches vowed to continue their mandated task while secretly hidden from man's sight until the time of Phycu."

"What's Phycu?" Mr. Wenstrom spoke up, completely fascinated by the young man's tale.

"It is the day that Satan is driven away from earth forever," the White Witch prince answered. "And God's children will live free of his evil once again."

Unable to hold back any longer, Mitch finally blurted out the question on everybody's mind, "Seriously?"

Mythical creatures being real, the beginning of the universe, and a person actually being unconsciously influenced by other beings—they were all having trouble believing any of it.

Realizing everything he had shared was all a little too fantastic for everyone in the class to accept, Kana decided to demonstrate. The only way they would be able to succeed with what was ahead of them was by everyone accepting reality now, before moving on.

Turning to his ward, the White Witch prince continued, calmly stating, "Ryon, I am what you would call your guardian angel."

Turning a little ashen in color, Ryon realized he could feel the prince's power inside of him. Panicking, he almost flipped his desk over backward.

"Get out of my head!"

Reaching over and tenderly taking Ryon's flailing hands in her own, Shilo tried soothing the young man's fear, while giving her brother a sharp look of disgust.

Calmly murmuring, "It's all right," the princess reached up and gently turned his head while looking him directly in the eye and explaining, "He can't get out. He has always been there, guiding you. The two of you grew up together this way, just like everyone in this room has, with their own White Witch guardian."

Noting that his sister's explanation did little to convince anyone else in the room, the prince decided to change tactics, moving on to an issue needing to be confronted sooner or later.

"Listen and take to heart what I say to you now." Kana stood up, raising a strong, white-gloved hand to gain their attention, his shimmering cape swirling behind him. "Be alert always for evil; it lurks everywhere. I say to you, it even resides in this room!" the prince gravely stated while turning to face Mádeohn. "Do not worry, Mádeohn, I do not challenge you. I have a feeling the battle would be more for your self-preservation than it would be for the cause."

"I am but a weary creature tortured by fate," Mádeohn replied, sighing with the relief of no longer having to hide the truth. "You have whatever help the Prince of Darkness can provide."

"Wait a minute!" Confused, Ryon slowly turned away from Shilo, interrupting loudly, "I don't understand!"

Looking gravely at his longtime best friend, Mádeohn dispassionately explained, "My real father is not dead, Ryon. My mother made a pact with the Devil, and here I am. Satan is my father."

MÁDEOHN'S TALE

"You? Are the son of Satan?"

Slumping back in his chair, stunned beyond disbelief at what just came out of his best friend's mouth, Ryon threw his hands up in the air, exclaiming, "This just keeps getting better and better!"

Sitting down next to Connie in the circle with everyone else, Kana patiently stated, "Ryon, you know deep down inside that what you have seen and heard here today is the truth."

Challenging the prince, Ryon retorted, "Do I, or is it just you inside my head saying so?"

"Actually, it is," Kana admitted, hammering away at his ward's doubt. "If you acknowledge that fact, then it stands to reason that the rest is also possible. Besides, how do you explain what you did at the lake the night of the party?"

That little dagger hit home. The entire class sat silently waiting for Ryon to respond, each dying to know what had really happened that night on the beach. Not giving him a chance to speak, the White Witch prince pressed on, dropping another bomb on him.

"As for Mádeohn, you owe him big time for saving your life after you passed out!"

After years of hanging out together, Ryon could tell when Mádeohn was telling the truth or bullshitting by the look in his eyes. Right now, his best friend's face said Kana was telling the truth.

Hesitantly, Ryon began relaxing, slowly accepting the White Witch's presence inside of him. Feeling the change, Kana sat back in his chair, letting up on the pressure he was applying to get his ward to believe. Sensing the change also, Shilo began gently releasing her grip on his arms.

Slowly exhaling, Ryon locked eyes with Mádeohn, asking his best friend point-blank, "You mean you knew all these years that your father was not really dead? Ever since you could remember, you knew who your father was, what he was? How could you live all this time as if nothing were wrong and always have that shadow hovering over you?"

Looking at his friend sympathetically, Mádeohn took up the instructing lead, addressing the whole class.

"Let me start by telling you a little about my father and Hell so that you can understand my story a little better."

Starting his tale, again images came to life in the center of the room, just like they had with the White Witch prince's narrative.

"As Kana told you, Satan and his followers were thrown into the farthest part of the VOID from Heaven, a place the Lord christened as Hell. A realm of dark holes, damp caves, swampy caverns, and eternal fire spat there by God's anger.

"Proclaiming himself king of the desolate domain, my father makes all he dominates bow in worship to him. His first attempt at creating life was a grotesque creature he called a dreg."

Mádeohn could feel the tension in the room increase tenfold after creating an image of one of the vile-looking demons from Hell in the center of the room. Standing erect like a man but with delicate web like wings, the creature's feet and hands were clawed, and its mouth had dozens of needle-sharp teeth.

"Like anything else Satan breathes his foul breath into," Mádeohn went on, "they are dark and hideous. During the ages, my father learned to disguise the grotesqueness of his creatures with illusions, but deep down, they all possess the ugly darkness of their master.

"When the Lord filled the VOID with the universes and all their wonders, it made Satan very jealous—obsessed, constantly searching for ways to corrupt or destroy what God had made. His mightiest attempt, during the First Age, was on a world called Caran."

The image in the center of the room slowly changed, depicting an ancient war-torn world. Forgetting about the White Witch prince's presence inside his head, Ryon sat forward in his seat, completely engrossed by the epic, mystical battle taking place in the middle of the classroom.

"Many years he spent establishing his evil forces on that world." Mádeohn went on, "His main objective was capturing of the soul of Karen, a mighty warlock who ruled on the planet centuries earlier. The warlock's soul was trapped in an emerald about the same size of a man's fist. The stone became known as Arein."

The class sat gazing in awe at the beautiful green jewel appearing before them as Mádeohn's tale continued.

"Controlling Caran also gave Satan a major stronghold in the center of the universe to spread his evil dark power from, but he lost that war. The Gray Witches put a stop to his plan, stealing Arein—and Karen's soul—and hiding it so that Satan would never be able to possess it.

"My father continues to hunt for the gem so that he can claim Karen's soul. However, when his dark spies informed him of the creation of God's children on earth, he quickly refocused his efforts on their corruption, aggressively pursuing that goal today."

Shifting his tale, the images of Caran began to fade.

"You're all familiar with those who have been corrupted by evil in earth's history."

Everyone became extremely uncomfortable, watching horrific images from the past fill the center of the room. The images

showed centuries of people being terrorized, brutally slaughtered, or enslaved by tyrants whose objectives were wealth and
power.

"What's concealed more often than not are the tragedies that
take place privately in our own homes."

The gruesome, historic scenes faded into a shockingly brutal
image of a man viciously pulling a young girl up a flight of stairs
by her hair. Savagely dragging the child, who was kicking and
screaming with terror, into a bedroom, he callously dumped her
on the floor before violently backhanding the little one across the
face.

Jumping at the sickening sound of the blow, Connie's breath
painfully caught in her throat. Watching the young one lie silently
dazed on the floor with a slow, crimson stream of blood trickling
from her swollen lip, Connie began feeling sick to her stomach.

"My mother was abused as a child," Mádeohn quietly
explained the ugly scene. "Running away from home at age fifteen
to get away from it, she quickly discovered life on the streets of a
big city wasn't much different.

"Starving for love and acceptance, my mom fell in with the
wrong crowd, becoming hooked on drugs and turning to prostitution to support her habit."

"That poor child," Rhonda's heart tore at the thought of what
Mrs. Cane must have been through. Looking at Mádeohn sympathetically, she lamented, "We never knew!"

"Until I told you today, no one in this town does. For her protection, it must remain that way to the rest of the world outside
this classroom. You will see why shortly."

Looking around the room, Mádeohn knew he had everyone's
unquestionable support in his request, continuing, "You all need
to realize, in spite of what I'm showing you, she's the same person
you have all come to know and love—the same woman who continually reaches out to the youth of this community, the way she
has always done since moving here."

Confidently speaking for the rest of the class, Ryon reassured his best friend, "No worries!"

Mádeohn silently nodded his thanks before continuing on with his narrative. "What I'm showing you right now is what you need to know about how I came to be."

The image of a handsome young man materialized in the center of the classroom.

"A youth named David, the son of the biggest drug syndicate lord in the city, became infatuated with my mom. He repeatedly asked for Maria, paying for her services just to be with her."

Confused, Connie interrupted, asking, "Wait a minute, I thought your mom's name was Sylvia?"

"It is," Mádeohn replied, "but wanting to forget her miserable childhood, she never told anyone her real name during this period of her life.

"Falling in love with the young prostitute, David took Maria off the streets, moving her in with him. They lived together in a penthouse at the top of one of the buildings his father owned, and David bought her anything she wanted. For the first time in her life, the pain and misery of her past were gone. She was happy!"

The class watched the young Maria cheerfully shopping in upscale clothing stores and enjoying being pampered at luxurious spas. Dining at extravagant restaurants, the couple held private parties in exclusive nightclubs that only the elite could afford to rent out. The new man in her life constantly provided Maria with all the money, jewelry, and drugs the young woman could ever want.

Walking in the rooftop garden of the penthouse one night, she thought to herself that life couldn't get any better. Then, under the full moon and with the lights of the city glowing in the background, David got down on one knee and romantically proposed.

A month later, in that same garden underneath a star-jeweled sky, David and Maria wed in a very expensive ceremony paid for by the young man's father. With hundreds of guest, thousands of flowers, a live band, and catering by a French chef, the night was a fairy-tale dream come true for the young woman.

"That's when everything changed," Mádeohn went on soberly. "Mom started suspecting David was cheating on her. One night, at a party they were hosting in the penthouse, she silently caught David with another woman. When the party was over and she was strung out on both drugs and alcohol, she finally confronted him!"

The class watched the two arguing in the middle of their living room, empty liquor bottles and drugs were everywhere, and the young man abruptly reached out and slapped the girl.

Jumping at the sound of the sudden attack, everyone in the classroom sat helplessly watching the two fight as David savagely tried raping his wife. With him tearing at her clothes, deeply buried memories of her father's sexual attacks began welling up inside Maria, and she viciously fought back. Trapped on the floor beneath her husband, she desperately reached for the first thing she could get her hands on, grabbing a carelessly discarded alcohol bottle. With all the pent-up rage from a childhood filled with physical abuse, she swung it, bashing it across the side of his head.

The whole class cheered. "Sorry," Connie apologized, looking embarrassingly at Mádeohn.

He smiled, nodding to the image in the center of the room.

Rolling the limp form off of her, Maria tried checking for a pulse before realizing he was dead. Head spinning from the alcohol and drugs, she knew that, along with her husband, she had just killed her perfect world. Panic gripped her, and she began sobbing hysterically.

"Quite a mess you've gotten yourself into, isn't it?"

Startled by the sound of the female voice, the young woman jumped, letting out a small screech. Two dark figures, a man and a woman, stood in the shadows.

Trying to cover herself up the best she could with her ripped clothing, Maria asked, "Who are you?"

Moving out of the darkness and stepping over the corpse, the very sensuous woman knelt down by the tattered girl on the floor.

Recognizing Lilith as the fallen angel stepped into view, shock spread through the classroom.

"Don't be frightened," Satan's wife cooed, "we are here to help."

"Help, how?" Maria asked between sobs.

Nodding to the dark figure still standing in the shadows, Lilith answered, "My husband is a very powerful man. More powerful than this piece of shit's father. He can make all this go away forever, but there is a price!"

Maria suspiciously looked at the woman through the fog of the drugs, replying, "There always is."

"That is right," Lilith agreed, smiling. "There always is, but this is such a small price for a lifetime of peace and prosperity—never worrying again about what happened here tonight, or about anyone ever hurting you again!"

"What do you want?" the girl asked suspiciously.

The figure in the shadows finally spoke.

"In your short life, child, you have learned the art of lovemaking very well. One night of passion beyond your wildest dreams is all we ask, and I promise you, this will all go away forever."

Maria looked at the woman kneeling next to her, asking, "How do I know you're telling me the truth and not just two sick people taking advantage of me?"

"I guess you don't," Lilith smiled, reaching out and gently brushing a tear from the girl's cheek.

Maria closed her eyes. There was something in the stranger's touch that felt warm and comforting, filling her with the sensation she could trust these two and that everything would be all right. It wasn't long after she had run away from home that Maria hardened herself to the idea of selling her body to get something in return. If these two told the truth, being free of everything in her life up to this night would certainly be worth it.

Opening her eyes, she slowly nodded agreement to the mysterious woman next to her.

Lilith stood up, gently helping the girl to her feet. With Lucifer's eyes glowing brightly in the shadows, his wife tenderly led Maria by the elbow toward her own bedroom suite.

"Don't go!" Rhonda whispered, dreadfully watching the three disappear from the front room of the penthouse.

"I was conceived during that night of lust." Mádeohn went on, "Revealing to my mother who they really were before the night was over, she remorsefully realized too late that she sold her soul to the Devil!"

The next morning, the two strangers were gone, and Maria was arrested for murdering her husband. The demon couple told the truth, though, because from that day on, it seemed the right people with the right opportunities came to her out of nowhere at just the right times. It eventually became evident during the trial that she was pregnant, and David's family vigorously fought to get custody of the child when it was born. Her appointed lawyer not only skillfully proved the murder was in self-defense and got her acquitted of all charges, but he also got her sole custody of the baby, along with all of David's money.

"What my mother has never known, and I didn't find out until later in life," Mádeohn explained, "was that the lawyer went to the syndicate family, showing them that he had all the evidence he needed to bring them down! He had everything he legally needed to put them in jail for the rest of their lives, convincing them that as long as they never searched for or went after my mother and I, the evidence would stay buried."

The images in the center of the room continued to shift as Mádeohn went on with his tale. With the lawyer's help, the young mother was able to relocate to the small college town and raise her child without the fear of David's family knowing where they were. It just so happened—conveniently—that, at the time the two moved, the pizzeria all of a sudden came up for sale. Using the inheritance, the young Mrs. Cane, the new name she went by, bought the business, even though she knew absolutely nothing about running a restaurant.

With the right people once again appearing at the perfect moment, the single mother was able to get the business back up and running, with the old employees staying on to help.

The scene in the center of the room then shifted to focus on Mádeohn as a child.

"All through my youth," he continued, "I had handlers come visit under the disguise of relatives from my father's side of the family, an aunt and uncle. Although not really related, they did come from my real father, denizens of Hell sent to begin my training. My mom was never happy about them coming, but there was nothing she could do to stop it."

The young Mádeohn quickly learned everything the two handlers taught: how to use his mind to move objects and simple hand-to-hand combat techniques to protect himself. One of the things drilled into the boy from the beginning was that he was never, ever to use what he was taught in front of other people. No one was to ever know what he was capable of doing while he was training. The only place the child was free to practice was when he was by himself or with just his mother around.

Scenes of little Mádeohn playing tricks on his mom, moving objects she was reaching for, or disappearing and reappearing when she went to grab him, had the whole class laughing uncontrollably.

"What a little monster!" Rhonda exclaimed while giggling hysterically.

Smiling at everyone's entertainment, Mádeohn replied, "Not yet."

The whole class quickly sobered up as they observed the two handlers take the youth away with them during summer break at age ten. Their amusement suddenly turned to dread as they watched the three disappear into the dark mouth of a cave everyone recognized as part of The Teeth.

"As you all know, every summer I supposedly started visiting my 'deceased father's family' in the city. In reality, I was taken to Hell, where I met my real father for the first time."

Satan sat upon his throne, with Lilith standing loyally by his side, both inspecting the youth standing before them.

"Down there, I was given the same training an archangel receives. By the end of high school, I had the knowledge and skills of a full-fledged warrior!

"At the end of each summer, I would come home, and each time, my mother would patiently teach me that there was another side to the story. Although I had been given great power and skills, she taught me that I did have the choice of how to use them. Good in the world existed too, and I didn't have to use what had been given to me for evil. Her lessons were the one thing that kept me grounded!

"Toward the end of high school came my first real test. Back in the city, after his father eventually died, David's brother took over the family business. Never able to let his brother's death go and no longer restrained by his father, he sought out and eventually found the location of mom and I. He personally was going to make the woman who killed David pay for what she did and bring me back to the city to learn the family business."

A very expensive sports car racing along the highway at night through the mountains just a few miles outside of town appeared in the center of the room. Screeching around a dark corner next to the shear drop-off of the canyon cliffs, Mádeohn, who was standing in the middle of the road, suddenly came into view in the speeding vehicle's headlights. Raising his arm and flipping it toward the deadly drop-off on the side of the road, Mádeohn used his power to throw the car over the cliff. Flicking his fingers at the automobile as it flew through the air, it exploded into a ball of flames, crashing down to the canyon floor below.

Turning to his two handlers standing next to the side of the highway, the youth saw both the man and woman smiling, nodding their approval of his accomplishment.

Mádeohn slowly walked over to the two dark figures, staring coldly at each, and stated, "For years, that family has left us alone. Then all of a sudden, out of the clear blue, you tell me David's brother has found us and is on his way here to kill my mom. Now I'm quite certain the only way that could have happened after all this time is if someone went to him, revealing where we live!"

The two handlers just stared at the boy silently.

"If I ever see either one of you again," Mádeohn continued through clenched teeth, "I'll kill you!"

One of the dark figures chuckled, asking, "Do you really think you are a match for either one of us halfling?"

"Doesn't matter if I am or not," Satan's son stated as a matter of fact, "I'll fight you to the death! If it's me that dies, it will be you standing before my father, explaining why!"

The man and woman stood there staring at the boy for a moment before nodding acquiescence and disappearing. The highway scene faded from the room, and Mádeohn continued as everyone sat in silence.

"From that moment on, I vowed never to use my powers for evil again, except to defend or protect my mother!"

Unable to keep quiet any longer, Ryon interrupted, asking, "That woman, your handler, she was the girl at the check-in booth at Rhonda's birthday party. I remember that you knew her. I also recall her being trapped on the beach during the storm. What ever happened to her?"

Staring at Ryon for a moment, contemplating how to answer his friend's question, Mádeohn finally decided on the truth, coldly stating, "I kept my promise."

Everyone sat in silence, not knowing how to respond to that.

Relieving them of their discomfort, Mádeohn moved on, wrapping up his tale. "This community was chosen for us to live in, after my father's spies learned that Kana's ward was born here. It was reasoned that the White Witch prince would naturally reveal himself to him on earth. In order for me to be near Ryon when that took place, our friendship was cultivated since childhood. Although this sounds like I have used you all our lives, Ryon, I swear to you, this part of Satan's plan was always concealed from me. I never knew who you were. My friendship with you has always been genuine.

"Then, on that day at the lake, my father tried to kill you. Watching that waterspout approach you on the beach, I understood who he was trying destroy! But somehow, Ryon, you stopped it! You destroyed the storm yourself. That was when I realized why he tried to kill you. I have never seen a human use mystical powers like that before."

The overwhelming fear and confusion he had been suppressing about what he did that night, suddenly surfaced full force in Ryon's mind. Turning to Kana, Ryon confessed, "I have no idea how I did that."

"You used what you always had in you," the prince explained, recreating the eerie image of the storm in the center of the room.

The shocking answer to the question on everyone's mind about what really happened to Ryon and Mádeohn that night began playing out for the entire class to see. Witnessing the jaw-dropping bombshell of Ryon destroying the storm and Mádeohn sheltering both of them from the resulting tide washing over the beach left the entire classed stunned by incredible feats of power performed by their two friends.

"This is something every one of you possess, buried deep inside!" Transitioning into why he was really there with them today, the White Witch prince continued explaining, "Ever since God created man and placed him on earth, there has been a battle between Heaven and Hell for complete control of this universe. That war is about to come to a head! Each of you will use the power you have in you to help me battle the Evil One, driving him from earth forever!"

The prince just kept dropping one bomb after another. Completely stunned, no one knew what to say about that shocker.

Breaking the silence, Mr. Wenstrom spoke up, rather doubtfully, asking, "And how are we supposed to battle the powerful black forces of the supernatural, especially the creator of all evil himself?"

"You will be taught," the White Witch prince said, revealing the group of young humans' future destiny.

"All White Witch warriors undergo years of archangel training, and as Mádeohn attested to, so do Satan's soldiers. This makes sense since both descend originally from real archangels. To prepare each of you for what is coming, I will be taking you through a condensed, very intense form of archangel boot camp, so to speak. Then, later, you will be taken to my world, where the Learned Ones will teach you. You will see many wonders there. I will take you to visit different universes and show you the *Tablets of Time*."

Leaning forward in his chair, Kana slowly began instructing the class in earnest, "First, you need to understand there is no such thing as magic as you define it. All of what you call magic, or supernatural powers, black or white, is nothing but a deeper understanding of the laws of nature. Once you are taught these laws, you will be able to use them yourselves."

"Go on," Mr. Wenstrom's scientific interest was aroused.

"As you know," Kana continued, "a lot of what your brain is capable of is still a mystery to you. Well, there is a portion of the brain connected to what is known as the fabric of the universe. It is a substance that literally connects everything together. Through this portion of the mind and with the knowledge of how to use it, you can work with almost anything that exists, in one way or another."

Together with Mádeohn and Shilo, Kana first began instructing the class on creating personal mind shields. The prince emphasized the importance of this ability, explaining, "Before you can learn to make your minds perform mystic feats, you must learn how to keep intruders out of it. A mystically active mind is a vulnerable target."

He began by showing them how to form the shields in small, overlapping triangles so as not to leave room for any intruder to get in between any gaps, explaining, "The triangle is the strongest geometric shape that exist."

The class continued meeting as scheduled by the college, with Kana teaching instead of Mr. Wenstrom. The instructor himself had a hard time recalling the last time he felt so energized to learn, eagerly joining his former students.

Although very pleased with everyone mastering his teachings at an astonishing speed, Kana had to sternly warn his pupils, "No matter how much you learn, or how good you get, always remember, Lucifer is smart and powerful. Give him credit for that, never underestimating what he can, or will, do. That mistake will be extremely fatal!"

MYSTIC ARTS 101

The merciless sun faithfully erupts upon the great Sahara Desert, inflaming the ageless sea of fluidly shifting sand with relentless heat. Long shadows of gigantic bronze-tinted dunes slowly begin stretching across the vast region of sand.

Awoken like clock-work by the intense rise in temperature, the wind eagerly began its sculpturing, staying true to the daily routine it developed over the centuries. Being very particular about its art, every little grain of sand had to be just so for the free-spirited force of nature. Starting out by generating great gusts of air for carving before appointing swirling dust devils to the lighter jobs, it finished up by creating small puffs of air for the personal, artistic touches.

As would happen once in a while though, by midafternoon, the natural artist grew more restless, throwing temper tantrums and destroying creations it had taken great care in shaping.

A dreadful sensation it hadn't felt for thousands of years suddenly overwhelmed the Sahara Desert. With growing apprehension, the mighty desert silently watched the wind stomping around in a very bad mood, kicking down every sand dune it came to.

Out of nowhere, big black, billowy clouds rolled across the sky from every direction, angrily forming a mighty storm. A storm similar to one the Sahara had witnessed centuries before.

With lightning streaking across the heavens, thunder booming through the air, and the wind blowing fiercely in every direction, fireballs erratically danced across the desert floor. In a wild frenzy, the wind began to cut down one particular dune it had built many centuries ago. Reaching its goal, the natural artist unearthed an object that was the aftermath of the last such storm: an egg.

An egg, protected and incubated for thousands of years by the desert, was silently waiting to be unearthed before finally hatching.

Suddenly, a bolt of lightning stretched down from the swarming ceiling of black clouds and struck the egg with a powerful explosion and a shower of sparks, cracking it open.

Finally, after hundreds of thousands of years, the Sahara learned what it had been nursing through the centuries. Born in the unnatural hell storm and then breaking its way out of the shell of its ancient egg, a reptilian creature made of pure electricity slowly emerged.

The desert had just given birth to the First Beast.

While staying on earth, Kana and Shilo shared an apartment a short distance away from the college, sometimes holding special classes there. Sitting cross-legged and facing each other in the front room, both White Witches floated a few feet above the floor, taunting each other, something the two siblings had been doing all their lives. The sudden appearance of a figure dressed in a gold White Witch outfit between the two arguing royalty brought their bickering to an abrupt end.

"Greetings from the White Witch World!"

"Argon," Shilo moaned, "what are you doing here?"

"I bring messages from your Father's throne room."

Turning to the prince, a veil of disgust suddenly swept across Kana's best friend's face.

"What are these?" Argon inquired, pointing to the earth clothes Kana and his sister were wearing.

Looking at his apparel, Kana replied, "I kind of like them, besides, is this any way to address your prince and princess?"

Kana's not-so-serious chastising brought a smile to both the young men's faces.

"Your Father says that what he has seen of your work, he personally feels is very good and also appears to please the council."

"Well, chalk one up for us!" Shilo sarcastically chimed in. "It's not often somebody does something that pleases those old fossils!"

"Tell him," Kana replied sincerely, ignoring his sister, "his faith and support are greatly appreciated."

Nodding acknowledgment, Argon turned to Shilo, delivering his second missive, "You, my pretty princess, your Father wishes to see in his throne room immediately! Something about running off without permission, I believe. Shall we?"

Sticking his arm out for her to take, Shilo refused, pouting, "I'm going! I'm in trouble now."

"Cheer up, little sister," Kana said while smugly smiling.

"I swear, your day is coming! I will get you!" With that, she turned out of earth's universe, disappearing from the room.

Looking at each other, Kana and Argon just shrugged their shoulders. "Eventually I hope she'll learn," the prince stated.

As his students began realizing they actually could accomplish feats using their minds, each one immediately began pleading with Kana to teach them how to move objects too. Adamant that they must be completely proficient with their protection shields first, the White Witch prince patiently continued pressing the class with their practice drills, ignoring the request. Eagerly working with that goal in mind, it only took a couple of weeks before Kana became truly satisfied in the quality and strength of each person's mind shield. With Mádeohn's help, he then began running them through exercises in constructing their shields instinctively, using simulated attacks, both physical and mystical.

"You're stalling," Mádeohn finally accused the White Witch prince after a week of monitoring his friends moving determinately through their rigorous practice exercises.

Thinking back to his own frustrating challenges and disappointments as a youth first learning to see the fabric of the universe in his mind, Kana nodded his head, admitting, "I guess I am."

Silently contemplating a few minutes more, the White Witch asked, "Did you have as much difficulty seeing it for the first time as I did?"

"Phsstt!" Mádeohn spat. "There were times when I thought my instructors were going to kill me just to put me out of their misery!"

Smiling, the two mystical instructors began amusing themselves by mentally swapping stories, depicting their own struggles with first detecting the fabric of the universe.

Choking between fits of laughter, "I thought I was bad!" Mádeohn said as he gestured for everyone who had stopped to see what was so funny to get back to practice.

Silently sitting at his desk, Ryon could feel Kana's presence in his mind, patiently guiding him in his search for the fabric of the universe. Concentrating on the task with both eyes closed, Ryon's thoughts began to wander, musing on how quite natural having the White Witch in there felt.

"That is because, as your, guardian angel, I have always been here."

"You heard that!"

Opening his eyes and losing all form of concentration, Ryon looked at the White Witch prince in shock.

Taking a deep breath, calming his annoyance at the sudden distraction, Kana gently smiled, divulging, "It is kind of hard to be your conscious without hearing everything in there. Now, let's start again."

Watching his best friend's face turn several shades of red, Mádeohn began chuckling with amusement, blurting out, "You're so busted!"

Closing his eyes and quickly pushing all thoughts of the princess aside, the voice of Shilo's brother sternly came flooding through Ryon's mind, "Everything!"

As the fabric of the universe suddenly came snapping into focus, Ryon jumped, falling over backward onto the floor. Both Kana and Mádeohn came racing to his side, with the rest of the class looking on in concern behind them. Slowly glancing all around the room from where he lay in his tipped-over chair, Ryon began trying to describe what he was seeing, whispering, as if relating a dream.

"It's crazy weird! I see a fluorescent, light-blue substance everywhere. It's a part of everything!"

"Don't touch it!" he heard Kana warning. "That is the fabric of the universe."

Cautiously backing away, the blue substance quickly disappeared, leaving just Mádeohn hovering over him and smiling.

"Good job, buddy!"

Reaching down, Mádeohn proudly helped his friend up off the floor.

Closing his eyes and quickly retracing the steps Kana had taught him, Ryon found himself once again gazing in wonder at the classroom, completely engulfed by the fabric of the universe. Marveling at how the fluorescent blue substance was not only entwined with everything in the room, he could see it inside of everyone, including himself.

Unable to verbalize his feelings of rapture, humility, and the pure beauty of the awesome power he was now envisioning, all Ryon could think of doing was whisper, "This is so...insane!"

Smiling at Ryon's reaction, Kana continued explaining his warning in regard to not touching the blue substance, "The fabric of the universe is pure power. I need to train you to work with the fabric safely."

Noticing that he was slowly pacing a circle around the center of the room with his hands clasped behind his back, Kana immediately forced himself to stop. The unconscious act reminded him too much of one of his own instructor's annoying daily performances in the classroom.

The White Witch prince went on, emphasizing, "You first need to learn to focus on exactly what it is you are trying to do, or else you wind up affecting everything around you."

Observing through his unique, enhanced perspective, Ryon intently watched Kana demonstrating his explanation with a beam of light emanating from the palm of the White Witch's hand. Curiously watching the red light beam expanding out across the room and intermingling with the blue fabric of the universe, he noticed it touching but not going through solid objects, including himself.

"See how the light hits everything? That is how an untrained mind inside the fabric of the universe operates." Kana continued, "It is touching, therefore, affecting, everything! You need to learn to dial it down."

Collapsing the beam down like an umbrella closing, the White Witch prince concentrated it into a narrow stream of light, zeroing in on a single object, Ryon's forehead.

"Bang!"

Jumping at Mádeohn's sudden exclamation, Ryon lost his focus and his view of the room inside his mind. Opening his eyes and glaring annoyingly over at his best friend, the rest of the class began snickering with amusement.

Smiling, Mádeohn blew make-believe smoke away from his fingers that were in the shape of a handgun, stating, "Game over."

"Funny!" Ryon snarled.

"Moving an object is actually a two-step process..."

Erupting into a spontaneous celebration, the class cut Kana off midsentence. The prince found pleasure in watching everyone's euphoric raving about finally getting to learn how to move things with their minds.

Understanding the sense of pride shining in the young prince's eyes, Mr. Wenstrom chose to share one of his own personal revelations with their young White Witch instructor. "I have discovered the most inspiring moments in an educator's life are when the students you are engaging eagerly proclaim their hunger for what you are teaching."

Reflecting on the instructor's word for a moment, Kana nodded, admitting to himself that he was currently feeling the sentiment Wenstrom was alluding to.

Beginning again, the White Witch prince brought the class back to order. "Moving an object with your mind is actually a two-step process. First is stretching gravity, making it thinner in order to move the object. Then you mentally take hold of that object and move it."

Starting them with exercises in detecting gravity—searching for its gray, elastic substance inside the fabric of the universe—proved to be just as difficult as first detecting the blue fabric. Once everyone could find it easily, Kana began drills of carefully focusing on reaching out with their mind, into the fabric of the universe, and touching the substance of gravity only, without disturbing anything else. After numerous failures and several odd events occurring inside the classroom because of them, the entire class finally mastered the procedure.

Illustrating with a demonstration, Kana continued with the next part of the process, explaining, "As you touch the gray substance of gravity, you can see that it is kind of rubbery, for a lack of a better description."

Everyone began to mentally poke at the gray substance to experience what Kana was indicating. Suddenly objects every-where in the room began to bounce in place as a result of the gray matter's juggling, startling everyone.

Recalling how he and his fellow classmates did the same thing as children, with the exact same results, Kana began chuck-ling at the humorous consequences of their inquisitive action. "Remember," the prince admonished with a grin, continuing with his demonstration, "everything you do inside the fabric of the universe has an effect on everything around it. You must focus on exactly what you are doing.

"Now that you all know you can touch gravity, you need to learn how to mentally grab the section you need. Then, by men-tally stretching the gravity around an object to make it thinner around what you wish to move, the item then becomes lighter. You can also compress it, making the gravity denser, thus, causing the object to get heavier."

Stretching the gravity around Mr. Wenstrom's desk so that everyone could see it this time, the huge piece of furniture began floating weightlessly in midair once again.

Moving on once everyone became comfortable with this, Kana showed the class how to mentally take hold of an object. Everyone found that controlling gravity and moving something at the same time took a great deal of concentration and coordination. It did not take long before almost everything that wasn't bolted down began flying back and forth across the room.

Nudging Ryon to get his attention, Mitch nodded over to where Connie and Rhonda were working through a practice exer-cise together. Grinning mischievously while pointing to Rhonda's back, Mitch reached out and mentally unsnapped her bra through her top. Both men high-fived each other without taking their eyes off the women, fully shielded just in case something suddenly came flying wildly across the room in their direction.

Moaning, "Seriously?" Rhonda turned to her boyfriend, glaring at him through her curly bangs.

"Your two years old, right?"

Totally ignoring her insult, Mitch just sat there, grinning proudly.

"Oh my God!" Connie could hear Rhonda whispering. "It's so beautiful!"

Stunned speechless by the amazing scene unfolding before them, all Connie could do was nod her own head, agreeing.

The two women, along with the rest of the class, sat observing Kana and Mádeohn performing a demonstration in the center of the classroom. The two mystical instructors were slowly showing how to join their personal shields, creating a larger, much stronger one.

Unaware that she was holding her breath while watching the mesmerizing sight, Connie marveled at the stunning vision, the triangles of their shields sparkling like diamonds in the fabric of the universe's blue light. As the triangles began slowly merging together, she could see them becoming denser, obviously stronger, eventually snapping into place as one large shield protecting both men.

Totally psyched by what they just saw, the entire class began diligently practicing until everyone was able to connect their personal shield with someone else's effortlessly.

Next came working together in small groups, quickly building upon the ability until the whole class was able to construct one massive shield in unison.

"Now," their White Witch instructor continued, "I will show you how to start working together. Reaching out to join forces with another mind is basically the same as reaching out to touch an object in order to move it."

The prince began by teaching them how to join minds one-on-one. This was taught in almost the same manner as the group shields. Being able to communicate mentally was an exciting bonus to connecting minds. This new perk spread like wildfire, dominating everyone's attention. Smiling, Kana let them run wild for a brief period of time so that they could play with their new psychic ability.

Figuring they were finally ready to stretch their wings outside the classroom, Kana had the class meet as scheduled at the school. Appearing together, the prince and Mádeohn both stood dressed in attire from their own, perspective worlds.

"Let's recap what we have learned so far before we move on to today's lesson," Kana began his instruction while picking up a baseball-shaped, metal paperweight from Mr. Wenstrom's desk.

Tossing the heavy ball back and forth between his hands, the prince began listing the class's accomplishments. "First, the most important thing you have learned is how to create your own personal protection shields. It doesn't matter what else you are capable of doing, if you can't protect yourself, the rest of what you learn is pretty much useless. I can't emphasize this enough!"

The White Witch prince took a moment to make eye contact with each one of them to be sure they all understood the magnitude of what he had just said.

"You now know how to see the fabric of the universe and plug into it, so to speak." He continued, requesting, "Please do so now."

Satisfied everybody could see him mystically in their minds, Kana held his hand out with the round paperweight sitting in his palm. "You all now know how to take hold of gravity around an object, stretching it to the thinness you need, and then grasping the object inside, moving it."

Stretching the gray matter of gravity around the metal ball, the prince grasped it mentally, slowly raising the heavy sphere in the air above his hand. He nonchalantly rotated a finger of his free hand above the paperweight, gradually spinning it.

The entire class sat transfixed, silently watching the metal ball rotating above Kana's hand while waiting for him to continue. Suddenly, without any warning, the heavy sphere went rocketing across the room on its own, slamming into Mádeohn's waiting palm with a loud smack. Jumping at the explosive sound of metal slapping against skin, the entire class sat gaping at Mádeohn in surprise.

Ryon was the first to break the silence of everyone's shock, exclaiming, "Dude! You just ripped that thing directly into your hand, never touching the gray stuff! How did you do that?"

Grinning at the class's response to his and Mádeohn's shock-and-awe demonstration, Kana explained, "That, my friends, is the gist of today's lesson."

After suggesting grabbing their coats, the prince and Mádeohn transported the class of students to a hill outside the city. Bare except for one lone, very large, dead tree, a bitterly cold wind blasted across the stark mound, cutting everyone straight to the bone.

Frowning at their bleak surroundings, Ryon stuffed his hands in his coat pockets for warmth. The White Witch prince just had to pick the day forecasted to have the first winter storm for a road trip outside the classroom.

Flipping his hood up and wrapping his cloak around himself, Kana directed everyone to form a wide circle around the tree. Mádeohn stood outside the circle, opposite the White Witch prince, watching patiently, his own black cloak whipping wildly behind him in the blistering wind.

"That's good," the prince continued once everyone was in place. "Next, plug into the fabric of the universe."

Closing his eyes, Ryon could see their surroundings perfectly with his mystical sight.

"Now I want you all to join minds with everyone here, except Mádeohn and myself," Kana continued. "Notice, by joining your minds, the mental web you are creating inside the circle?"

The prince was right.

Completely forgetting about the icy wind pounding against his back, Ryon silently gazed across the stunning vision unfolding before him. With everybody's minds uniting together mentally, a massive web of dark-blue lines running through the fabric of the universe spread out across the interior of their circle.

Kana continued by pointing out how their mystical net was entrapping the tree at its center. He instructed them, "Use your one mind, together, lift the tree! Pull it up out of the ground by its roots!"

Shouting, "Let's do this!" Ryon began focusing on the tree with all his might.

Several moments passed with Kana and Mádeohn quietly monitoring the class concentrating on their task. The tree slowly began rocking back and forth, moaning and creaking, causing the ground beneath it to vibrate intensely. Inch by inch, the tree started rising up into the air, crying out, protesting, its ancient roots tearing loose from the ground holding it in place for hundreds of years. Suddenly breaking free from the Earth, the huge tree slowly began rising several feet up into the air. Loose dirt continued falling from gigantic roots while hovering overhead, trapped in the class's mental grasp.

Kana looked at Mádeohn and smiled. Mentally taking the tree from the class, the White Witch threw it aside, away from the barren hill. They all began to cheer in triumph, jumping up and high-fiving each other in celebration of their huge accomplishment.

While giving Connie a hug of congratulations, the prince of the White Witches proudly announced, "I think now you are ready!"

Later that afternoon, a light snow gently began falling upon the quiet little college town, replacing the morning's bitter, cold wind.

Suspending training for the rest of the day, Kana met the class at Mrs. Cane's Pizza to celebrate the morning's achievement. Both working, Ryon and Mádeohn caught a few moments of celebrating with their friends when they could, sitting down and joining in during their breaks.

Watching his students enjoying themselves, the White Witch prince smiled with satisfaction. Seeing them completely unconcerned about anything at the moment—except loud music, laughing, joking, more pizza, and beer—meant that the grim reality of the future was not weighing them down mentally. A concern he was keeping a close eye on. Normal life was about to come crashing to an abrupt end.

Joining the young adults' celebration for a few moments, Mrs. Cane sat down with the class during one of Ryon and Mádeohn's breaks. Mádeohn told her about the White Witch prince and what he was teaching the class. To her, it was like living her son's childhood all over again, and she wanted to voice her concerns to the prince.

"I know they all feel as if they are fully matured at this age." The concern in Silvia's voice was unmistakable as she looked around the table at each one of the students while addressing Kana. "When I was their age, God knows I thought I was. Each one of them thinks that they're fully capable of making the right decision all the time. The truth is, though, they're young adults; they have much to learn yet! Thanks to the choices I made at their age, because I didn't know any better at that time, Mádeohn is trapped in his fate. My heart breaks every day at what I have brought down upon him."

Everyone sat in silence as Mrs. Cane spoke while clearly fighting back tears.

Turning once again to Kana, the woman continued, "What you're doing here is exposing them all to a side of life no one ever sees, putting their lives—their entire futures—in danger!"

The White Witch prince looked at the woman as reassuringly as he could, trying to calm her concerns. "Mrs. Cane, you are right, but you have always known they had a reason for putting Mádeohn here. The time is almost upon us where everyone in this world will be a slave to that side of life unless it is stopped. Don't you think it would be better if they learned how to fight it now, instead of waiting until it is too late and not be able to resist?"

Silvia knew the White Witch was right. Standing up, she gave Mádeohn a kiss on the cheek and said, "I've known each of you since you were children. Please be careful."

Looking directly at the prince, she added challengingly, "I don't want to lose any of you!"

The students of the Mystic Arts Class sat in silence, watching Mádeohn's mom work her way across the room toward the kitchen, stopping now and again at a table to greet people enjoying their meal. What she said was true; they all had known her since they could remember. Growing up, it was always a special affair to go out and eat pizza at Mrs. Cane's. The woman always had a way of making everyone she met just naturally grow fond of her, especially the kids. To see her so emotional about each of them truly tore at their hearts.

"Well, on that note," Mitch broke the silence, standing up and pulling on Rhonda's arm, "it's getting late. We need to get going."

Sighing in agreement, Rhonda grabbed her coat, preparing to leave. After saying their good-byes, the two headed out into the snowy night.

Not long after, the rest of the class followed suit, leaving just Ryon, Mádeohn, Connie, and Kana at the table.

Ryon could clearly see the deep worry on Mádeohn's face for his mother. Standing up and patting his best friend compassionately on the shoulder, he softly urged, "Come on, buddy, break is over. We need to get back to work."

Turning away from the door to the kitchen where his mother had just disappeared, Mádeohn waved to Ryon, responding, "You go ahead, I'll be just a minute."

"Yes, boss," Ryon smiled, turning to head back to the kitchen himself. That brought a smile to Mádeohn's face as he watched his friend go.

"You know," the son of Satan sighed, "as worried about all of us as she is, it isn't the only concern on Mom's mind. She's always known she would have to pay for her sin...for making a deal with my father. What's happening right now only makes it seem that the day to pay that price might be almost here!"

"I can't speak for God," Kana replied compassionately, "so I'm going to tell you what I believe. Your mom may have made some poor decisions in her youth, but she has done nothing but devote her life to helping other people for the last two decades. Look at everything she has done for this community, for the kids going to school here. Then there is you. You yourself have said that if not for her you would have never known that you could use what you have learned for good instead of evil. I know you are taking a great risk helping us. I think if God can forgive the angels who did not stand by Him, the ones who were truly sorry for their mistake, he can forgive one woman for hers also. *I truly believe your mom is going to be all right!*"

After sitting there momentarily while quietly contemplating the White Witch prince's words, Mádeohn finally nodded he understood before standing up to go back to work.

That left just Kana and Connie sitting at the table, silently watching Mádeohn disappearing into the kitchen.

Reaching over, placing her hand upon his, she softly said, "That was a very compassionate thing you did for him."

Locking eyes and tenderly entwining their fingers, the two sat in silence, enjoying being alone for the moment.

"You realize, don't you," the White Witch spoke to Connie mentally, "that this is the first time we have been alone."

"Yeah," she responded back with just her thoughts. "What's up with that?"

"Well," he replied out loud, "with all the training I have been doing for all of you, there hasn't been much free time to just do what I want."

"Uh-huh," Connie teased, grinning. "And here I thought you were just too afraid to ask me out."

Looking annoyed, the prince responded, "I'm a White Witch warrior! In my training, I have faced demons from Hell. Do you really think I get afraid?"

"I don't know, do you?"

"Only a fool with a death wish does not have fear," Kana said, reciting his own mystical warfare instructor. "Enough about me," changing the subject, the White Witch prince said, "I want to know more about you."

"Can't you just go into my mind and learn all about me that way?" Connie asked mischievously.

"Yes, I can," Kana admitted, smiling. "But I won't, not without your permission. The only time I do that is in battle. Besides, do you really want me to see what is in there right now?"

Turning a little red with embarrassment while raising her eyes to look at the ceiling, Connie let out a deep breath, admitting, "Maybe not."

"OK," returning her gaze to the prince, she continued, "much to my Daddy's personal pleasure, and a great pain to his wallet, I decided to become a doctor. I'm getting all my prerequisites done here, and when I graduate, I'll be enrolling in med school."

"That is a very noble profession to get into," Kana complimented Connie while giving her hand an affectionate squeeze, a gesture that sent the young woman's heart racing.

"In fact," he continued, "you and my mother will get along great! That is what she studied—becoming a healer."

Leaning forward, gazing intimately into her eyes, he asked enticingly, "How would you like to learn how to heal a wound or mend a broken bone with just your mind?"

"Oh my God!" Connie exclaimed, her excitement not only showing on her beautiful face but also through the tight grip she had on the prince's hand. "That would be so awesome!"

"You will make a wonderful healer," Kana said softly, reaching up with his free hand and tenderly brushing the back of his finger across her cheek.

Connie could perceive the same intense emotion deep in the prince's eyes that she felt welling up inside of her. She had never before felt longing for someone the way she did for this amazing man from a different universe. Her lips became hypersensitive, tingling beyond tolerance as he bent closer to kiss her. Closing her eyes, all life and all sound—the whole world—faded down in her mind, leaving just the two of them. An involuntary whimper escaped her lips as she felt the warmth of his mouth almost upon hers.

"Get a room," Ryon mocked walking past with a hot pizza on his way to a table by the front window of the restaurant.

Startled, Connie jumped back, and the two freshmen girls Ryon delivered the pizza to began giggling with amusement at her embarrassment. Irritably glaring at Ryon's back, she felt Kana gently squeeze her hand. Turning back to the prince, her ire faded at the obvious look of love for her in his eyes.

"It is getting late," Kana commented softly.

Nodding agreement, the young woman's face brightened back up while putting her coat on. "You can walk me home and meet Daddy!"

Kana sat back in his chair with a look of pain on his face, moaning, "Oh no! The dreaded meet-the-dad moment!"

Connie stopped with her coat half on and looked at the White Witch prince quizzically. "Don't tell me the guys where you're from are as afraid to meet a girl's father as they are here."

"Sweetheart," the prince pointed out, "it doesn't matter what universe you are in, daddy's little girl is daddy's little girl!"

"Oh, that explains everything, doesn't it?" she asked sarcastically, grabbing him by the arm and pulling him up to go.

"Bye guys!" Ryon called on his way back to the kitchen.

Connie just glared coldly at him again.

Raising his arms questioningly, Ryon tried to fake innocence while disappearing through the kitchen door and asking, "What?"

Putting her hood up and stepping out into the gently falling snow, Connie pointed in the direction they needed to go. Crossing the parking lot, the couple strolled hand in hand into the park across the street from the pizzeria.

"Will your parents still be up this late?" Kana asked.

"It's just Daddy and me; Mom died when I was a little girl," Connie stated simply.

"I'm sorry," the prince apologized, gently squeezing her hand.

"It's OK. Daddy and I get along real great. I pretty much have him wrapped around my finger."

Rolling his eyes, Kana stressed his point, "That's what I am afraid of. They are the ones who are the hardest to let go."

"Oh, stop it!" Connie exclaimed, hitting him in the chest with her free hand. Her only reward for the playful gesture was sharp pain shooting through the back of her hand. Adding insult to her injury, the White Witch prince didn't even flinch at the sudden blow.

Leaning her head on his shoulder while rubbing her sore hand behind her back so that he couldn't see it, Connie asked, "Aren't you cold with just that trench coat? It's freezing out here."

"I'm sorry, I'm being rude not thinking about you," the prince apologized. Stopping, he wrapped his arms around her and explained, "I am able to regulate the air temperature around me."

Extending the field of warm air surrounding him to include his shivering companion, Connie exclaimed, "That feels so awesome! How do you do that?"

"It is a survival trick we are taught."

Looking up at the prince, the young woman pleaded, "You have to teach me it!"

Smiling down at her, he tenderly replied, "You will learn it in your training, just like I did."

"It feels so good," she whispered, raising herself up as the young White Witch prince bent down to kiss her. Moaning with the pleasure of finally fulfilling her desire, Kana's magic shot through her whole body, making it tingle with fire as his lips met hers. Surprised by the sensation, Connie's legs gave way, and the prince had to hold her up to keep her from collapsing.

When it ended, she looked up at him, gulping for air.

"Oh my God! What did you do? That was so awesome!"

Smiling, Kana chuckled, amused at her reaction to his magic.

Grabbing his head, she hungrily pulled him back to her, begging, "Do it again!"

The snow continued to gently fall around the young lovers locked in a passionate embrace in the center of the park.

"Well now, if this isn't a pretty picture!"

Connie yelped in surprise at the intrusion of the male voice. Kana released her, turning to put himself between her and the two guys approaching them.

"Well, well, Connie," the one who spoke first chided, "I see you lost no time throwing yourself on the new guy in town. I guess us *locals* just aren't good enough for you."

"That is enough!" Kana calmly commanded. "Just move along. We don't want any trouble."

"Oh, I think there's going to be trouble!" the second intruder cackled.

"Connie, I want you to put up a force field and keep it up," the White Witch prince spoke to her mentally. After sensing that she did as requested, Kana stepped forward challengingly, stating coolly, "I said, just leave us be."

"Ooh, he thinks he's tough," the first thug mocked, suddenly brandishing a knife in his hand. "Let's see how tough you are against this!"

Both intruders attacked the White Witch warrior at once. As the blade was thrust toward him, Kana spun away from the path of the weapon, following through as the first attacker's momentum brought him in close with an elbow to the side of his head. Continuing with his spin, the prince placed a well-aimed kick into the chest of the second antagonist. That thug flew a few feet through the air, flipping over a park bench and collapsing in the snow on the other side.

"You just made a big mistake!" the first attacker shouted as Kana turned to face him again and Connie screamed.

The thug launched his knife straight at the prince's head.

Faster than the blade, the White Witch warrior easily snatched it out of the air just before it reached his face, flinging it right back where it had come from. Stopping the blade mentally a hair's width from plunging into its owner, he left it hanging in midair right between the thug's eyes.

The guy stood frozen with fear, staring at his own weapon hovering before his face. Stepping over to the ruffian's side, Kana looked at the space between the tip of the blade and his opponent's skull.

"Whew, that was close," he commented nonchalantly, watching a bead of sweat roll down the guy's nose in spite of the freezing temperature outside.

"You know," the prince continued calmly, "I'm holding the knife from piercing into that pea brain of yours, but I'm not holding you. What I don't get is why you're still here."

Realizing what the White Witch said was true, the antagonist stumbled off across the park as fast as he could.

Grabbing the knife out of the air and placing it in his coat pocket, Kana turned to take care of the second thug. To his surprise, he discovered the idiot kneeling in the snow and Connie standing behind him. She had the guy's arm twisted behind his back in such a manner that he couldn't move without her breaking it. Giving her an annoyed look, the White Witch prince walked over to join the two.

"Hey," she explained with a look of triumph on her face, "you don't grow up a cop's daughter and not learn how to defend yourself!"

Surprised, Kana asked, "Your dad's a cop?"

He bent down to look the second assailant in the eye. "Seems to me, you have two choices: join your friend, or I leave you to her."

"I'll go! I'll go! Just tell the bitch not to break my arm!"

Turning him loose, Connie grinned with pleasure as she watched him jump up and sprint away in the direction of his friend.

Looking up at the prince, her smile faded. She could see it in his eyes: disappointment. Her heart sank. Wounded by his look of annoyance, she said, "I thought you would be proud of what I could do to defend myself."

Seeing the hurt look on the young woman's face, Kana explained, "Remember earlier today when I said, 'Now you are ready?'"

Confused, Connie nodded yes.

"Mrs. Cane was right. When I began teaching all of you how to develop your minds and connect to the fabric of the universe, it opened you all up to attack from anyone else also able to do so. You haven't learned how to detect evil yet. That is what you will learn next. So far I have been protecting all of you from that kind of attack, but there will come a time when I won't always be able to. That is why I told you to put up a force field—for your own protection. You had no idea if those two where demons from Hell or just two idiots. When you dropped your shield, you exposed yourself to a mystical attack! Do you understand my concern?"

Noticing she was about to cry, the White Witch prince placed his hand under her chin. Gently lifting it and looking directly into her tear-filled eyes, he compassionately added with a smile, "You sure kicked his butt, though, didn't you?"

Connie laughed as he gently wiped a tear away from her face. She began patting her cheeks to make sure there were no more.

Noticing her shivering again, Kana invited, "Come here," and put his arm around the girl while extending his field of warm air to include her.

"Oh my God! That feels so good!" she exclaimed, snuggling into the White Witch's embrace. "I can't wait until you teach me how to do that!"

"You will learn," Kana repeated, raising his eyebrows at a new thought.

Questioning the look on his face, Connie asked, "What?"

"I was just thinking," the prince replied, "a healer that can kick ass! How would Ryon put it? Su-weet!"

Bumping him with her hip, she responded with a smirk, "And don't you forget it! Now come on, I want you to meet my father," she said as she tugged on his hand to go.

"I was hoping you had forgotten that," Kana sighed, standing his ground.

"Unbelievable!" Connie cried incredibly. "The mighty White Witch warrior is afraid!"

"I just don't have a death wish," the prince responded matter-of-factly.

Dragging the reluctant White Witch prince away into the snowy night, Connie rolled her eyes, chiding him, "Come on, you big baby!"

PUBLIC EXPOSURE

Hell has been described as a fiery pit in the bowels of existence. Satan's throne room was just one of many caverns beneath the mountain range in Hell known as The Teeth. The demon had hand carved the throne upon which he sat out of the stone walls of the huge room. Flickering fires from both torches and the perpetual flame spat there in God's anger were his kingdom of darkness's only means of light.

The lord of sin sat silently upon his royal chair with his wife standing quietly next to him. Powerfully built, as were all archangels, layers of bulging muscles flowed under his jet-black skin. He had no eyes, just sockets filled with white fire, and his mouth housed rows of pearly, needlelike fangs. His entire body was completely hairless. Massive, black, leathery wings draped over the arms of the stone throne chair, the tips resting upon the cavern floor.

Soon, another very beautiful female soul entered the room with her head down and carrying a large goblet of drink. She knelt before her master and offered her burden to him. Taking it, Satan noticed Kon, a dreg general in his army of darkness, had also entered the room.

Kon stepped forward, bowing to his creator. Satan took a sip of his drink as the female servant, with head bowed, exited the throne room.

"It begins, Master."

"I know, Kon. The young prince is already upon the earth and causing a lot of trouble."

"Mádeohn is with him."

"Yes, I know this also. That may prove to be useful in the future though. How are your forces advancing?"

"Not as well as they should, but they are moving forward. Kana is the strongest White Witch we have ever encountered. We continue to attack and test him constantly but have so far found no limit to his power. Even while he teaches that group of humans to play with their minds, he protects them from our probes and is out searching and destroying us. So far, though, he has limited himself to our hidden cults and demons, not exposing himself publicly."

"Yes," Satan pondered, taking another drink of the goblet. "God is very smart; never forget that, Kon. He would only send his strongest. The prince is wise too. He knows what public reaction to him would be in that world if he exposed himself too dramatically. We may be able to use that to our advantage also. I will take care of Mádeohn. You keep you forces advancing, and continue your assault on Kana. We will strike at him from every angle!"

Turning to his wife, the lord of Hell asked, "Is the bitch ready?"

"I finished her last conditioning session today," Lilith answered with a smile.

"Bring her to me."

The demon queen turned to the doorway of the throne room and ordered, "Na-amah, come stand before your king!"

A very beautiful creature entered the room and stood with head bowed before the devil.

Satan sat his goblet down on the arm of his throne chair and got up to walk around the luscious wench, inspecting her. The young woman was long-legged and full breasted, with blonde hair that reached down below her shoulders. A very revealing gold outfit barely covered her breasts and round bottom. Boots of the same color reached up to her knees.

"Beautiful as her mother," Satan complimented his wife.

"She has some of your traits as well," Lilith responded, grateful that he was pleased.

Satan stopped in front of her and raised the girl's head. Her eyes were of white fire like his, and her lovely smile exposed rows of needlelike fangs. He ran the back of his hand gently down her silky, blonde hair.

Lilith knew her husband was remembering his own head of hair very similar to the girl's and just how much it had meant to him.

To take his mind away from those distant memories, she asked, "Do you wish to try her?"

"No, I will save that for her reward when she completes her task," Hell's master responded, dropping his hand and returning to his throne.

"Go now, my child," Lilith commanded the young woman. "It is time. Make your mother proud!"

The next few days for the Mystic Arts Class were intensely grueling and mentally exhausting. Kana made good on his promise to Connie, teaching them how to detect someone else with mystical abilities.

"What you will see is a little more complex than the obvious lines detectable in a mind connection."

As usual, Ryon was the first one to accomplish the feat, mentally seeing the others in the class actually connecting to the fabric of the universe.

"This is so cool!" he exclaimed, seeing everyone in a whole new way.

It wasn't long before the whole class was amazed at detecting the connection in each other.

"Now," their White Witch instructor went on, "you still need to realize that just because you see the mystical coupling doesn't mean you can detect evil that exists in some who can make the connection. We will work on that next. It is much harder. For your own protection, just assume that anyone you detect could very well be in league with Satan. I want you all to keep yourselves fully protected mentally and go out and practice what you have learned. You will see just how many others in this world are already able to mentally join with the fabric of the universe to one degree or another. Use caution! Remember, you also can be detected if you do not have your mind shielded the way I taught you to do!"

The very next Saturday night, Prince Kana appeared inside the mystic arts classroom, wearing his now familiar trench coat. Almost all of his students were already assembled, waiting to take the prince to a nightclub for an evening out.

"Isn't Mr. Wenstrom coming with us?" he asked innocently.

Grinning with amusement at the thought of Wenstrom in a nightclub, Connie replied, "He said he had more important things to do."

Sauntering over next to Kana, she casually took his hand, enjoying the feeling of his strong fingers intertwining with hers and tenderly squeezing.

Noticing one side of her long brown hair pulled back and pinned, Kana reached up with his free hand, running it along the side of her head. A glowing glass flower appeared in place of the plastic barrette holding her hair.

"Oh! It's beautiful, Connie!" Rhonda exclaimed.

Ryon and Mádeohn entered the room just then, apologizing for being late.

"Are we ready then?" the prince of the White Witches asked enthusiastically.

Suddenly, a flash of light came streaking through the room, wrapping itself around Kana like a neon boa constrictor. Stepping through a mystical doorway, Shilo appeared, triumphantly grinning at her bound brother.

Everyone was stunned at the princess's sudden, goddess-like appearance and surprise attack on her brother.

"You will never learn, will you, little sister?" Kana shook his head, mentally grabbing the neon trap and unwrapping it from himself effortlessly. Smiling mischievously, he quickly flung the mystical ambush back, wrapping it around his sister before she knew what had hit her.

"Kana!" she screamed furiously. Everyone had to struggle to keep from laughing at the princess's comical and completely futile efforts to get free of her own trap.

Snapping his fingers, Kana's sister's bonds disappeared.

"I suppose Daddy's little girl sweet-talked her way out of being in trouble again?" the prince asked snidely, taking Connie's arm into his own.

With a huge grin, Shilo mockingly replied, "Jealous?"

"I'm just glad she came back for tonight," Ryon said, taking Shilo by the hand.

"Shilo, I love your outfit!" exclaimed Connie, admiring the princess's White Witch apparel.

"Thank you, but it probably is a little too much for here on earth, isn't it?"

Connie and Rhonda both nodded their heads in unison, agreeing.

With a wave of her hand, the princess's outfit quickly changed into something more in style with Earthly fashion.

"Much better," Rhonda approved.

"Let's go! Rock 'n' roll!" Ryon shouted.

"Where are we going?" the prince asked.

Almost in unison, the whole class shouted, "TWKW!"

"TWKW?" Kana looked at Connie quizzically.

"It's the most popular nightclub in town," Connie explained to him. "The Who-Knows-Who, or TWKW for short."

"All right," the prince replied. "Show me mentally where it is."

Mentally picturing the club, Connie could feel the White Witch prince touch her mind. Although not a new sensation to her, it still felt weird.

After seeing for himself what she was visualizing, the prince shared the information with Shilo and Mádeohn in the same manner.

"Grab your coats," Kana instructed. "Get ready to go!"

Nodding to his sister and Mádeohn, the three combined their mystical abilities, transporting the whole class at once. They all appeared in an almost unused section of a parking lot, across the street from the nightclub.

Almost unused. One vehicle sat in a remote section of the parking area, occupied by two guys sharing a bottle of whiskey, smoking, laughing, and joking while listening to the music blaring from car's sound system. Upon seeing the group of people materialize out of thin air next to their car, both immediately froze, staring in disbelief.

Reaching up, Connie grabbed Kana's arm in alarm, realizing the two thugs were the guys that had attacked them in the park.

Both occupants of the vehicle also recognized the White Witch prince, who stood boldly glaring back at them. The driver's knife slowly came floating out of the prince's coat pocket, where he had stashed it, and hung suspended in the air between Kana and the car. Everyone stood in silence, watching the blade slowly rotate in midair, tip down and light glinting off it from one of the parking lot's floodlights.

Throwing the car in gear, the owner of the weapon sent his vehicle screeching out of the parking area, leaving a cloud of smoke behind.

The whole class suddenly broke out laughing at the comical exit.

Reaching out mentally, the White Witch prince shorted out the speeding automobile's electrical system, causing the engine to lose power and die.

Watching the car coast to a halt down the street, Kana mused out loud, "I wonder how many more toys I'm going to have to take away from him in order to keep him from hurting somebody?"

"What are you going to do with this one?" Ryon asked, observing the knife still hanging suspended before them.

The White Witch prince reached out to retrieve the blade, and Connie tugged on his arm, informing him, "You can't take that inside with us."

Nodding, the prince ushered everyone toward the nightclub.

Two extremely large bouncers stood chatting with each other at the entrance of The Who-Knows-Who. Filing up the walkway together, one of them began waving the group on inside, not pausing in his conversation with his coworker. Upon reaching the large fellow, Kana grabbed his waving hand, casually placing the knife in it and then walking right on by with Connie at his side.

"What the..." the bouncer exclaimed, glaring at the prince's back.

Patting one of the guy's massive shoulders while walking past without stopping, Ryon teased, "Don't hurt yourself with that, big dude."

Proceeding into the main dance room, a wave of hard, driving music, blinding lights, and the sound of a whole lot of people having fun slammed into them like thunder.

"This is how we humans create a little fantasy of our own," Rhonda shouted, dancing across the room with Mitch in tow.

"Hey, Ryon," one of the cocktail waitresses walking by smiled seductively.

"Hey!" he smiled back until he saw the look on Shilo's face. Sensing her connect to the fabric of the universe, he mentally shouted to the princess, "Shilo, no!"

It was too late. One of the spaghetti straps holding the girl's top up snapped, briefly exposing her breast. With a screech of embarrassment, the pretty little waitress ran from the room to repair her sudden wardrobe malfunction.

Ryon gave Shilo a look of annoyance, but she just grinned proudly back at him.

"You know," he explained to the princess mentally so that she could hear him above the loud music, "you have absolutely nothing to be worried about. There is no one else in the whole wide world for me since I met you."

Pursing her lips and with a mischievous glint in her eye, Shilo reached up, patted him on the cheek, and replied, "Just don't forget it."

The princess then turned, grabbing Connie's arm. Both women took off across the room in the direction Rhonda and Mitch had gone, giggling about Shilo's little stunt the whole way.

Without saying it out loud, Ryon mouthed the word, "Right," while turning to the prince for some help. Grinning, Kana wordlessly took off also, pretty much indicating to Ryon that he was on his own in this one.

Watching the White Witch walk away, with a look of dejection he shouted above the music, "Great! Some guardian you are!"

The music and lights died down as the group found a place to sit, and they were finally able to hear themselves talk without shouting.

A slow song came on, and Connie gently squeezed Kana's hand, softly inviting, "Come on."

Out on the dance floor, Connie held her prince from another universe close. His arms tenderly wrapping around her, gave her a very warm feeling. Taking her head off of his shoulder, Connie looked up into his smiling eyes. Slowly bending down and softly kissing her, Connie's entire body began tingling with fire as Kana's magic suddenly engulfed her from head to toe. When their lips parted, the prince had to hold her up to keep her from falling.

Kana gave her a wink. Once again, he startled her with his mystical power, just like the first time they kissed on that cold, snowy night in the park.

"You keep doing that," Connie teased, "and I won't be able to walk!"

The dance floor was surrounded on three sides by seating space, and on the fourth was the DJ booth. To either side of it was a glass cubicle with a lighted dance pole and a girl performing in it. Big-screen TVs hung everywhere, some showing random shots of the crowd and others focused on the girls in the dance booths. A few displayed video games that some of the patrons were engaged in playing.

Backstage, one of the club's dance girls prepared to relieve a coworker out front, making some last-minute makeup and costume adjustments. Turning around, she almost ran into one of the most beautiful women she had ever seen, who was scantily dressed in a gold outfit and knee-high boots.

Realizing the woman's eyes were pure white fire, the nightclub entertainer tried to scream in fear.

Two beams of blue energy shot from Na-amah's eyes into the young dancer's, immediately stifling the scream before turning the girl into a pile of ash on the floor.

Stepping into the glass dance booth, Na-amah seductively began swinging around the lighted pole in the center of it. Her lustful moves and provocative gestures brought entertainment to the entire room.

Turning his attention away from Connie for a moment, Kana looked to see what everyone was so interested in. His face immediately went blank when his eyes met those of the she beast. All of a sudden, he stopped dancing, working his way through the crowd toward the demon. The little whore from Hell had caught the White Witch prince by surprise and now had him under her spell.

"What's wrong?" Connie tried to shout over the music, but the prince just kept right on walking. She couldn't even reach him mentally. Frightened, all she could think to do was chase after him.

Shilo didn't turn Ryon loose all night. No one came between the White Witch princess and her man, until Kana came blundering through and kept right on walking. Ready to angrily zap her brother but suddenly noticing Connie vainly trying to stop him confused her.

Looking up in the direction where Kana seemed to be blindly heading, Shilo immediately recognized what was in the dance booth, exclaiming, "Oh my God!"

Leaving Ryon standing there in puzzlement, she began shoving her way through the crowd, trying to catch Kana before it was too late.

Sitting at their table, laughing, and enjoying himself with his friends almost seemed like old times to Mádeohn. Everything was so much simpler back before the storm at Mitch's house and before the White Witch prince arrived. Although, he had to admit, not hiding who he truly was from his friends anymore did feel pretty good.

Looking up at one of the big-screen TVs, Mádeohn saw one of his father's corrupt creations dancing for the crowd. Exploding from his chair, he quickly began worming his way across the crowded dance floor.

"Ryon!" Satan's son shouted mentally. "Gather everyone around Kana, and form a force field! Protect the prince! Now!"

Without hesitation, Ryon immediately had the whole class shoving their way toward the White Witch prince.

Just as Kana reached the small stage, Na-amah extended her hand, offering herself to the prince. She had the White Witch entrapped in her power. He was hers to use however she wished, and oh, how she would use him. Her body began quivering at the thought of the pleasure he would give her. When she was done with him, she would receive her reward: pleasing the master. That thought turned her on even more.

Encircling the prince, the Mystic Arts Class formed a shield around him, immediately severing the she beast's mental grasp. At the same time, a white light flashed in front of her, and the demon was hurled to the floor at the back of the glass booth.

Argon stood before Kana, ready for whatever the she beast might do next.

The creature cringed at the sight of Mádeohn leaping upon the stage. Recognizing Satan's son, she snarled viciously at him, revealing rows of pearly, needlelike teeth.

"Back to the dark hole you crept out of!" Mádeohn ordered, and Na-amah quickly disappeared, melting into the floor as if there truly were a hole there.

"You all right?" Argon asked his best friend.

"Yes," Kana replied, obviously a little dazed. "That's the strongest one yet. We have already caused enough of a spectacle. Go out the back."

Nodding, Argon turned away, exiting through the door at the back of the dance booth. Kana slowly began walking away from the small stage, followed by the rest of the class. As they did so, the whole room began cheering and applauding at the performance they had just witnessed. Obviously the whole incident was an amazing performance staged by the management.

"What was that?" Ryon asked his best friend.

Still glaring at the spot the she beast had just disappeared into, Mádeohn soberly replied, "My sister!"

Turning, the prince of Hell left it at that, silently following everyone else back to their table.

"Sister!" Ryon exclaimed, stunned. Trying to keep up with his best friend, his efforts were impeded by the crowd on the dance floor.

"Wait! You have a sister?"

Stopping Shilo as they worked their way back across the dance floor, Connie asked, "What did he mean by the strongest one yet?"

Replying mentally, the princess explained, "From the time Kana first arrived here, the evil one has been testing his strength. Not only was this encounter the strongest one yet, but it is also the first time there has been a confrontation in public. The rest have been hidden from humans."

Nodding that she understood, Connie silently stood there, fearfully contemplating just how much was going on around them that no one really knew about.

Stopping only long enough to raise the small head upon its long neck to sniff the air, the First Beast, the Electrical Beast, continued lumbering across the harsh desert. Day and night, always in the same direction, it pushed on and on toward a specific goal. Tasting its objective on the wind and never diverting for one moment, no matter what kind of distraction the desert threw in its way, it tirelessly trekked on mile after mile until it finally came to a dirt track used as a road.

Lowering its head to the ground, the beast sniffed its way across the dirt track to a power pole on the opposite side. Raising its head in the air, the Electrical Beast carefully began sniffing one of the power lines. Suddenly excited about finding what it had been searching for, it began stomping the ground, letting out a loud roar.

Turning back to the pole, he threw his weight against it, snapping the pole in two at the bottom. The post came crashing to the ground in a shower of wooden splinters and sparks from the broken electrical lines.

Standing there mesmerized by one of the charged cables dancing across the ground like a snake, the creature's head began weaving back and forth while watching it. Then, like a bolt of lightning, Electrical Beast shot for one of the whipping power lines, snapping it up in its jaws. Immediately it began sucking the electrical juice from the cable, consuming the sweet, sweet nourishment. Slowly the creature began glowing brighter and brighter. Finally dropping the line and raising its head to the sky, the First Beast let out a thundering roar, shaking the land for miles.

Turning again to the electrically charged cable, the hell-spawned creature caught it up once again. This time, though, the Electrical Beast merged with the power flowing through the line, becoming a part of the world's power grid.

The look of frustration on Kana's face tore at Connie's heart, and she had no idea how to help. Looking helplessly across the room at Rhonda for suggestions, her best friend shrugged back, indicating she had no clue what to do either. Resting her head against his shoulder to indicate she was there for him was the only thing Connie could think of to help.

Without turning, the prince responded by tenderly reaching for her hand and gently squeezing it to indicate he appreciated her comforting gesture.

Taking a deep breath, trying to release her own frustration, Connie looked down again at the panic and turmoil below. There were literally hundreds of people curiously crowding the main parking lot of the campus, right below the mystical-arts classroom. Red and blue strobe lights flashing from several emergency vehicles intermediately lit up the dark classroom as the mystical-arts students all silently observed the mad chaos.

A circle of police in the center of the crowd continuously struggled to keep the curious mob of onlookers outside their human wall. Inside the closed-off area, another mysterious phenomenon was once again focusing the world's attention on the small college town. Television networks from all over the world were calling it a sick, evil mystery. Unexplainable by experts, from scientific to psychic, everyone just stood silently observing, scratching their heads in puzzlement.

The center of attention was a unique fire burning unlike anything ever seen before. There was no apparent origin, nothing fueling it, yet it existed, intensely blazing a baby-blue color. They tried to extinguish the flame, but nothing they used could put it out—either water or chemicals. Amazingly though, any nonliving material, such as plastics and metal, immediately froze upon entering the fire. However, living tissue did not freeze in the strange blaze, it burned, made evident by the charred body suspended above the blue flames.

The corpse hung by itself in midair, with no apparent support, rotating slowly like a pig on a barbecue spit. When anyone tried to get near the body to take it down, the fire would flare up.

Staring out the glass wall at the crowd below, Argon was bent down on one knee, and next to him, the White Witch prince methodically probed the strange fire mentally. Finally giving in to his findings, Kana stated frustratingly, "I can find only one hole."

"Same here, I am afraid," replied Argon, standing up and stretching the cramps out of his legs.

"I don't understand," Connie said, looking at Kana puzzled.

The prince tried explaining, "Satan has designed his little display down there very well. The only way to get that boy's body out is for me personally to carry it out of the blue flame."

"Won't you get burned in the fire? They said it burns all living matter."

"The evil one left it open so he could use a shield against it. He doesn't want Kana destroyed, just exposed," Argon clarified.

"He's right, the whole thing is just to get me out into the eyes of the public and let the humans know I'm here. Then they will have someone tangible to blame for all of the Hell and destruction Satan is about to unleash upon the world."

"That's not fair!" Rhonda blurted out.

Argon and Kana both turned, looking at her pathetically.

"Fair does not exist in Hell," the prince coldly stated.

Mádeohn suddenly appeared in the room, turning to the two White Witches and apologetically proclaiming, "I'm sorry, Kana, you have the only opening. I am completely locked out!"

The sudden appearance of a strange, angelic-looking creature inside the police perimeter immediately attracted everyone's attention.

"You!" Sheriff Tanner exclaimed, recognizing his daughter's new boyfriend. "How did you do that? Where's Connie?"

"Right here, Daddy!"

He barely heard the girl's shouting over the crowd noise. Turning to the sound of his daughter's voice, he spotted her struggling to shove her way through the crowd. Stopping at the line of police, the sheriff commanded, "Let her in!"

Rushing up to her father, Connie franticly appealed to him, "Daddy, let him be, he's here to help!"

The prince of the White Witches definitely glared at the sheriff for a second before silently turning toward the blue fire. Shocking everyone, he boldly stepped into the flames, grabbing the floating, charred body in his arms and returning unharmed.

Gently laying the body on the ground before a group of mystified paramedics, Kana informed them, "You will find his teeth have been left intact so that you may identify the boy."

Turning away, he stopped abruptly, coming face to face with Connie's dad.

"Who are you?" the sheriff asked coldly. "How is it that you were able to do what no one else could and do it unharmed?"

Without answering the sheriff, Kana turned to Connie, soberly stating, "It is our friend with the knife from the park."

"Oh my God!" Connie exclaimed, suddenly covering her mouth with her hands and staring back at the White Witch prince in shock.

"Who?" the sheriff asked sharply.

"We were attacked by this guy with a knife in the park the night it snowed," Connie explained.

"You were attacked at knifepoint, and didn't tell me?" her father exclaimed.

"There was no need!" Connie defended herself. "Kana took care of it!"

"He did?" the sheriff asked, changing his tone and looking at the silent White Witch suspiciously. Abruptly raising his voice, he exploded, "What the hell have you got my daughter mixed up in?"

Realizing what her father was implying, Connie grabbed him by the arm, trying to get her stubborn father to listen. "No Daddy! It's not like that!"

Coldly returning the sheriff's menacing glare, the prince calmly replied, "Right now, I'm the one standing in Hell's way. Be prepared, this is only the beginning."

"Beginning! Beginning of what?" Sheriff Tanner snapped.

Looking at all the cameras focusing on the three of them, Kana turned to Connie, speaking to her mentally, "I need to go, this has gone on long enough. Will you be all right?"

Nodding, Connie silently watched the White Witch prince disappear, right before everyone's eyes.

"Where the hell did he go?" the sheriff shouted, looking questioningly at his daughter for an answer.

"I will explain everything," Connie threw her arms up in surrender, trying to calm her father down.

Without taking his eyes off her, the sheriff raised his hand, motioning to one of his deputies. "Escort my daughter to my car, and make sure she stays in it till I get there," he commanded.

"No, Daddy!" Connie defiantly stood her ground, demanding, "He can take me home, and I'll wait for you there."

Glaring at his daughter for a moment, Tanner nodded approval, charging, "Don't leave her till I get there!"

The two began making their way through the crowd, and the sheriff turned to another one of his officers, ordering, "I want an APB out on her new boyfriend. I don't know how he pulled that disappearing act, but he can't have gone far."

Walking over to where the medical people were working on the charred body, Sheriff Tanner looked at it and sighed, "Shit, it's going to be a long night!"

Mádeohn struggled not to laugh while watching Ryon reach for his can of soda, which, mysteriously, was no longer sitting where he had left it.

"Dude!" Ryon sighed, turning to confront his friend. "You know, back in the day, before I knew you could move stuff with your mind, you were totally able to mess with me like that. Not so much anymore. Where is it?"

Feigning innocence, Mádeohn simply shrugged.

Taking a short break from putting away the morning's supply deliveries, the two sat idly harassing each other in the closed pizzeria's stockroom. Suddenly, a bloodcurdling scream sent both of them bolting through the empty kitchen and out into the dining room. Bursting through the kitchen door, Mádeohn's heart leapt into his throat at the sight of a dreg viciously looming over his mother.

Screaming again, Sylvia Cane continued trying to back away from the slimy, foul creature but was unable to do so with her back already against a wall. Sick to her stomach, she could feel the heat of the demon's rancid breath blasting her face inches away. Choking on her own acidic bile burning in her throat, Sylvia's stomach churned, as she knew Satan was finally collecting on the debt she owed him—her soul.

Throwing himself between the demon and his mom, Mádeohn roughly shoved the dreg across the dining room, screaming at Ryon, "Get her out of here!"

Quickly grabbing Mrs. Cane, Ryon put a force field around himself and Mádeohn's mom and hastily shoved the woman out the front door.

Hissing with rage while watching its prey escape, the hell-spawned creature moved to intercept. A blast of energy from the palm of Mádeohn's hand grazed the beast's shoulder, diverting the beast's attention away from his mother and back to him. The enraged dreg attacked Mádeohn, sending the two rolling across the room, locked in hand-to-hand combat and crushing tables and chairs along the way.

Two more dregs suddenly appeared, grabbing Mádeohn and brutally beating him into semi consciousness before holding his limp body up between them.

The first creature slowly stood back up, growling, with slobber dripping from its razor-lined jaws. Methodically raising a claw, the beast grinned at the prospect of digging it into the soft flesh of Mádeohn's face.

It never got the pleasure. An intense burst of energy unexpectedly exploded against its chest, knocking the beast across the room.

Turning in surprise, the other two dregs discovered Kana and Argon calmly standing next to the kitchen door.

Dropping Satan's son without hesitation, the two demons quickly attacked the White Witches.

The first dreg slowly stood up half-dazed, roughly grabbing Mádeohn's limp form from where he had collapsed on the floor. Quickly disappearing through a universal door, the beast made its escape while the two White Witches were occupied defending themselves from its brother demons.

Kana blasted the dreg charging at him, knocking it completely through the front door of the restaurant. Turning, he made sure that Argon was doing all right before stepping outside via the new hole in the glass door. The dreg lay on the ground just outside the restaurant, groggily trying to roll over to get up. Creating a laser beam that emanated from his hand, Kana calmly cut the beast's head off, killing it.

Looking up, the prince noticed a crowd of people already forming, curious to see what all the commotion was taking place at the closed pizzeria.

Something all of a sudden came exploding out of the front window of the building, landing at his feet.

Reaching down to help his friend up, Kana chided, "Argon, a little itty-bitty ol' dreg?"

"You tell him that!" Argon exclaimed.

The restaurant exploded, and debris began raining down everywhere, sending the growing crowd of onlookers scuttling for safety. In the middle of the destroyed building's rubble, the dreg stood twenty feet tall, murderously gazing out at the stunned crowd. Fully extending its wings, it gave a pitiful, piercing screech.

"That's new!" Argon commented, the creature's changing size surprising him.

The two White Witches quickly dove apart, dodging an energy blast emanating from the beast's fiery red eyes.

"Argon, the people!" Kana ordered, scrambling up to attack back.

With the precision of a well-trained fighting team, the White Witch warriors went to work. Creating a shield enclosing the dreg and the prince, Argon kept the people outside safe. The beast itself stood no chance against the White Witch prince. In a few short minutes, the creature lay dead in the rubble that used to be Mrs. Cane's Pizza, a lethal hole smoldering in the center of its massive chest.

"Argon!" Kana immediately commanded as reporters and police began closing in on him, "take Mrs. Cane back to Lysta'cu'mha. Ryon, gather everyone in the classroom immediately!"

With that, the four suddenly disappeared, leaving behind a group of puzzled bystanders milling about in front of a building destroyed in a mystical battle. People were completely baffled by what they had just witnessed and the two dead monsters left behind in the rubble.

"Mádeohn?" Kana inquired sympathetically.

"Never saw him come out of the pizzeria before it went boom!" Ryon shrugged nonchalantly.

Not buying Ryon's unconcerned response, the White Witch prince stated, "He is alive, Mádeohn is too powerful not have escaped the blast."

"I know," Ryon sighed, letting his guard down. "I keep telling myself, he saved both of us from a demonic title wave, he can survive an explosion."

Satisfied with that response, standing in the middle of the circle of desks, Kana calmly addressed the rest of the class.

"Satan has succeeded in accomplishing what he wanted. He has twice brought us to the public's attention. Today at Mrs. Cane's and before, out in the parking lot. I have taught everything I can teach you here. My presence on earth has become both a distraction and a liability. As long as I'm with you, Satan will continue to focus on attacking me and every one of you, hindering what you all need to accomplish next.

"You all must go out in the world and teach others what I have taught you. Split up, go everywhere, gather followers. You now need to build armies of people willing to learn what you've been taught, appointing leaders of your own choosing to continue to do the same. Later on in the future, this army will do the work of resisting Satan while you yourselves will resume your own schooling in Lysta'cu'mha.

"God's blessings be with you all until I return."

Then, without any further explanation, the class silently watched the White Witch tenderly kiss Connie good-bye before completely disappearing from their world.

RYON'S DREAM

"OK," Ryon declared to himself, "it's official. I'm an idiot! A totally screwed idiot!"

The blazing orb in the sky beat down upon him like a relentless hammer, slowly pounding every ounce of strength he had out of his blistering body. Stumbling for the millionth time, he fell face-first, gulping in a mouth full of hot sand. Unable to produce the saliva to spit it back out, he lay there for a minute, choking and coughing up the fine dirt.

He needed to get up; he had to keep moving. Clenching fists full of the fine gravel, he painfully pushed himself to his feet. Forcing his legs to move, Ryon continued stumbling forward, trying to put more distance between himself and his pursuers.

He had screwed himself epically this time. There he was, crusading heroically out into the world, preparing it for an apocalyptic battle against Hell. Earth's hero.

Well, not so much anymore. Now, ironically, he was about to become a nameless corpse in the desert, running from a bunch of ordinary thugs. He wanted to laugh at how pathetic that was but didn't have the strength to do it.

Following through with Kana's instructions, the class sent the message out, and people everywhere slowly became interested in learning about the mystical world. Intrigued at first by the power they could possibly possess and then learning about the impending war against Satan motivated each into teaching others to also get involved.

So their little movement slowly grew.

Answering an inquiry in a small desert town, Ryon found several people who were willing to join them. Even though his success there was solid, his opposition was just as great. Following Kana's lead, for everyone's safety, he hid his teaching sessions from the public.

Successfully developing the group's skills to the point of self-sufficiency, he quietly packed up to return home, leaving one of them in charge. Conveying his good-byes, he left them with his final instructions before heading for the bus stop: "A great calling will be made, and you will be summoned. You will know the time when it comes. Until then, keep the faith, and remember what you have been taught. Your foes are many here; resist them. Try to bring more into your fold."

Making his way on foot across an empty dirt lot at the edge of town, Ryon was suddenly attacked by a pickup full of gunmen. Speeding past him, the truck came to a halt in a cloud of dust just a few feet away. Quickly jumping out of the back and silently surrounding Ryon, each one menacingly displayed some sort of firearm.

"You know, boy," the driver calmly began addressing Ryon while casually walking around the truck with a shotgun. "You come into our peaceful little town and start raising all kinds of hell with your strange preaching, disturbing decent folk and leaving a few twisted souls behind in your wake who foolishly believe your rhetoric, and then you just walk away like nothing's changed.

"Well, I'm glad you're leaving. The boys and I just came out to say good-bye and make sure you understand not to come back here again!"

"Just let me pass," Ryon said calmly, trying to walk around the big guy.

Not finished yet, the group's leader reached out and roughly shoved Ryon backward to the ground.

Ryon immediately put up a shield while closing his eyes and plugging into the fabric of the universe. The connection enhanced his vision, giving him a unique perspective on his situation. He could actually see who was definitely enjoying himself and who was just standing there, nervously playing along.

Looking confused by the latticework of the force field, the group's leader reached out to examine it, asking, "What the hell is this?"

Touching the shield, he received an electrical shock that sent him painfully recoiling backward a couple of steps.

Chuckling at the idiot standing there flapping his arm and trying to relieve the pain in his hand, Ryon noticed the keys still in the pickup's ignition. Reaching out mentally, he started the truck up, and everyone jumped at the sound of the engine.

"What the hell!" the truck's owner turned accusingly to Ryon while still massaging his sore hand.

Grinning mischievously, Ryon mentally popped the vehicle into gear, sending it crashing driverless across the empty lot.

The entire group of gunmen stood slack-jawed, helplessly watching as Ryon mercilessly sent the truck ramming head-on into a power pole.

Satisfied they couldn't use the vehicle to pursue him, Ryon returned his attention to his ring of tormentors.

"Damn you!" the pickup owner shouted, leveling the shotgun at Ryon.

"That was my truck you just totaled!"

He angrily squeezed the trigger, but the gun's buckshot just bounced off Ryon's shield, spraying back at the large man. The rest of the antagonists immediately began firing also, but nothing got through Ryon's shield. When they finally quit, they found him calmly staring back at them, unharmed.

"Well, that tickled," Ryon commented, trying to shake them up even more by being a smart ass. Slowly stepping past the group, he left them standing there, staring at his back in disbelief.

Figuring he stood a better chance of getting away by disappearing out in the desert, he had been running ever since.

Absolute brilliance.

"Really!" Ryon moaned, finding himself face-first on the ground again. "How long have I been lying here this time?"

Something was different; he wasn't lying on sand.

Attempting to open his eyes, he was only able to crack them enough to see his face pressing against a hot, black surface. "A road!" he thought just before passing out again.

Ryon felt peaceful, calmly floating in his endless sea of tranquil darkness. He had no clue how he had gotten there. He had no desire to even try remembering. All he knew or cared about was... he was.

Was what?

Something started tugging at the back of Ryon's mind. He found it irritating, disrupting the comfort of his darkness. He felt content in there, feeling no pain and experiencing no desires. Everything he needed was right here in the darkness. What else could possibly matter?

The persistent irritation disturbing his peaceful bliss grew stronger, but he continued fighting, keeping it at bay. Soon, though, it became an endless struggle. So consumed by this internal battle that even his beloved darkness began fading away.

Images started flashing through Ryon's mind: black clouds, lightning, and a storm by a lake; Kana personally tutoring him; Mádeohn and his mother laughing about something in her office; Connie and Rhonda coming into class together; Shilo flashing her beautiful smile across the room; and Kana telling him, "I am your conscience!" Ryon could feel the storm pressing his body to the ground, pinning it there. Kana was suddenly in his face shouting, "Now, Ryon! Now!" Watching himself, he struggled to his knees in the storm, every muscle in his body straining to point a finger to the churning chaos in the sky. From his extended appendage leaped a bolt of lightning, smacking the angry, boiling clouds.

In a blaze of bright white light, everything exploded, completely shattering what little was left of his comforting darkness. His internal battle was finally over.

Ryon suddenly found himself standing in a dimly lit basement. How did he know that?

What little illumination there was in the room came from several candles scattered about.

What the hell is going on? How did he get here?

After escaping out into the desert like a bonehead, he was pretty sure when he passed out by the road that it was game over. Then he was struggling with something while floating in some sort of dark sea.

So where was he now? Something started tugging at the back of his mind.

Looking around the dimly lit chamber, he noticed a stairway leading up and out at one end of the rectangular room. In the wall opposite the stairway, he could see a dark recess, but he wasn't able to see anything inside it. A twenty-foot-square pit was sunk three feet deep in the center of the room. What appeared to be a severely charred alter rose up in the middle of the pit. A huge oven hood hung over the top of the sacrificial table, disappearing into the ceiling. At each end of the alter, metal pipes rising out of the floor to just above the black alter bent ninety degrees to face each other in a perpetual, silent duel.

A noise that sounded like a stifled growl suddenly startled Ryon. Pressing himself back into the shadows farther, footsteps on the stairway caught his attention. Silently watching a hooded figure in a red cloak sweep quickly down the stairs, he followed the newcomer as he marched around the opposite side of the pit from him. Reaching the dark recess in the opposite wall, the shadowy character dropped to his knees, reverently bowing his head to the floor.

"I feel a presence in the room with us!" a low scratchy voice stated from the darkness of the alcove. The cloaked figure sprang to his feet, swirling around to face the room, searching.

"Where?"

"I do not know," the voice from the darkness hoarsely replied. "I cannot see anything, but I can barely sense there is someone near!"

Not see him? Ryon found it hard to believe they couldn't see him. There was nothing in the bare room to hide behind except the shadows. Surely if they looked hard enough they would find him.

Ryon didn't understand. Something kept tugging at the back of his mind.

"Is everything in readiness for tonight?" he heard the rough voice cough.

The nagging in Ryon's mind continued hammering at him, like he was on the verge of remembering something but couldn't get it to come to mind.

"Yes," replied the cloaked one. "The girl is upstairs. She will be completely prepared by this evening."

Girl? Upstairs? This evening? What was going on?

All of a sudden, Ryon was no longer in the basement. Instead he found himself standing in the living room of a house. Not the same house with the dingy basement, though, that he was sure of.

How could he tell?

Something in the back of his mind was trying to be recognized, but he couldn't place it.

A small group of people were quietly mulling about the room. Connie sat with them, softly calling to him. He could hear urgency in her voice.

"Ryon, can you hear me? Please answer! Ryon, do you hear me? Come to us, Ryon!"

Her pleading wasn't the source of the nagging going on in the back of his mind.

"I'm here," he answered flatly, and everyone in the room jumped.

Startled, Connie opened her eyes, searching the room.

"Ryon?"

"Here!" Ryon answered. "In front of you. Connie, how did I get here?"

"Ryon?" Connie asked again, still searching. "I can hear you, but I can't see you!"

"Can't see me? I'm right here. I can see you plain as day!"

Connie quickly realized what was going on. The main reason she was calling him for help was because he happened to be the strongest of everyone in the Mystic Arts Class. That had to be the reason he probably could see and hear her, whereas she could only hear him.

"All that can wait till later," she said, pushing it aside for the moment. "Right now I need you to listen to me! Time is running out, and I need your help! This house belongs to a friend of mine. I came here in response to her inquiry, and she learned eagerly. With her help, I've been able to gather the following you see here."

Ryon took a good look around at Connie's students, who were quietly listening to the mystical conversation.

"Satan also has a strong force here," Connie went on explaining. "A force that goes so far as to secretly sacrifice people. A young girl by the name of Rylee became part of the evil cult, but we were able to persuade her to our side. She was leaving the occult to be with us, but they found out and now are holding her prisoner. She is to be sacrificed to Satan tonight."

"Girl? Sacrifice tonight? I was there!" Ryon shouted.

"What? Where?" Connie asked, surprised by Ryon's sudden outburst.

"They said she was upstairs being prepared for tonight. I've seen the sacrificial altar!"

"Ryon," Connie pleaded, trying to get him to make sense.

Deliberately calming himself down, Ryon asked, "Connie, why me? How can I help you when I don't even know how I got here or where here is?"

He could hear the exhaustion and anxiety in her voice as she tried to convince him. "Because of your close mental link with Kana, you've always surpassed us in learning what he taught. You're the most powerful one of us all!"

Click. That was the trigger he needed. The nagging thought in the back of his mind finally came flooding through like a tidal wave. Understanding engulfed him as he partially realized what was happening.

He now knew he wasn't physically in the house with Connie. His body was somewhere else, only his mind's eye was there.

Suddenly, Kana's voice came to him, "You have finally broken the barrier between us. Actually, it was more of a restriction than a barrier. We have always been able to reach each other across the universes to a degree. You know, guardian angel and all."

"I still don't understand what's really going on," Ryon honestly admitted.

"Do you remember the storm at the lake last fall? Do you remember what happened? What you did?"

"Of course I remember, vividly!" That was something he would never forget, or understand.

"On that day," the White Witch explained, "you unconsciously broke through the barrier, reaching out to me, taking from my mind what you needed to stop the storm. Once again you have broken that barrier, allowing you to connect to me whenever you wish. Use the vast reserve of my knowledge, and go do what must be done. The life of a girl depends on your fast action!"

Looking down at his own body lying like a corpse in a hospital bed was just crazy. From his out-of-body vantage point, Ryon patiently watched the nurse go through her routine, monitoring his condition. When she left the room, under

Kana's mental guidance, he began examining the half-dead figure lying in the bed. He could see second-degree burns covering his face, neck, and arms, the obvious result of wandering through the desert. Going deeper, he began examining himself internally, starting from his head and then slowly working down. Relieved at seeing no brain damage, he did detect severely deteriorating muscle tissue everywhere. Thankfully, for the most part, everything else was pretty much undamaged. Severe dehydration and lack nourishment appeared to be his worst internal problems.

How long was he out there?

Returning to his brain and using knowledge obtained from Kana's mind, Ryon began the healing process. Starting at his head and then working his way down, he began returning his skin to its normal condition.

Mesmerized by his transformation, Ryon exclaimed mentally, "How cool is that!"

"This is nothing compared to what else you can learn from me."

Ryon detected a hint of amusement in the White Witch prince's voice.

"Do you recall after we had an intense practice session how exhausted you were?" Kana asked him.

"Yeah, pretty much."

"Performing feats like this takes a lot energy," Kana explained. "You'll be pretty drained when you're done here."

"Great. Thanks for the heads up."

While his muscle tissue slowly began rejuvenating, Ryon took a moment to reach into the unconscious portion of his mind. Searching carefully, he was able to discover what did happen after he fell unconscious on the road. After finding his half-dead body on the highway he had stumbled upon, a motorist rushed him to this hospital's emergency room. While the doctors were struggling to stabilize his condition, a computer check on his ID revealed an APB for assault had been issued for him.

Seriously, who assaulted whom?

The sheriff from the small town he was fleeing from was currently on his way to the hospital now.

The nurse reentered the room with new medication to place in Ryon's IV. Discovering the metamorphosis his body was going through sent the poor woman into hysteria. Several people began dashing in to see what all the screaming was about. Witnessing the shocking transformation, everyone stopped dead in their tracks. Ryon's recuperation process was moving over his shoulders and down his chest.

"Get her out of here!" a doctor commanded, indicating the hysterical nurse. Stepping over to the bed, he tore the bedding from Ryon's body. Repaired flesh spread down to his waist.

"My God!" the physician exclaimed. Looking up to the monitors attached to Ryon's body, he noticed everything reading normal. Reaching down to curiously touch where the flesh was repairing itself, he received an electrical shock for the effort. Startled and confused, he tried again. Again he was shocked.

"Apparently you're not supposed to touch him," someone commented.

Completing the healing process, Ryon mentally gave himself a once-over, just to make sure everything was all right. Satisfied, he opened his eyes. The small crowd surrounding him held their breath all at once. Slowly swinging his feet over the edge of the bed and sitting up, he quietly gazed around at the shocked audience he was attracting.

"How did you do that?" the doctor asked, staring at him in amazement.

The sheriff would be there any minute, and he had a life to save. Deciding not to hang around the severely crowded hospital room any longer, Ryon silently vanished, right before everyone's bewildered eyes.

Trever's mind was racing wildly, a stark contrast to the cool demeanor he was currently displaying for all to see while stepping down the stairs into the ceremonial chamber. The occult leader found the fact that his master, Seren, could feel another presence in the chamber earlier today puzzling. Specifically troubling was the demon admitting he couldn't clearly detect where the intruder was hiding. There really was nothing in the sacrificial chamber to hide behind.

Someone as powerful as the hell spawn being incapable of penetrating a defense shield was highly unusual—unless the intruder happened to be more powerful than Seren.

That thought alone conjured up very serious concerns. As human leader of his cult, Trever was fully briefed on the White Which prince and how powerful he was.

More powerful than Seren? Realistically, that just wasn't fathomable.

Trever was also informed that the prince was no longer on earth.

Could he be back?

Forcing himself to clear the perplexing issue from his mind, he began to fully focus on the upcoming sacrifice. The ceremony would be an important lesson to all who might be harboring thoughts of betrayal, like the young lady upstairs. Killing such a sweet morsel was, admittedly, going to be a shame, but a crystal-clear precedent needed to be established.

Cloaked in the red robe of his rank as high priest to personally preside over the sacrifice, Trever took his position down in the pit. The room suddenly lit up as the flame throwers at each end of the altar spit fire at one another like combating dragons.

Jumping in surprise when the flame throwers suddenly came to life, Connie silently took a deep breath. Terrified out of her mind, she returned to concentrating on the chanting, calming herself.

In spite of her own fear, there was no way she was going to abandon Rylee. Sharing the same commitment, even though they knew they would be in way over their heads, her new friends were with her to rescue the young woman. Concealing themselves in gray cloaks, they quietly infiltrated the ceremony, scattering themselves among the rest of the cult members.

Connie still had no idea what they were going to do; she just knew they had to do something. No way was she going to let these sick animals justify their own twisted dogma by butchering her friend. Not without a fight.

What choice did she have? She had no clue what had happened to Ryon this afternoon. One minute they were communicating mentally, with him making absolutely no sense, the next there was nothing but silence. No matter how hard she tried, she was unable to reconnect with him again.

What was really confusing about the whole incident was Ryon's babbling about being here and seeing the sacrificial alter.

Is that possible? Could he have really been here before?

The chanting took on a dramatic change, bringing Connie's mind back to the present. Everyone's attention turned to six women slowly descending down the stairs in pairs. They carried a platform between them, upon which sat a painted-up, oiled, and heavily drugged Rylee. Connie's heart leapt into her throat at the sight of the young girl.

After parading her around the room, the women placed Rylee on the floor in front of Trever in the altar pit. Taking her by the hand, the high priest gently helped the drugged girl to her feet, guiding her over to the altar. Easily sweeping Rylee up in his arms, he placed her face up, between the two flamethrowers.

Trever brought silence to the underground chamber by raising his arms in prayer to start the ceremony. "Oh mighty dark one," he began, "we, your children, gather to pay you homage. To you, who knows all, has seen all, and does not tolerate sacrilege, we offer you the pretty one who sought to betray you..."

"She is not the only betrayer here!" A rough voice coughed from the dark end of the room, opposite the stairway. "Others are here to interfere!"

"Now!" Connie shouted, leaping into the pit.

Throwing off their gray cloaks, the rest of her friends followed her. Surrounding Trever and the altar, the group formed a shield between themselves, trapping the occult priest.

Turning slowly, Trever carefully looked at each one of them before bursting out in laughter. An explosion of energy suddenly erupted from his body, blasting through their shield, knocking the entire group off their feet. Several powerful gray-robed figures stepped forward, pinning them to the floor mystically.

"If this is the best they can do," Trever chuckled," they are the ones in need of help! Start the sacrifice!"

To Connie's horror, when the chanting began again, the dueling serpents at each end of the altar came to life, spitting fire at each other with their victim between them.

"No!" Connie cried, struggling to free herself from the mystical bonds.

Abruptly the chanting stopped and was replaced by sounds of confusion. Looking up again, Connie's heart leaped with joy.

He had made it. A concave field of blue energy appeared by Rylee's head and feet, stopping the flames from reaching its victim. Slowly encasing her, like a blue cocoon, the energy field rose up into the air, safely floating away from the flame-covered altar.

With a cry of anger, Trever launched a blast of energy at the cocoon in an effort to destroy it. Shockingly, the blue energy field absorbed his high-intensity bombardment. Then the mystical bonds holding the intruders down was abruptly severed, releasing them.

"Connie!" Ryon's voice suddenly boomed throughout the room, "behind the cocoon!"

The small group of rescuers quickly did as they were told. Ryon appeared between them and the cocoon of blue energy, protecting everyone with his own shield.

"Thank God you made it!" Connie exclaimed, giving him a big hug.

"Get the girl and your friends out of here," Ryon coldly ordered.

"What about you?" Connie asked, concerned about leaving him behind in a basement full of Satan's worshippers.

"I've more work to finish here. Now go!"

Ryon's tone left Connie with no doubt his command was not up for debate. Turning around, she immediately began pushing her people up the stairs.

"You will pay for that act of sacrilege with your life!" Trever venomously hissed, raising his arm and preparing to attack Ryon.

"Let him be," the hoarse voice from the dark recess ordered. "He is beyond you."

Glaring at Ryon, the occult leader hesitated, obviously debating whether or not to obey the order before finally stepping back.

Seren came lumbering out of the dark recess in full view of the entire room. Ryon recognized the demon from his encounter with the one at Mrs. Cane's Pizza. It was a dreg.

"So, the White Witch prince did accomplish something during his brief time upon earth," Seren hissed with saliva dripping from his mouth. "No matter, you are still just a human. No match for, hell spawn!"

When the beast first emerged out of his dark hole, its wings were tucked in along its back. With his sudden outburst, he flexed them to their full span, bowling over gray-robed figures as he did. Others in the chamber began bowing in homage at the beast's unexpected show of physical power.

Pointing a bony, clawed finger at Ryon, Seren sent a blast of energy into the latter's shield, forcing the human backward a couple of steps. A slimy smile spread across the dreg's lizard-like face at Ryon's show of weakness. He continued the assault, slowly pushing the human back until he tripped, falling on the bottom step of the stairs.

Ryon, in all honesty, had to admit to himself that the demon was delivering him a severe beat down. Wiping away the sweat pouring down into his eyes, he strained with everything he had to keep his shield up against the relentless attack. He could hear Seren laughing as the beast continued wearing him down.

Not knowing how much longer he could hold out, Ryon wanted to end it as soon as possible. Reaching out mentally to Kana, he began searching the White Witch's mind for what he needed. He had unconsciously made a similar search once before, pinned down at that time by an evil power at a friend's birthday party. Slowly raising his hand and pointing a finger at the dreg, just like on that night by the lake, he let loose a powerful bolt of pure white lightening. Breaking right through the demon's shield, the concentrated beam of energy smacked the beast square in the chest, causing a small explosion. The shock wave from the blast threw gray-robed figures everywhere.

Ryon's own shield protected him from the explosion. Slowly standing, he surveyed the aftermath of his blast throughout the room. The dreg itself was totally destroyed. He could see smoldering chunks of it scattered all about the basement. The altar was a twisted pile of metal in the room's center. Bodies were strewn around the destroyed room, some moving and some not. Trever, the red-robed high priest, however, was nowhere to be found.

Completely drained of all energy, Ryon left the occult members to fend for themselves. He would have Connie and her friends tend to them. Maybe, with time, they might be able to successfully straighten out some of the demon worshippers' twisted minds.

PART II

THE WHITE WITCH WORLD

For the first time in several months, the Mystic Arts Class assembled all together in Wenstrom's classroom. Looking out across the room, the instructor smiled to himself. It was good to see the whole class together once again. Everyone sat in the circle of desks Kana had formed the day he formally arrived, and each shared the various events they had experienced during their travels around the world.

Relaxing back in his chair, Wenstrom laid his glasses down on the book he was reading, reminiscing on how much he and the class had accomplished over the last several months. "Progress was definitely sluggish at best, in the beginning," he thought to himself while slowly exhaling. Resuming his role as instructor to help them get going, he encouraged the class to brainstorm for ways they could get the word out and start developing new recruits. Settling on a strategy utilizing the known success of social sites on the Internet, they began by enticing people into learning how to develop mystical powers. Wenstrom was amazed at how many people in the modern world were genuinely interested in learning mystical skills. Three months after the Internet launch, the class slowly began spreading out across the country, meeting and training new recruits. As agreed upon by the entire class from the beginning, that training came with a price. Each new student had to commit their lives to the new fledgling army, swearing an oath to defend mankind in the inevitable war against Hell.

The new students were then instructed to go out and gather followers of their own, teaching them what they had learned, thus, continuing to spread that knowledge to others all around the world. Wenstrom was impressed by the fact that after just a few months, the network of people the Mystical Arts Class developed across the planet became pretty substantial.

Wenstrom remained based at the college, coordinating everyone's efforts and movements from there via computer. He continued to developed new students of his own, teaching them the mystical arts he knew. He also instructed them on how to run the new army's base of operations he had created to keep things running smoothly for everyone. With help from students in the IT department of the school, the college instructor constructed a website for general information, and text messaging was used as the main source of communication between everybody.

Carrying on with the charade of teaching an academic curriculum for the college to see was the biggest challenge Wenstrom dealt with daily. Otherwise, he would not have been able to utilize the necessary resources available at the school to help accomplish their mission.

As the human resistance to Satan's army slowly grew, so did Wenstrom's concern. He began receiving increasing reports of assaults upon them by the evil forces on earth. After Ryon's breakthrough with his connection to Kana, he became the most mystically powerful one of them all. It wasn't long before Ryon could no longer concern himself with finding and teaching new people. Instead, Wenstrom had him concentrate on defending the new army from the ever increasing attacks by Hell's minions.

After being on their own for almost a year, Ryon sent word to Wenstrom that the White Witch prince finally wanted the Mystical Arts Class to all meet together back at the college. The instructor sent out a broadcast, summoning everyone to return to the school, and once again, there they all were. All except Mádeohn, Shilo, and Kana.

Staring at his cluttered desk, Wenstrom smiled to himself, recalling the day the prince had revealed himself to the class. The instructor chuckled as he envisioned himself sitting at the same desk, floating in the air and terrified out of his mind. Thinking back on it, he had to admit that the sight must have been pretty comical. Now even he could easily perform the same feat.

Placing both hands down on the desktop and closing his eyes, Wenstrom easily made the connection with the fabric of the universe in his mind. Stretching the gravity around himself just like the prince had taught, he began levitating both the desk and the chair he was sitting in, just like Kana had. Grinning at his former ignorance, he recalled how excited he had been about moving a chess piece with his mind. Today it was his desk and chair—with him in it.

"How's that working for you?"

Wenstrom lost all concentration at the sound of Kana's voice, and everything he was mentally levitating fell. The instructor's face turned from delight in his accomplishment to a grimace while anticipating the inevitable crash coming when he hit the floor.

The White Witch prince mentally caught Wenstrom and his furniture and gently set them down without so much as a bump.

"Awkward!" the instructor heard someone declare.

Embarrassed, Wenstrom sat there with his eyes closed, taking a moment to calm his racing heart. Cautiously opening one eye, he peered out at everyone silently staring at him for a moment.

He knew it. Once again, he had made a fool of himself.

Taking a deep breath and then reaching for his glasses, he slowly placed them back on his face, trying to restore some semblance of dignity.

Formally addressing Kana, who was standing in the center of the classroom and closely embracing Connie, the instructor greeted the prince, "Welcome back, Your Highness."

"Thank you, Mr. Wenstrom," Kana smiled. Giving Connie a gentle hug, he added, "It is good to be back!" Looking around the room, the prince asked Ryon, "Still no word from Mádeohn?"

Ryon shook his head, clearly displaying concern for his missing friend.

"That's not good," the White Witch prince replied sympathetically. "My guess is that his father probably has him, and there is nothing we can do about that. I'm sorry."

Turning to address the rest of the class, he continued, "The work you all have done is excellent! When you put together the following each one of you has developed, it creates a sizable army here on earth. For now, though, the leaders you have selected will have to run things here. I am taking you to Lysta'cu'mha, where your training will continue under the supervision of the Learned Ones."

Cheers of excitement filled the room, and Connie gave the prince a big hug and a kiss, thoroughly pleased at the thought of seeing Kana's home.

"Settle down now," the White Witch shouted. "It's not going to be all fun and games. You've got a lot of work—studying and training—ahead of you. Shilo and I have been working to prepare for your stay in the White Witch World."

Connie looked at the prince incredulously and asked, "You and Shilo working together?"

Smiling, Kana replied, "Yeah, try not to ponder on that too long. Mr. Wenstrom, are you coming with us?"

"Are you kidding?" Wenstrom exclaimed getting up. "I wouldn't miss this for the world!"

"Let's go then," Kana said calmly. Raising his arms, the whole group faded from the room.

"Oh! Wow!" Connie almost fell over before Kana caught her. "Where are we?"

"We are now in what is called the null corridor," the White Witch prince explained. "It's what separates the universes from the Space of Doors."

Looking around them, Connie could see that they stood in what appeared to be a pure white hallway. As far as she could see, there were no visible floor, walls, or ceiling, although she could sense that they were there.

"What is the Space of Doors?" Mr. Wenstrom asked.

"This way," the prince instructed the class to follow him.

They all walked toward a black square boldly standing out in contrast to the white nothingness surrounding the group. Upon reaching the dark opening, Kana kept right on walking. Connie screamed as she saw the endless drop below the prince, but he did not fall. He just floated where he stood, in midair.

"This is the Space of Doors!" their White Witch guide explained while raising his hands and indicating his surroundings.

Offering his hand to Connie, she carefully followed her prince and, to her delight, found she too was floating by his side. She watched the rest of the class emerge out of the null corridor, each looking around in wide-eyed wonder and totally amazed by what they saw.

To Connie, it appeared as if they were floating in the center of a large room with four walls disappearing into a dauntingly end-less drop of pitch-black darkness below. Looking up, the walls of the room extended over her head, vanishing into a beautiful, bright light above.

"Stay away from the light!" Ryon joked, gazing up into the alluring radiance that felt like it was beckoning his very soul.

Connie smiled at his reference to the near-death stories they all had heard about. Tales of people brought back from death claiming to be drawn to a brilliant light before waking up.

Tearing her eyes away from the bewitching radiance, she then became fascinated by doorways on each one of the walls. Similar to the one they had just come out of, she took a moment to watch them all randomly move about. When her gaze brought her to the far wall, across from where they all stood floating, Connie could see an alcove supporting doorways of its own.

When he figured they all had had a good enough look around, Kana began to explain about the huge room, "The Space of Doors is all that is left of the VOID. Within each of these walls lies the multitude of universes God created, filling the VOID. Just like the one we came out of, what you see on the walls are the doorways into each of those universes. The light you see above us is Heaven. The darkness you see below, in the farthest part of the VOID away from Heaven, is Hell."

"If this is how you travel in and out of the universes," Mr. Wenstrom asked, "why don't you just post guards by the door we just came out of to prevent Satan's minions from entering?"

"That is an excellent question," the White Witch prince responded. "One of the first things Satan did after his exile, and after God filled the VOID, was develop back doors into the universes so that he could use them to sneak his evil minions in and out undetected. Guarding the main entrance to a universe is pretty much useless with these back doors.

"That is why you will see very little traffic out here." Kana went on to explain, "Satan has no need to use these doors. Besides, White Witches simply don't have the resources to guard the multitude of doors that exist. There could also be thousands of Satan's alternate entrances that we don't know about!

"Now," the prince went on with his instruction, moving to a new subject, "remember me teaching you how to connect to the fabric of the universe and that it is a part of everything around you?"

The class all nodded affirmatively, and Kana continued, "The walls you see here, and everything inside them, *is* the fabric of the universe."

"Wow, that does make more sense," Connie commented, now able to physically see how everything was connected together, just like Kana had explained to them in the beginning.

Smiling back at the beautiful earth girl he loved, the White Witch took her by the hand and began to float toward the alcove in the far wall, with the whole group in tow.

"This is Myshunar, the section of the VOID that God has banned Satan, or any of his evil, from entering," he said as they entered the alcove.

"The doorway in the center is my world, Lysta'cu'mha," the prince announced with pride. "Get ready, you get your weight back when you step into the null corridor."

Upon entering the White Witch World, Rhonda exclaimed, "Oh my God!"

She tightened her grip on Mitch's arm as her free hand involuntarily rose up to cover her mouth. Completely overcome with emotion, her eyes began welling up with tears, blurring her vision. The beauty of this alien world was beyond anything she had ever imagined.

Standing at the edge of a park like forest, the scenic vista that spread out all around the Mystic Arts Class had the entire group of earthlings completely stunned.

Opening his cloak, Kana put his arm around Connie. Attempting to clear her blurry vision, she leaned against the prince, gazing up in wonder at the strange, beautifully colored creatures flying through a pink-tinted twilight sky. Looking off in the distance, she could see an orange sun slipping down behind a range of majestic purple mountains. It had to be the most gorgeous sunset Connie had ever seen.

Slowly tearing her eyes away from the breathtaking vista in the distance, she wiped a new stream of uncontrollable tears of joy away from her face. Trying to focus on any one thing in this beautiful world was difficult. Beneath her feet, a multitude of colored flowers sprung up through a lawn of soft, violet-colored grass.

At least she thought it was grass. It looked like grass to her.

Releasing herself from Kana's embrace, Connie wiped her tear-soaked hands on her jeans. Then, bending down, she curiously ran her fingers through the soft purple blades, enjoying the familiar feel of grass.

Twisting around and peering into the trees behind them, she could see shoots of various-sized ferns peppering the forest floor. Each plant displayed a unique pigment of its own, hues totally inconceivable to the earth woman. The leaves of the trees were a kaleidoscope of colors that beautifully reflected the setting sun.

As if in a dream, Connie watched Ryon reach out and run his hand along the trunk of one of the trees.

"The bark, it feels like velvet!" he proclaimed in amazement to his mesmerized friends.

Turning back to gaze up at Kana, Connie noticed the White Witch prince's head tilted to one side, as if listening to something. Nodding, the prince reached down, offering his hand to help her back up to her feet.

"We must go now," Kana's voice drew everyone's attention back to their White Witch guide. "The king awaits our arrival."

Swiftly following the prince into the alien forest, the colorful foliage closed in around Connie, blocking the White Witch setting sun. To her amazement, mysteriously beautiful, glowing flowers illuminated the path beneath her feet, which made trekking the narrow footpath easy. Stepping back out into the evening sun after a surprisingly short distance, an enchanting vision spread out before her.

The ivory towers of an enormous palace majestically rising up into the pink sky brought Connie to an abrupt halt.

"Oh my Lord!" Rhonda whispered, stopping next to Connie. "It's like something out of a fairy tale."

Emerging from the trees, each member of the class spread out around the two women, taking a good look at the beautiful fortress.

"Wow!" Ryon exclaimed, stepping up next to the girls. "It looks like the buildings in the archangel city."

"He's right," Connie thought to herself, marveling at the beauty of the royal structure awash with the light of the setting sun. To her, the enormous palace looked more like a small city sitting on an island in a vast lake of deep-blue water. A crystal bridge reflecting a rainbow of colors stretched from the main shore to what appeared to be a jeweled gate in the ivory-white walls surrounding the entire island.

"Come," the White Witch prince invited with a smile of pride, "enter Shycoma, my father's house."

Thus began a trip that the class would never forget: a tour through worlds where the mind rules, where time, fate, and universes are made and destroyed. Worlds that God specifically set aside for their pure, innocent beauty.

Hand in hand, Kana and Connie led the rest of the group through the jeweled gates of the palace and into a great violet-colored park. The road they stood on inside the palace walls sparkled like diamonds in the evening light. The gates began closing behind them, and seemingly out of nowhere, six chariots drawn by milk-white, winged unicorns suddenly appeared on the road.

"Are these some kind of cross breed between unicorns and Pegasus?" Mr. Wenstrom inquired, amazed by the animals.

"Like I said," the prince replied, "a lot of your myths and legends are based on what people saw when the White Witches use to roam freely on earth."

Climbing into one of the chariots, Mitch asked, "How do you drive one of these?" while looking for the unicorns' reins.

Kana smiled with amusement as the animals drawing the chariot he, Connie, and Ryon stood in took off without any physical prompting. Mitch quickly grabbed his chariot's railing in alarm, almost falling out when it started to move. He grinned at Rhonda, but she just rolled her eyes while shaking her head in disbelief.

The White Witch prince's chariot led the class down the beautiful but strange highway toward the main palace.

After disembarking from the chariots upon reaching the palace doors, the chariots quietly vanished in the same manner as when they first appeared.

The massive bronze doors looked like they reached the sky. "This place is so unreal," Connie said.

Kana smiled at her. "No dear, everything imaginable is real in this world. Look up there." He pointed to one of the strange flying creatures in the sky. "That is called a Falgon—part bird, part dragon—and, yes, there is such a thing as a dragon."

The prince looked at the great bronze doors, and they majestically began opening on their own to an enormous hall forty feet wide.

Peering down the hallway, Ryon noticed its walls pulsating and glowing in a pearly white hue. At the far end of the corridor, he could see another massive set of doors.

Connie looked at the red carpet floating a foot above the floor and reaching all the way down to the brass doors at the hall's end.

"How?" she asked curiously.

"I couldn't begin to explain it so that you would understand," Kana said. Stepping aside, he gestured into the doorway, inviting, "After you."

Hesitating for a moment, she cautiously placed one foot on the carpet, and it surprisingly held firm.

Nonchalantly walking past her, Kana headed down the hallway saying, "Come on."

Following the White Witch along the extraordinary passage into the interior of the mystical palace, the whole class marveled at each of the artifacts appearing to float on the pulsating walls.

Inquisitively touching the glowing surface, it felt warm under Ryon's fingertips.

"It's almost as if they're alive," he commented to no one in particular.

"They are," Kana responded. "That's how the doors open by themselves: the walls do it."

Reaching the second set of doors, the prince added, "This, my friends, is the throne room of the White Witches."

The brass doors began opening, and the throne room that came into view, like everything else so far, was grander than any the earthlings could imagine.

On the far side of the chamber, Kana's parents occupied two throne chairs on a dais. The two elders watched as their son led the group across the room. Halfway to the throne, Shilo appeared, joining the rest of her friends. As their daughter gave Ryon a very affectionate hug, both stood mutely watching him enthusiastically return the embrace.

Stopping everyone at the foot of the throne platform and mounting the steps himself, Kana knelt in front of his father. Bowing his head respectfully, he reverently kissed the king's ring.

"Are we supposed to curtsy, or kneel, or something?" Rhonda whispered to Connie.

Whispering back out of the corner of her mouth, Connie replied, "How am I supposed to know?"

"You're the one dating a prince!"

Connie gave her friend a get-real look, whispering again through her teeth, "Please! Like I've ever bowed to him!"

Rhonda gave her friend a brief smile while shrugging her shoulders, indicating she had no idea what the two of them did alone.

The prince stood up, facing his parents, formally beginning his introductions, "Father, Mother, these are the leaders of my army."

Turning, he waved a hand over his earth friends, continuing, "Mr. Wenstrom, Ryon, Connie, and the Mystic Arts Class, my parents, King Marcan and his queen, Mirha."

Graciously smiling down at the group of young adults before her, the queen bid her guests, "Welcome to our home. This is a very monumental occasion! You are the first of God's children to ever grace Lysta'cu'mha. We hope your stay with us is not only productive but also pleasurable."

"Mr. Wenstrom!"

The instructor stood a little taller as the king addressed him.

"The path you and your students have embarked on," Marcan continued gravely, "is a very dangerous one. You all are very brave for taking on this dangerous but necessary task. Necessary for the salvation of your world!"

Then the king stood, raised his hand to his forehead, and touched it with his fingertips, sincerely adding, "On behalf of every White Witch, I salute you all!"

There were no words to describe the depth of pride each member of the Mystic Arts Class was feeling at that moment.

This honor was not the greeting Connie was expecting upon their arrival to the White Witch prince's home. Having the monarch of an entire universe, the descendant of former angels, humbly paying tribute to you was beyond her wildest dreams. With tears of pride rolling down her face and not knowing what else to do to show her appreciation to the king's humble words, Connie bent down on one knee, bowing to Kana's parents.

Sniffing and attempting to dry her own cheeks, Rhonda joined Connie, kneeling down beside her best friend. One by one, each member of the Mystic Arts Class followed the girls' lead, bowing down to honor the royal family.

Kana turned to his parents, smiling with pride.

Marcan nodded his approval to his son as Mirha stood, bidding the class, "Please, rise. I have prepared a small reception in your honor. Relax, and enjoy yourselves. Shilo or Kana will answer any questions you might have about the White Witch cuisine."

Stepping up next to his queen, Marcan offered her his arm. Taking it, the two turned and regally exited through a private doorway behind their throne chairs.

While mingling and sampling the queen's food, every one of the guests of honor experienced a very emotional meeting with their guardian angel. Each class member spent quite a bit of time getting acquainted with his or her personal White Witch guardian during the reception.

Later that evening, Kana gathered all of them on a terrace adjoining the throne room and overlooking the palace courtyard. "You will start your schooling in three days," he informed the group. "Your White Witch guardian will assist you in your training. I suggest you get to know them well; they will be your greatest assets as you learn. It's not going to be easy for any of you, so get some rest for the next couple of days. You all have the run of the palace and any part of the park inside of the wall. Everyone is at your disposal, just ask if you need something. Ladies, you have girls in your room to assist you in your bath needs."

"Gosh, we're going to be spoiled and never want to leave," Connie said cheerfully, snuggling up to her prince.

"It's so beautiful here," Rhonda sighed contentedly while leaning out over the balcony. Taking a deep breath of the clear air, she let her eyes roam around the moonlit, violet grass of the park. In several places, she could see benches sitting under multi-colored trees, some of which had small lights glowing along their branches. At least they appeared to be lights at first. Then, to her delight, one swarm of the lights suddenly took flight, disappearing over the palace's outer wall.

"Oh my gosh! *That was so awesome!*" Rhonda exclaimed.

The next day, Shilo escorted the Mystic Arts Class to the palace's huge outdoor arena. Ushering them through the royal family's entrance so they could avoid the crowds, she led the way to the guest of honor box. Located just below the royalty seats, the princess explained that the special suite of seats had a perfect view of the stadium. The entire class was overwhelmed with fascination at the size and architecture of the huge amphitheater. They watched curiously as vendors with refreshments and souvenirs strolled about, shouting what they were offering to the thousands of people flocking into the huge arena.

"This is like a giant version of the Coliseum in Rome," Ryon commented out loud as he took a seat next to Shilo.

The princess smiled and asked him, "Who do you think helped design the Coliseum, along with a lot of other structures during that era on earth?"

"Let's see," Ryon quipped, "the gods?"

Shilo backhanded him in the chest.

"Ouch!" Ryon moaned, rubbing his chest where she had stuck him.

"Oh, please!" Shilo admonished. "Like that really hurt!"

He smiled and asked, "What's going on today?"

This was the very question running through the rest of the Earthling's minds.

"Today is the annual White Witch Army Mystical Tournament," was the only explanation the princess gave. They all had to content themselves with watching a variety of small competitions held on the arena floor. The class was entirely mesmerized by the displays of mystical-art warfare.

"A lot of what you see down there," Shilo informed her friends, "you will be taught by the Learned Ones before you return to earth."

After almost two of hours watching the events below, the class observed the arena floor clear of all contestants, except for one lone person. A wave of anticipation swept through the crowd. Suddenly trumpets blared, and the crowd rose to its feet, cheering. King Marcan and Queen Mirha stepped into the royalty box above the class, followed by Zaia, Cyphis, and the rest of the council.

Raising his hand, the king silenced the crowd.

"Arena master," he shouted

"Here, my lord," came a voice from the figure standing in the center of the field below.

"Prepare the battleground!" the king commanded.

The arena master slowly raised his arms up and held them outstretched from his sides. The class watched in amazement as the two outer halves of the arena floor began to silently rise up into the air and then break apart into sixteen smaller sections, leaving only the center strip the entire length of the arena behind.

"Awesome!" Ryon exclaimed as each of the sections expanded upward and down, with each becoming unique islands of rock, the upper part supporting bushes, trees, and other forms of vegetation growing out of the stony mound. One of them, to his delight, even had a waterfall flowing down its side, the water disappearing into thin air after tumbling off the side of the floating island of rock.

"That is so cool!" Rhonda yelled to Shilo. The White Witch princess stood there smiling at her new friends, completely amused by the childlike looks of fascination on each one of their faces. Looking up to her father in the box above, he winked at her, acknowledging that he was equally entertained by her earth friends' enthrallment.

Completely captivated, the class watched as nine of the center islands began to rise up above the seven outer ones. Of those nine, the four in the middle of that group floated up even higher. Then the center island, the one with the waterfalls, climbed up high above the rest, the apex of four levels of islands floating in midair.

"Everyone link minds so I can talk to you mentally," Shilo shouted over the crowd noise. "That way all of you can hear me as I explain what is going on!"

After doing so, the class watched as each level of the islands began to rotate in a circle. At the same time, each individually spun slowly on its axis, some clockwise, others in the opposite direction.

"The reason for everything rotating is so the people can get a view of each island, no matter where in the stands they are sitting," Shilo explained. "It will also make the battle a little more difficult for the warriors, as you will see after they get started."

"How do they do that?" Mr. Wenstrom asked, totally intrigued by the chunks of rock floating in midair.

"It is a similar technology used to make the carpet float in the palace halls, but a lot more sophisticated," Shilo answered. "When they get started, you will also notice that each island has its own gravity field. That field is just strong enough to allow a contestant to stand on it but so weak that it takes very little force to knock them off, an important factor in the game, you will notice"

"Battlefield complete!" the arena master shouted.

"Bring in the contestants!" Marcan commanded.

Once again, the crowd went wild. From opposite ends, across the remaining section of the arena floor still on the ground, two groups of warriors advanced toward the arena master. Connie's heart leaped when she saw Kana, Argon at his side, leading his warriors as the two teams paraded toward the center of the arena. She noticed Kana's team was dressed in red and white and riding unicorns. The opposing team, on the other hand, wore gold and blue. Unlike Kana's team, their warriors were riding a birdlike creature that stood on long, powerful legs at about seven feet tall. The huge bird's mostly brown plumage had various other colors mixed in.

"Now that's what I'm talking about!" Mitch shouted. Standing next to Rhonda and smiling with delight at the fierce-looking birds, he exclaimed, "Those are wicked!"

Both teams had their battle mounts decked out in jeweled dress armor that sparkled brilliantly in the bright, midday sun.

"The uniform colors," Shilo continued to explain, "are team colors, and the mounts are team's choice. Kana and Argon have always preferred unicorns to kyterns, what the gold-and-blue team is riding, although the latter are considered by most as the better battle mount. Kana is riding on Cloudrunner, and Argon has Gray Wind. The two animals shared the same womb together."

Intrigued by what the princess said about the pair of unicorns, Connie took a closer look at the two lead animals. Cloudrunner's coat was white. The feathers of his wings started out blue at the body, changing to red and then pink at the ends. Gray Wind, on the other hand, was completely gray, thus, his name, but his body sparkled in the sunlight as if his coat were covered with shiny crystals.

"They're so beautiful," Connie commented mentally so everyone could hear over the roar of the crowd. She stood there, proudly watching her prince and completely enchanted by the unicorns as they marched toward the center of the arena.

The two teams consisted of twenty warriors riding in twos. Upon reaching the arena center, they halted. Kana and the opposing team captain advanced before the arena master. While seated atop their mounts, each ceremoniously bowed to the arena master and then respectfully bowed to each other.

"I will briefly remind you of the rules," the arena master shouted, and the cheering crowd quieted down.

The official continued, "Your first objective is for your team to gain the majority control of the islands on each level. That team will be declared conquerors of that level. Once a team accomplishes that, both teams will advance to the next level to battle for majority control of that level, and so on until the uppermost island is won. Each island under a team's control is worth two points, except the top level, which is worth five points. Control of an island is declared when a team has five members on it at the same time, for a count of five on the first level, and three warriors on the next two levels, for a count of five. On the last level, the first team to have only its warriors on that island wins it. Any excessive force will be assessed as a foul. That team will lose one point, and that team member must drop to the defender position on a lower island for a period of one level battle.

"Turn now, and await final instructions from your king."

All the warriors, and the entire crowd of spectators turned and faced Marcan.

"You are all White Witch warriors, I expect you to battle honorably today." King Marcan's voice resonated throughout the arena. "At the first trumpet blast, all warriors are to take starting positions, at the second trumpet, begin."

The first trumpet sounded, and the Mystic Arts Class watched in amazement as all the warriors levitated up to the bottom level of islands. Each entire team landed on an island floating on the opposite sides of the circle. The rock on the bottom of Kana's island turned red, the other team's turned blue.

"This starting position is the team's home island. When a team has control, or conquers an island, it will turn that team's color, just like those two did. That way, the crowd not only can keep track of who controls what but each team's score as well," the White Witch princess said.

One member of each team then moved over to the two adjacent islands on each side of their home island, leaving only one of the seven bottom islands with no one on it at all. Next, three warriors of each team levitated up to the next level. All three of those team members took up positions on one island also on the opposite sides of the circle of that level from the opposing three competitors.

"Starting positions achieved!" the arena master shouted.

"Get ready!" Shilo told everyone, her own excitement obvious in the tone of her mental voice.

King Marcan nodded his head, and the brass horns blasted once again. The crowd exploded as the battle began.

As soon as the starting horn sounded, the entire Mystic Arts Class leaped to their feet, cheering on Kana's team, even though none of them had any idea as to what was going on.

First they observed each warrior erect a personal shield around themselves. Then all but four from each home island launched into the air. Blasts of energy started to crisscross back and forth between the islands as warriors began shooting at opponents, knocking them off the islands that both teams were trying to conquer. Fortunately for the class, the personal shields and the discharges of energy were colored: red for Kana's team and blue for the other. This made following who was who just a little easier in the confusion of the battle.

Within moments of the contest beginning, each team took control of the two islands adjacent to their home island, the bottoms turning red and blue respectively, giving both teams three islands each. That left only one to go. The class watched with anticipation as the warriors who did not remain on their conquered islands to defend them swarmed the remaining one. Bodies flew everywhere as blasts of energy were hurled at opponents, knocking them away from their goal in the low gravity. Even those in the next level up were bombarding opposing team members from their elevated position.

Suddenly the last island turned red, and all fighting stopped. The Mystic Arts Class joined the rest of the crowd cheering as Kana's team was declared the conquerors of the first level. Connie grabbed Rhonda by the arm, and both girls jumped up and down, celebrating and chanting, "Yes! Yes! Yes!"

"Don't get too excited about winning that level," Shilo warned. "When you have watched as many tournaments as I have, you can see when one team lets the other one win. It is part of their battle strategy."

"What do you mean they let Kana's team win?" Ryon asked confused. "Why?"

"Watch as they set up for the next level," the White Witch princess went on explaining.

Warriors from both teams began levitating up to the next level of islands.

"See how two members of each team remain on each one of their conquered islands below? They must do that according to the rules on each level, reducing the number of warriors able to participate in the levels above. So now, even though Kana's team has more points, he has fewer warriors than the opposing team advancing up to fight. Part of your game strategy is that you have to balance out earning points with how many team members you have to battle with. I would not be surprised to see Kana allow the other team to win this next level."

"Why go through all the effort of fighting if you're going to just give up a level?" Wenstrom asked. "Why not stand back and just let the other team take the winning island?"

"Because it is against the rules," Shilo answered. "Every player on a battle level must be actively engaged in attacking or achieving a foothold on an island."

"Kana and Argon stayed below," Connie observed, frowning.

"That's right," the princess went on, explaining the White Witch prince's thinking, "it is also a requirement for every team member to sit out one level of battle by defending a lower island. Kana has chosen to take the first break in order to participate in the upper two levels. Once again, it is a battle strategy."

With all players reset, the trumpets blared again, and the crowd once more exploded into cheering on their team. The colorful blast of energy once again crisscrossed back and forth, exploding against personal shields and sending warriors flying through the air. Just as Shilo predicted, within minutes, the blue-and-gold team was announced conquerors of the second level.

Watching as the two teams quickly set up for the third level, the class saw warriors from both teams drop down and replace those defending conquered islands on the first level. Kana and Argon rose up and took positions on the third one with their teammates. With only three islands in the third level, it only left one to fight for, just like on the first two levels since both teams automatically had a home island. The trumpets sounded once again, and the battle began.

This time, with so few warriors fighting for the third island, it was easier to keep track of an individual player. From the beginning, the whole thing didn't seem fair to Connie. The battle was nothing but a two-man slaughter. Everywhere Kana and Argon went—wherever one was, the other was somewhere near—opposing warriors were knocked around like rag dolls. The blue-and-gold team had no answer for the duo's clearly superior battle skills, something that was quite evident to Connie, though no one else in the arena appeared to mind it. In fact, to her mind, it actually fueled the crowd's excitement even more.

In less than a minute, Kana's team had control of the third island.

"Yes!" Ryon shouted. "Sixteen to fourteen, we're in the lead!"

Shilo smiled up to him and commented, "That may be so, but that only leaves two warriors from his team who can advance to the final level, while they have five."

Ryon's excitement was replaced by a perplexed look of concern.

"OK, I see what you mean. This is why the other team let us have the first level. They can win in points, taking the last one, and they have more warriors to do it!"

"That's right, my dear," Shilo replied while tenderly patting Ryon's chest.

Smiling once again, he reached up, taking her hand in his. Lifting it to his lips, he gently began kissing her fingers. She responded by raising herself up on her toes and softly kissing his cheek.

Kana and Argon rose up to the island that was the final level. As Shilo pointed out, five of the blue-and-gold team members also levitated up to the top island. The horn blasted once more, and the battle for the last level began. Rhonda had a tight grip on Mitch's arm as she bounced up and down, every time Kana or Argon scored a hit. It wasn't long before they had their opponents whittled down to two. Glancing at Connie and seeing the grim look on her friend's face, she stopped to see what the matter was.

"What's wrong, sweetie? Are you all right?"

"I'm fine," Connie replied but then retorted, "it isn't fair!"

"What isn't fair?" Rhonda asked, totally confused.

"As good as the warriors on the other team are," Connie tried to explain, "none of them are on the same level as Kana and Argon in battle skills. It isn't a fair contest!"

"Your man is out there kicking butt, on the verge of winning," Rhonda reproached her friend, "and you're worried whether the other side is being treated fairly? You need to get your priorities straight, girlfriend!"

A sudden change in the tone of the crowd brought both girls' attention back to the battle. As the top island slowly rotated around, Argon and one of the blue-and-gold team members came back into view of the class and were floating away from it. That left only one last opponent for the White Witch prince to eliminate for victory. The two adversaries carefully circled each other near the waterfall, making absolutely certain they were anchored down by using whatever they could get their hands on or their feet hooked under. Every now and then, there would be an exchange of energy blasts as each tried to dislodge the other from the floating island. The two disappeared again as the island's rotation continued, leaving the entire Mystic Arts Class tense with anticipation at not being able to see what was happening. When they came back around into view, both warriors were still firmly anchored in place, exchanging a series of energy blasts at each other.

Suddenly Kana dropped his shield, and the crowd cheered.

"Why did he drop his shield?" Ryon asked, shocked.

"It is forbidden to strike anyone who does not have a shield up to protect themselves with an energy blast," Shilo explained. "Kana is inviting him to hand-to-hand combat."

The blue-and-gold team member dropped his shield, and the two warriors approached each other carefully in the low gravity.

"Fighting hand-to-hand in the low gravity is very difficult," Shilo continued with a little anxiety clearly in her own voice.

The crowd waited with anticipation to see how well the two could do without losing their hold on the island. What Kana did next took everyone by surprise, including his opponent. With his own feet firmly lodged under a rock overhang, the White Witch prince shot an energy blast at a root next to where the other warrior had his foot hooked under it, breaking that anchor. Immediately the prince followed up with a second blast into the trunk of a tree behind his opponent. The blue-and-gold warrior was clinging to vines hanging down from it. The tree broke from its base as it was pushed over by the blast and slowly tumbled into the waterfall. Realizing that the tree he was holding onto was about to be swept away from the island by the rapidly falling water, the blue-and-gold warrior quickly released the vines and scrambled to connect his feet under something solid. His efforts were to no avail, though, as he too drifted away from the island, propelled by the momentum of the tree he hadn't released his grip from quickly enough.

"I thought you said they couldn't use energy blasts?" Ryon looked at Shilo, confused.

"I said they could not shoot at someone with their shield down," the princess replied with a smirk of satisfaction. "I never said they couldn't shoot at something else!"

The rock under the uppermost island turned red, and the crowd erupted with cheering. Kana carefully climbed to the top and stood where everyone could see him, raising his fist in victory to the roaring crowd.

All the other warriors dropped back down to where their battle mounts were waiting quietly. Cloudrunner spread his massive wings and launched himself into the air, flying up to where Kana stood. Leaping off the top of the island as the unicorn glided by, the prince grabbed the reins and mounted the beast on the fly.

The crowd exploded once more as the prince guided Cloudrunner around the arena in a victory lap, waving at Connie and his earth friends while flying by the guest box. Argon, with the rest of the red-and-white team, joined Kana on his second victory trip around, which ended back on the center strip of the arena floor with the blue-and-gold team. Both teams began to intermingle, discussing different events that took place during the battle as the islands began their slow decent, retracting back into their original positions as the arena floor.

When it was complete, Shilo dragged the Mystic Arts Class down onto the field and over to the mingling group of warriors. Seeing Connie, Kana turned from the other team captain to share his victory with her, but the smile left his face as he looked into her eyes.

"What's the matter?" he asked.

"It wasn't fair," she claimed with a clear hint of frustration in her voice. "They had no chance of winning from the beginning with you in there. There was no competition at all. Is it like that all the time? Do you always win?"

"Of course, I win," Kana smiled while replying matter-of-factly. "I was not trained to lose!"

That evening, Queen Mirha opened her home to all the visiting guests by hosting a banquet in Shycoma. Standing with Kana and Argon in the palace's main lobby, Ryon was totally spellbound by the decor of the huge room the trio stepped into.

One of the things that continually fascinated Ryon since their arrival into the White Witch World was the palace lighting. All the interior lighting came from the walls, floor, or ceiling. Kana explained to him that the desired atmosphere or mood dictated the color and intensity of the light.

To his amazement, Ryon now stood in the totally alien jungle of Lysta'cu'mha at night, lavishly recreated in the large room

Also completely mesmerized by what he saw, Kana stood next to his ward and commented, "Wow! Mom really outdid herself this time!"

Ryon smiled with delight at the ceiling, which sparkled as if it were a clear, star-filled sky. Looking around him, he noticed the glowing walls were no longer pearly white but a dark chocolate brown, with splashes every now and then of luminescent blues, greens, and white mixed with vibrant purples and hot pink.

What really drew Ryon's attention was the main focal point of the huge room. Staring awestruck, he marveled at a majestic, semicircular, marble stairway designed so that the bottom steps expanded to twice the width of those at the top as they descended. Watching a white mist gently roll over each step like a stream tumbling down a waterfall, he followed it spellbound as it continued to flood out across the entire lobby floor. The river of fog was glowing white while cascading down the stairway and across the huge room. The source of light, Ryon assumed, was the floor underneath the captivating vapor.

The mist churned and swirled around several tables scattered about the room. Ryon stood completely fascinated by the jungle of exotic fruits and vegetables adorning each table, creating tropical islands floating in the sea of glowing vapor. To his delight, strange flowers and leafy plants glowing brightly in the dimly lit room provided illumination of the edible delicacies on each tropical island.

Discovering fountains of bright-blue liquid flowing freely in the midst of the luminescent vegetation, Ryon noticed the other guest wandering about the room while drinking it. Tasting the exotic-looking beverage, he was pleasantly surprised to find it tasted a lot like champagne.

Mitch and the other members of the Mystic Arts Class slowly arrived, one at a time, escorted by their White Witch guardian angel. It wasn't long before everyone was there, except Connie and Rhonda.

The two women were getting ready together for the banquet with Shilo. The guys occupied themselves while waiting by meandering around the room, sampling the exotic cuisine and mingling with the guests. Kana introduced Ryon and the other members of the Mystic Arts Class to his fellow teammates, as well as different members of the blue-and-gold team. The entire lobby was buzzing with conversation over an undertone of music that drifted in through an archway leading to the park outside the palace.

Reminiscing about different events that took place earlier during the tournament, Kana and Argon stood facing each other with their hands in the air, demonstrating a particular maneuver the two had made. The prince noticed that his best friend had stopped talking and was staring at something behind him. As Kana turned to see what had caught Argon's attention, the White Witch prince noticed a hush had fallen all throughout the lobby. Upon glimpsing the heavenly vision at the top of the stairs, Kana immediately became as spellbound as the rest of the room.

Like three angelic creatures, Shilo, Connie, and Rhonda appeared beautifully attired in stunning evening dresses at the top of the waterfall of mist. Their floor-touching gowns, uniquely different in cut and color, elegantly complemented each girl's every curve. With sensuously open backs; alluring, plunging necklines; and thigh-high slits, all three women had the entire room enchantingly mesmerized.

The White Witch prince watched transfixed as the three captivating women gracefully began descending the fog-covered stairway. To him, they looked like celestial beings majestically floating down a gently tumbling waterfall.

Upon reaching the lobby floor, Shilo brushed past Kana on her way to where Ryon stood while mentally chiding her brother, "Close your mouth, you look like an idiot!"

Annoyingly realizing his sister was right, the White Witch prince stopped gaping and smiled down at the angel who stood in front of him.

Stammering, he tried to speak, "I...ah...there are no words... you are so beautiful...just...doesn't seem adequate!"

Blushing, Connie smiled back. Rising up on her toes, she whispered in his ear, "The look on your face—that was adequate enough."

Arm in arm, the two followed Ryon, Shilo, Rhonda, and Mitch as they worked their way across the lobby from table to table. While snacking along the way, the princess shared her intimate knowledge of how the entire room was conceived and set up. The two earth women were totally fascinated by her tale and asked many questions.

"You think this is awesome," Shilo stated enthusiastically, "wait till you see the park outside!"

The music drifting into the palace grew distinctively louder as the three couples approached the archway leading outside. Stepping through the opening, Rhonda stopped abruptly and exclaimed, "Oh my God!"

The sight before them took Connie's breath away as well. She watched, fascinated, as beautiful fountains of water scattered throughout the park fluctuated with various colors pulsing and spraying in time to the music. She also noticed the little glowing bugs adorning trees and bushes everywhere, setting the ambiance in the palace park. The alien stars sparkling in the moonless sky above only added to the overwhelming wonder Connie was feeling at the moment while standing on a foreign planet in a completely different universe from her own.

The multitude of guests filling the park before her gyrated with the primal beat of what sounded like very primitive music blended perfectly with the heavenly melodies of an angelic choir. It all looked and sounded very ancient, very ritualistic, and somewhat barbaric. This rave-style behavior was not at all what Connie expected to see from former angels.

Suddenly, Queen Mirha stood next to the small group. "You ladies look very beautiful tonight." She smiled at the girls.

Each blushed, bowing to the queen's gracious compliment.

Looking directly at her son, Mirha then emphasized, "I hope the men take time out of their self-edification over today's events to appreciate the time it took you to prepare for this evening. Now I want all of you to go enjoy yourselves!"

With that, the queen disappeared into the crowd, gracefully greeting guests as she went.

Connie looked up at the prince, clearly trying not burst out giggling.

"What?" he asked of her obvious amusement.

Raising her eyebrows, she teased, "Guess you got told!"

Kana replied back with a sarcastic smile, then asked, "Would you like to dance, or just continue to emotionally dagger me?"

"Hmm," Connie pretended to chew on her thumbnail, "that's a hard one!"

"Fine!" the prince gazed out at the crowd over her head.

"You *are* a big baby!" she exclaimed while taking his hand and pulling him out onto the park lawn.

Upon reaching a section surrounded by three of the lighted fountains and occupied by several other couples dancing, Kana stopped Connie by pulling her into his arms. With her back to the prince, the two lovers began to fluidly sway to the music, their bodies molded perfectly together as one. Connie lifted an arm up and wrapped it around Kana's neck while he bent forward over her shoulder, gently breathing down upon her neck.

Closing her eyes, Connie was having a hard time believing where she was—dancing to music that sounded like it was being performed by a heavenly choir and in an alien world. Holding her was the most beautiful man she had ever seen in her life, who also happened to be a warrior prince, and she was dancing with him in the sexiest, most revealing evening gown she had ever worn. Happy and content, the woman wanted to savor the moment forever.

The fountains exploded with a blinding shower of light at the end of the song, turning crimson, to Connie's delight, and highlighted with streaks of blue. The water began to pulsate in time with what sounded like a heart beating.

Turning around so they could face each other, Connie could feel her own heart beat in time with the sound filling the park air. She laid her head upon Kana's massive chest and listened to his heart. It too pulsed in time to the music. The angelic choir began to softly chant in the background, and the couple slowly swayed to the drumbeat.

While she was growing up, Connie always knew guys were interested in her, at least until they found out that her father was a cop. That intimidation usually put a screeching halt to any serious relationship. Quite frankly, Connie was all right with that. None of them sparked any real desire for something lasting in her, not until Kana came into her life. He was the first one she truly cared deeply about. The first one she ached for—heart, body, and soul.

The prince made it obvious that he cared for her. She just couldn't tell how deep his feelings ran. As deep as hers? The White Witch warrior's mind was always carefully shielded, and so far, she had no clear idea what his true, inner emotions were.

Connie could hear a beautiful female voice fill the air, melding in with the choir and the sound of the heartbeat rhythm. The angelic words spoke straight to her soul, telling her to close her eyes, which she did, and listen to the voice deep inside her. That voice grew ever louder, bidding her to open her heart to love. Welling up with emotion, she could feel her closed eyes begin to tear up. Opening them to look up at Kana, she saw stars surrounding them through her blurred vision. After blinking the mist away, the little spots of light turned out to be the glowing bugs from the trees, gracefully floating all around the two of them. It was beautiful. Then she realized, to her amazement, they no longer stood on the lawn but were floating in the air above the park, inside the swarm of fluttering lights.

The chanting of the choir became louder and more intense.

While looking up at the White Witch prince, Connie was unable to express the depth of love that painfully surged through her heart at that moment—her desire to always be with him, to stand at his side forever. She completely opened her mind up to Kana so that he could see what she was feeling. He was there, anxiously waiting to come inside. She saw in him the same fervid yearning that burned inside her. With their minds so intimately entwined, she could now feel the same impassioned commitment and deep love in his heart that she felt in hers. Ravenously locking her lips with her love, she began to moan and convulse uncontrollably as the White Witch's intense magic repeatedly shot back and forth through her body.

The music escalated to a dramatic climax, and the heavenly voices of the choir abruptly became silent as Kana reluctantly released her.

Panting hard, desperate for air, Connie completely collapsed in his arms. Unable to do so on her own, the prince had to literally hold her up while she continued to slowly catch her breath. Once again, she rested her head upon Kana's now heaving chest, listening to his heart race wildly. Relishing the sensations her body was experiencing at the moment, she listened to the throbbing heartbeat sound of a lingering drumbeat as the song they were dancing to came to a close. It was pulsating through the night air, alive with little fluttering glow bugs.

Connie was truly floating with her prince among the stars.

MYSTICAL TOUR

Mádeohn sat quietly in the dark, cold room, methodically running through the series of mental exercises he had developed to keep his mind sharp. This mental workout was the only thing keeping him sane after several months of isolation. Imprisoned in a dark, damp, rocky chamber ever since his capture, he had given up on trying to escape a long time ago. The son of Satan was not strong enough to break through whatever force shielded the dark cave to keep him in.

Ever since Mádeohn could remember, he had given very little thought to any of his father's ambitions, even when he was fully immersed in his archangel-warrior studies. His only concern was always for his mom's safety. That was the one motivation he used to excel in his studies. It had nothing to do with whatever his father had planned for him.

Now, after months of solitary confinement, and continually going over the events that led up to his capture, all that changed. Realizing how ineffective he had been in protecting his mother from Hell's minions and not knowing what had happened to her, Mádeohn slowly developed a raging hatred for his father. Just the thought that she might be suffering some unimaginable fate somewhere in Hell almost made him violently sick. This slow-burning malice toward everything associated with Satan and his evil kingdom and his desire to rescue or avenge his mother continually fueled Mádeohn's need to stay focused and alert. Using that helped keep him from sinking into complete despondency as he quietly waited in solitude.

His isolation was broken every now and then by a visit from his sister. Apparently Na-amah was charged with bringing him his meals and making sure he stayed healthy. For what reason, Mádeohn had no idea, nor did he care. He rebuffed the she demon's attempts to befriend him, making absolutely no effort to hide his disgust and loathing for the hell-spawn beast. At one point, she even tried to break through his cold demeanor by attempting to seductively entice him. Thoroughly repulsed by the mere thought, Mádeohn blasted the abomination completely across the rocky prison chamber. It was a couple of days later before Na-amah returned again. Leaving the bowl of food she brought, the she demon immediately left and never made the mistake of trying to seduce her brother again.

Mádeohn's mystically bound seclusion finally came to an end one day when two dregs entered his dark prison chamber. Escorted through the rocky tunnels of Hell, he was forcibly shoved to his knees before his father upon reaching Satan's throne room. Looking around, he noticed the place hadn't changed much since the last time he was there during his training. Lilith stood quietly next to her husband's throne chair, with Na-amah right by her side. The demon king's dark body glistened from the glow of fires scattered about the throne chamber. His eyes, pits of white fire, bore down upon his son.

"Well now, if this isn't a cozy family reunion?" Hell's master began softly. "My two children," Satan went on, "both I spawned to accomplish a specific purpose, and neither one has succeeded!"

"At least my daughter has stayed loyal to her father and tried," Lilith defended Na-amah. "That is more than you can say for your son!"

Seeing the annoyance in her husband's face at her outburst, Lilith bowed her head in submission to her lord's authority. She held her tongue from further comment, fearing more than an unpleasant look from him.

Turning back to Mádeohn, Satan's voice boomed through the rocky chambers. "I cannot believe that you thought you could thwart my plans!"

The fires that were scattered everywhere seemed to rise with his anger.

"Not only do I find you helping those who are plotting against me, but you don't have enough brains to assemble a strong force to work with you, just a pathetic group of kids!"

"Power?" Satan's son grinned. "You have not seen power until you've matched up with the White Witch prince! Besides, the *Tablets of Time* say that a group of *kids* is to be your downfall on earth, and I aim to do everything in my power to see that happen!"

The contempt in Mádeohn's voice was abundantly clear.

"The *Tablets of Time*," Satan sneered, "are just an old man's babbling from several eons ago. Your power...it's such a shame to waste all that power. It could easily lead my forces on earth."

Hell's lord stood over Mádeohn and extended a powerful black hand over his son. Grabbing the top of the young man's head, a form of electrical energy began flowing down the demon king's arm and out his fingertips. Engulfing Mádeohn with the discharge of energy, the youth began convulsing in his father's grip. Satan ceased his bombardment, and the dark prince doubled over in pain. Collapsing onto the cavern's stone floor, he continued jerking with spasms. After the pain subsided and he regained control of the muscles in his body once again, Mádeohn slowly rose to his feet.

Lilith stood next to the throne chair, completely in shock at the young man's transformation. With eyes glowing white like Satan's, the youth's skin was now a deep red color. He was trapped inside his own mind, and she could see the prince of Hell was now completely under his father's control.

"Master."

Satan looked up from his son to see Kon standing at the entrance to the subterranean throne room.

"Enter!"

The dreg general hustled into the throne chamber, bowing before the demon king.

"Master," the beast reported, "the force leaders on earth report that everything is now in full readiness. The First Beast is in the world electrical grid, in place, and ready to strike."

"Good," Lucifer replied, "Mitch reports Kana and the Mystic Arts Class are in Lysta'cu'mha. All that is left on earth is their feeble little army."

"Mitch?" Mádeohn questioned, surprised.

"Yes, Mitch!" Satan smiled. "Mitch has been mine ever since the first time my spies reported Cyphis snooping around your school. Kon! Tell the force leaders to prepare! Mádeohn will join them shortly to take command of the first strike!"

Bowing again, the dreg immediately left the rocky chamber.

Racing down the hall from his room to the main lobby, Ryon once again marveled at the carpet floating a foot above the floor. This one simple feat of White Witch technology still totally blew him away. He could feel the carpet holding firm, even at this fast pace.

He needed to hurry. He was psyched about starting their instructions with the Learned Ones, and being late for his first day of class in Lysta'cu'mha would not be cool.

Surpassing everyone else in the class with his mystical abilities, every lesson he mastered clearly drove home just how little he knew of the mystical arts. With the entire class constantly looking up to him for leadership in Kana's absence, Ryon refused to let them down with his ignorance. This single passion continually pushed him to absolutely crush, without flaw, everything the White Witch prince taught him. He fully committed himself to dominating all the White Witch master's lessons.

As he approached the palace's lobby, Ryon noticed he wasn't the only one anxious to get started. Mr. Wenstrom and the rest of the Mystic Arts Class were already mulling about, waiting for Kana. Connie and Rhonda stood chatting, with Mitch at his girlfriend's side, silently listening to the two women.

Ryon's heart leaped with joy at the sudden appearance of Kana and Shilo at the top of the circular stairway. Descending down to the lobby, the princess cheerfully smiled up at him as he took her hand.

Kana's face lit up with his own grin while joining Connie. Chivalrously bowing his head, he offered his arm for her to take while announcing to everyone, "Let's get started. Follow me!"

With that, the prince began escorting the group through a series of hallways and inner courtyards within the palace. Ryon tried unsuccessfully to pay attention to the route they were taking, giving up entirely after the fourth turn.

Finally stopping, Kana had the group assembled in a large glass atrium.

The White Witch prince took pleasure in watching the entire class being overwhelmed with amazement by what they saw before them. Blazing like fire in the warm Lysta'cu'mha sun shining down through the atrium's crystal clear glass roof stood two massive golden doors.

Gaping in awe, Ryon began examining the various pictographs and symbols covering the two enormous metal slabs, even though he had no idea of the meaning of any of them.

"This is where your classes shall begin," Kana explained. "The White Witch Cathedral, our house of worship, lies on the other side of these two doors."

The White Witch prince then turned, nodding at the doorway, and the two golden slabs silently began swinging inward. The class stood mesmerized. It was like watching the gates to Heaven opening.

Inside the doorway, a central aisle the width of the golden doors extended through the temple, stretching to the sanctuary at the front of the cathedral. Vacant, white pews silently lined each side of the walkway, patiently awaiting its congregation.

Kana stood aside, pleasantly watching as the class slowly shuffled into the main aisle and gaze in wonder at the cathedral's majestic architecture. Their imposable attempt to walk quietly across the marble floor amused the White Witch prince. Spreading out along the aisle, each stopped, marveling at the massive white columns rising up to form wide archways, upon which rested a stadium-style balcony on each side of the holy structure. Craning their necks, the human eyes continued to follow the huge columns soaring high into the vaulted ceiling above. There, the mighty supports narrowed to form a new arch perpendicular to the ones below.

Ryon became transfixed with a massive metal sculpture dominating the wall right behind the altar. Mesmerized by the enormous piece of art, it appeared to be a conceptual image of angel wings swooping out and upward. This same symbol was something he noticed appearing everywhere throughout the palace.

Sensing the question on his ward's mind, Kana moved up to stand at Ryon's side, quietly staring at the metal sculpture also. After a couple minutes of silently contemplating, the White Witch prince explained out loud what the artifact represented, his voice echoing throughout the cathedral for everyone to hear.

"It symbolizes what we, as fallen angels, have lost and the goal each one of us strives to achieve upon Judgment Day. The return of our wings!"

"Wow!" Ryon thought to himself as the meaning of what Kana said sank in. He couldn't even begin to imagine what it would be like, stripped of who and what you are, let alone living with the constant longing to get back what had been lost. It would be no different than he himself being turned into an animal of some kind and constantly longing to be human again.

Silence reigned throughout the temple after the echoes of Kana's words faded until Mr. Wenstrom's curiosity got the better of him.

"I've seen these other symbols everywhere," the earth instructor said. "If I'm not mistaken, aren't they angelic script?"

"Since it was former angels who built this place," an elderly voice boomed through the temple, "that would be a very logical deduction, Mr. Wenstrom!"

Everyone turned to see Zaia quietly striding down the main aisle toward them, his footsteps falling silent upon the marble floor. Turning to Kana, Connie mouthed the question, "How?"

Shrugging, the White Witch prince replied mentally, "No one has a clue. It is one of the many mysteries about the high priest that amuses him to know nobody can figure out."

Grinning, Connie replied back telegraphically, "At least now we know he *does* have a sense of humor!"

Smiling as the old priest approached, Kana bowed to him while announcing to the class, "High Priest Zaia will be your first instructor today."

"Yes," the old priest smiled, "welcome to everyone."

Then turning serious, he continued, "Well, you have a lot to learn, and a short time to do it in. Shall we get started?"

With a swirl of his priestly robes, Zaia spun around and began striding along between two pews, heading for a door beneath one of the balconies.

Chuckling to himself while watching everyone, except his sister, stand there in dumbfounded silence, Kana suddenly barked, "The high priest has spoken! What are you standing here for? Let's go!"

Jumping at the prince's voice booming throughout the cathedral, the group quickly began filing along after the old priest.

Sensing the class leaping into motion, a grin lit up Zaia's wrinkled face. The high priest passed through the cathedral's side door as it silently opened before him with his new students following close behind.

Stepping through the doorway and back out into Lysta'cu'mha's sun, Ryon began blinking to adjust his eyes to the sudden bright change in light. Standing next to Shilo, he found himself in another one of the palace's many courtyards, this one rather large compared to the others. His attention immediately became riveted to a marble structure occupying the far side of the park like area. Noticing Shilo uncharacteristically quiet and following her lead, he began examining the building.

At first glance, Ryon thought it to be a large crypt or a small temple. Stone steps led up to a landing across the front of the building. White columns rose up, supporting an overhang shading the landing. The statue of an angel silently standing guard towered up above the structure as if protecting it and the surrounding area.

Between two of the white pillars, Ryon could see the ornate slabs of two brass doors adorned with the angelic script he saw everywhere else. A massive round seal protruded from the center of the two doors, embossed with the same winged symbol hanging behind the altar in the cathedral.

Clasping Kana's hand, Connie began wandering about, admiring the multitude of colorful flowers growing everywhere and nestled amid fernlike foliage. She found the virtual cornucopia of fragrances filling the air very pleasing, tenderly squeezing the prince's hand to express her contentment.

Rhonda and Mitch slowly strode over to a small pool surrounding a fountain in the center of the courtyard. Reaching down and slowly dragging her finger through the crystal-clear liquid, she found it to feel pleasantly cool to her touch. Smiling with joy, she closed her eyes while listening to the relaxing sound of water flowing over the marble, leaf-shaped bowls of the fountain.

Next to the bottom step of the small temple, Zaia stood quietly examining his new group of pupils. Each brought with them individual strengths and talents that, at the moment, not even they were aware of. Everything appeared to be falling into place, just as was written. Following protocol, the high priest let the serenity of the garden take effect on the class, preparing them for what they were about to see. Nodding to the White Witch prince when he felt sufficient time had passed, Zaia began mounting the steps, approaching the two brass doors.

Gently urging Connie toward the marble structure. Shilo and Ryon fell in behind them as they climbed the stairs, with the rest of the class following.

Zaia stood quietly facing the two brass doors, waiting for the entire class to finish assembling behind him. Bowing his head, the high priest began praying aloud, "Lord, please bless all who enter this holy place."

Reaching out, the old priest placed his gnarled hand upon the seal. It, and each of the runes upon the doors, suddenly flared to life with a flash of blue light, causing the entire class to jump. With the whisper of a click, Ryon could hear the ornate lock behind the seal release. The two doors then silently swung inward, revealing nothing beyond but pitch-black darkness.

Fully intrigued, Ryon curiously observed Zaia stepping through the dark doorway. Within seconds of the priest disappearing inside, he could detect a bluish-green light slowly growing in intensity as it lit up the mysterious inner chamber. The now visible high priest slowly strode to the far side of a small altar in center of the room.

"Do as I do," Kana instructed everyone, tenderly moving Connie forward while stepping just inside the doorway.

Watching the pair bending down upon one knee, Ryon intently observed Kana's gestures and Connie silently echoing each of them. Gently touching the palms of his hands to his forehead, the prince then slowly moved them down to his chest, covering his heart. The White Witch prince then placed both hands over his ears before extending his arms in front of him with his palms up.

Standing together, the prince continued escorting Connie into the room, stopping before the altar.

Stepping through the door with Shilo and genuflecting down on his own knee, the princess's voice gently filtered into Ryon's mind as he carefully began mimicking Kana's reverent gestures.

"Lord, open my mind and my heart that I might hear and understand, the words of your most holy prophet. Amen."

Quietly joining Kana and Connie standing before the altar, Ryon took a good look around while waiting for everyone else to enter. The first things to catch his eye were the four glowing orbs lighting up the room. Each shining sphere sat carefully perched atop the outstretched hands and wings of sconces carved like angels soaring upward toward Heaven. Mounted upon all four walls, Ryon noticed hundreds of stone tablets, each covered with the angelic script.

Shock swept across his face as he suddenly realized what it was lining the walls of the small chamber: the *Tablets of Time*.

"Very good!" Kana's mental voice filled Ryon's mind.

Once everyone else was assembled inside the small room, Ryon's attention was brought back to the high priest as Zaia began to explain where they were.

"The room we stand in is called Sunoma," the old priest calmly began instructing. Slowly waving his hand around to indicate the walls, Zaia continued, "The stones you see mounted upon the walls, some of you may have already guessed, are the *Tablets of Time*. Each tablet was personally hand carved by the great prophet Zephrom, depicting his visions of the future."

Wenstrom carefully raised his hand to indicate that he had a question.

"Yes, Mr. Wenstrom?" Zaia acknowledged the instructor.

"With all the power White Witches possess," Wenstrom inquired, "why would he spend his life writing on stone and not parchment or something else easier to handle?"

"Excellent question," the old priest said and smiled. "It is one that the White Witches have been struggling with for years. If you are the first to see Zephrom after the resurrection on Judgment

Day, please ask him. Then be so kind to share what you learn with the rest of us."

Everyone got a small chuckle out of the fact that the holy priest made a joke in such a sanctified setting.

Once they had settled down, the entire class stood silently watching as Zaia then reverently placed his hands together in front of himself in silent prayer. Slowly bowing to the altar, the high priest then stood up, and turning to his left, he respectably bowed once again to the stone tablets upon the wall. To everyone's surprise, one of the sacred stones dislodged itself, silently floating across the room and coming to rest in the high priest's waiting hands.

Placing the consecrated text upon the altar in front of the waiting Mystic Arts Class, Zaia broke the silence inquiring, "Prince Kana, would you please read the passage upon the tablet for everyone?"

Connie could tell that the elderly priest's request took Kana by surprise.

Recovering quickly and nodding, the prince stepped up to the altar. Laying his hands on the edges of the ancient tablet, Connie was dazzled by the angelic script leaping up about an inch off the surface in a blaze of blue light.

She stood silently with the rest of her friends as Kana read aloud the short, ancient passage from the *Tablets of Time*:

PRIOR TO THE DAWNING OF THE THIRD AGE, SATAN'S WEB OF EVIL UPON THE WORLD OF GOD'S CHILDREN WILL BE COMPLETE. KNOWING THIS WORLD WAS VERY SPECIAL TO THE LORD, THE KING OF HELL MADE CONTROLLING THE EARTH HIS MOST FEVERISH OBSESSION. HE CONTINUOUSLY USED HIS VILE CORRUPTION TO DESTROY THE GOODNESS GOD PLACED THERE. ONE DAY, THOUGH, THERE WILL

COME A YOUNG *W*HITE *W*ITCH, *K*ANA
BY NAME, WHO SHALL BE MORE POWER-
FUL THAN ANY *W*HITE *W*ITCH BEFORE
HIM. *T*OGETHER, WITH THE WEAPONS OF
*G*OD AND AN ARMY OF YOUTH RECRUITED
FROM THE EARTH, HE WILL DRIVE *S*ATAN
FROM THAT WORLD FOREVER!

—Zephrom

"I don't know about anybody else," Rhonda said, shivering as they all stepped out of Sunoma, "but even though it never mentioned anyone by name, except Kana, I personally find all of *us* being in that book just a little bit creepy!"

"Zaia?" Connie asked thoughtfully. "Rhonda's right. Why were we chosen to be the ones in the prophecy? I mean, each one of us specifically?"

"Aw, my dear," the old priest responded, raising a finger for emphasis, "the answer to that question lies within your next lesson for today. I want you all to meet Master Gabriel, our head FOTUS."

A middle-aged White Witch suddenly appeared next to the high priest.

"Please, everyone," the new White Witch invited, "just call me Gabe. We are not quite as formal in my department as our esteemed high priest."

"Yes," Zaia acknowledged. Wrinkling his brow in an effort to look sterner while continuing, he said, "I have been meaning to address that issue."

Grinning at the old priest, Gabe countered, "You have been telling me that for years."

"Don't mistake my lack of focus on you as forgetting!"

"Gabe," the ever-so-curious Wenstrom asked, interrupting the two White Witch's verbal sparring, "what exactly is a FOTUS?"

"Mr. Wenstrom." Gabe smiled, bowing to Zaia as he took over instructing, and said, "First off, it's so nice to finally get a chance to meet the first group of God's children visiting us here in Lysta'cu'mha."

Stepping down to the lawn between the marble stairs and the fountain, he continued, "Second, *your* question is an excellent place to start to better understand the answer to the prince's lady friend's question."

Pacing back and forth in front of the fountain, Gabriel began his dissertation, "FOTUS is an acronym for Fabric of the Universe Specialist. A FOTUS specializes in studying the cause and results of movements inside the fabric of the universe. Charting those movements and their effects allows us to understand why things happen and lets us predict possible outcomes in the future."

"Kind of like thinking ahead of different moves in a game of chess?" Ryon asked.

"Chess?" Gabriel looked confused.

"It is similar to Karn." Kana explained.

"Ah, I see!" Gabe responded and then continued explaining. "Yes, very similar to that. We are also able with what we know to reverse study, or start at an event, then work backwards to the original incident leading up to what caused it, ascertaining how or why it happened.

"You will see from my example we will follow through together that there are a multitude of factors continuously influencing the outcome of your life."

Stopping in front of the fountain, Gabriel took a quick look at each of his new pupil's faces, ascertaining that they looked no more confused than any other first-year student. This was a good sign.

"So," swinging his arms around, palms up, indicating everyone, the FOTUS master asked, "what about Connie's question, why each one of you *specifically*?"

Pausing a moment, as if really expecting someone to answer, Gabe allowed the class's silence to linger uncomfortably for a dramatic effect.

Bringing an end to everyone's anxiety over not being able to answer the question, Gabe proposed a new one, "What one thing do you all have in common?"

"We're all here," Mitch braved a response.

"This is true," the White Witch instructor acknowledged, "but I want all of you to think back to just before you met Prince Kana. What one thing did you all have in common then?"

After several moments of only the sound of falling water from the fountain, Connie finally ventured a guess. "We are all in Mr. Wenstrom's class together?"

"That is it!" Gabriel said and smiled. "You each have your own story of what brought you to his class and why," he went on explaining, "and I will be happy to meet with any of you who wish to see that story at some other time. Today we don't have enough time to explore each one."

Resuming his pacing, Gabe went on, "Mr. Wenstrom's class is your focal point in time.

"Now," stopping again and raising a finger into the air for emphasis, he went on, "let's research this a little deeper. We know what the focal point is, so what brought it about?"

Turning and looking at the earth instructor, Gabriel proposed the question, "Why was Mr. Wenstrom's class even available at your school to begin with?"

Wenstrom shrugged while explaining, "There was an opening in social studies at the school when I was looking for a new job. When I presented my curriculum on the study of ancient religions and mysticism of the world and how they shaped society at that particular time in history, the board liked it."

"Excellent." Gabe continued, "Based on that one simple explanation, there are three different threads we can follow.

"One: 'the board liked it.' We could track each of the board members back and see what events took place in their lives that would have influenced a positive decision.

"Two: why was there an opening? What events took place to create that opening, and right when Mr. Wenstrom needed it?

"Three: why did Mr. Wenstrom need the job and happen to need it right when there was an opening?"

Stopping and looking around, the White Witch instructor could see the beginning of understanding in the complexities of all the different possibilities in each of their faces.

"Let's go back even further," Gabe went on. "Mr. Wenstrom, the study of ancient religions and mysticism and their influence on society at that point in history; why that particularly study?"

"Well," the earth instructor thought for a moment before answering. "Both my parents were archaeologists. I grew up with them working at different, ancient sights all around the world. I remember watching them work and listening to them tell me stories about the people who used to live where we were excavating. I guess I was drawn to their different religious beliefs because their temples and shrines dedicated to their deities fascinated me the most. Who were these gods, what powers did they possess, and how did they interact with mortals? Those were the questions I had to know the answer to! That pretty much is what led me to this career."

"So, basically," Gabriel drew the conclusion for everyone, "your parents' careers had a major influence on your own. If they had not brought you with them to their excavations and exposed you to that environment, you may have never developed the interest you have today."

"I've never thought of that," Wenstrom had to admit, "but I suppose that's true."

"So the next logical step for us would be to see what influenced them to choose their careers. Do you see where this is going?" Gabe asked, looking from face to face.

"Each one of you are here," he continued, "because Mr. Wenstrom's parents decided to be archaeologists and he developed an interest in ancient religions and mythology, leading him to his present career. Circumstances we did not explore put him in a position to need a job at the same time one just happened to be available at your school. That availability was brought about by totally different events. The circumstances leading him to need a job and the job opening, when both are traced back, could possibly have the same roots. This is something a FOTUS would definitely explore. What about the board liking his presentation enough to hire him? Does it have roots linking back to the job need and job opening? Then you add each one of you and your own story, bringing you together all at the same time in his class, and we arrive at our focal point!" Gabriel stopped to let that example fully sink into their minds.

Breaking the silence after a while, Mitch solemnly stated, "It sounds to me like we've had no choice in our future."

"On the contrary, young man!" Gabe countered gravely. "I stated there are many factors influencing the outcome of your life. The most important one of them being *free will,* your ability to choose for yourself how *you* respond to those influences!"

The class spent the rest of the day meeting their instructors, masters in both mystical and physical combat. After beginning the next morning again with Zaia for spiritual training, it was then off to Master Gabriel for more in-depth FOTUS instruction. Concluding the first half of their day with a mental-discipline course designed to enhance the control and protection of their mind, they finally broke for a much-needed lunch. The rest of their afternoon the earthlings exhaustingly dubbed "mystical arts boot camp" classes on personal battle training. Thus became their normal, daily education regiment.

Accompanying the high priest to their weekly council meeting reaffirmed for Gabriel the one constant in the universe that every White Witch knew for certain: nothing could get Zaia to move any faster than the old man wished to. Although there were rumors floating around about an instance of him jumping when

Queen Mirha frustratingly snapped at the old priest during one of their disagreements.

"I would have loved to have seen that!" the FOTUS master thought to himself with an amusing grin.

"Do you find something particularly entertaining?" Zaia brought Gabriel back to the present.

Continuing to smirk with pleasure, Gabe replied, "Indeed!"

"Care to share?" Zaia curiously inquired.

Finding perverse pleasure in keeping his former mentor in the dark, Gabriel lightheartedly replied, "No, I'm good!"

Dismissing his subordinate's obvious disrespectful amusement at the high priest's expense with a side glance of annoyance, Zaia changed the subject, inquiring, "How have your classes with our young guests been going?"

The FOTUS master's face lit up brightly as he responded, "Very enlightening! The prince prepared them very well. They all absorb what is being taught like a sponge. I am especially impressed with Mr. Wenstrom. Once fully credited, he will make a fine addition to the academic community. Let me show you..."

Continuing their Zaia-paced journey down the hall, a scene of the White Witch instructor's classroom appeared, floating in front of the two masters.

Walking to the front of the room between desks, the image of Gabriel concluded the lesson for the day, asking, "Can everyone now see why knowing how the fabric of the universe works actually helps you to better master the mystical arts?"

Glancing around the room, the White Witch instructor saw understanding of his lesson clearly reflected in their eyes. "Good," he continued, "any questions before you go?"

Raising his hand and proclaiming, "I have one!" everybody's attention, including Zaia's in the real world, turned to Mr. Wenstrom.

"Go ahead," Gabriel's image acknowledged the Earthly professor.

"From day one on earth, Kana has been teaching us about mystical powers. Fast-forward to the present and our instruction here in the White Witch World, and it's pretty evident that both your and Satan's forces wield some intense power."

Agreeing with Wenstrom so far, Gabriel curiously pressed for his question, "True, yet?"

Continuing his inquiry, the Mystic Arts Class instructor came to his point, asking, "When Kana showed us Lucifer's war in Heaven, we witnessed a lot of primitive, conventional combat and very little mystical. Why?"

Raising his eyebrow, impressed with the question, Zaia turned to the real Master Gabriel, stating, "Our Mr. Wenstrom is very observant to fine details."

Agreeing, "Exactly!" Gabe went on, stating his own point, "When this is over and he has accomplished what he is destined to do, maybe our earth instructor can be persuaded to join my team. We can definitely use his kind of microscopic attention to detail, reexamining our work from an outsider's point of view!"

Cocking his head, seriously considering the proposal, Zaia's attention was brought back to the scene playing out before him by the voice of the White Witch instructor's image.

"So," placing his hands on his desk and leaning forward toward the class, Gabriel inquired, "since the powers we possess here, out here in the universes, originally came from Heaven when created by God, you summarize that the powers of the inhabitants of Heaven would be just as great, if not more, than those we have here?"

Concurring, Wenstrom stated, "Pretty much, at least based on the facts presented to me so far, that would be my theory."

Walking around his desk, hands clasped behind his back while thinking how to best answer the question, Gabe began pacing back and forth across the front of the classroom.

Carefully choosing his words, the White Witch instructor slowly began explaining, "The story Prince Kana showed you is the exact same one that has been taught generation after generation since our first ancestors were exiled here by God. Being mortal, obviously they are no longer around for us to ask why we seem more powerful out here in the universes than most of the inhabitants of Heaven in the story. It is a question our own scholars have been pondering for eons. The original White Witches, former angels from Heaven, for some reason chose not to leave any kind of explanation, written or otherwise. The only other beings who would know the answer are the other fallen angels. Throughout history, the Gray Witches pretty much have kept to themselves, with very limited communication between us, so no help there. That leaves the Black Witches. Satan and his followers have been pretty tight-lipped about the subject also.

"So, the question is still debated by White Witches to this day; are we more powerful than they were?"

Stopping and looking Wenstrom directly in the eye, Gabriel concluded his explanation, pondering, "Or are they so powerful in Heaven that, as mortals, we would never be able to envision what the war would truly look like, thus, our forefathers had to dumb the story down so we would comprehend it?"

No one spoke.

Slowly looking around the silent room, Gabe finally asked, "Anyone else?"

Raising his hand, Ryon replied, "I have one."

"Go ahead," Gabriel said.

Leaning forward, Ryon thought for a moment while scratching his forehead.

"You all keep calling us God's children." Leaning back in his chair and spreading his arms, indicating the rest of the class, Ryon went on, asking, "Why us? Out of all the universes you say are out there, why are we God's children? What makes us so special, and what's with Satan's insane obsession with our world?"

Raising an eyebrow, Zaia continued watching the classroom scene, curious to hear the White Witch instructor's response to the inquiry.

Exhaling dramatically, Gabriel could see the same question on everyone's face. Sitting back on the edge of his desk, contemplating how to best answer Ryon, he ran a hand through his hair while thinking.

"Wow! Tough crowd today," he began. "The high priest and your history instructors would be better suited to tackle that question, but I'll give it a shot.

"Throughout all of White Witch history, the people of earth have always been referred to as God's children. The only two clues we have as to why you are so special to the Lord, are, one," Gabriel raised a finger into the air, "Satan's relentless passion throughout the ages to corrupt, conquer, and destroy you. The reason for that, we assume is, he knows why."

Continuing, he raised a second figure for emphasis, "And, two, the last known prophecy of Zephrom. Only one sentence long, stated: 'From the womb of a descendant of God's children will come the One who will conquer all evil in the end.' That's it. After countless centuries, to this day, that one, prophetic line is the only answer we have. From your world will come the one who will defeat Satan!"

Dropping his hand into his lap, the White Witch instructor silently gazed out across his room full of pupils, carefully gauging their reaction to his explanation.

"Well," Wenstrom thoughtfully mused, "that certainly does make earth unique from all the other universes out there, not to mention giving the devil plenty of motive to destroy us."

Agreeing, Gabriel replied, "It does, doesn't it?"

Continuing on down the hall in silence with the image of the classroom dissipating behind them, the high priest grunted his approval of Gabriel's explanation.

For the next several weeks, the Mystical Arts Class went through some of the most intense and exhausting training any of them had ever experienced.

"You have a lot to learn in a very short period of time!" their instructors kept drumming into them.

Day by day, and with the help of their White Witch guardian angels, the power and knowledge of each one of the earthlings painfully grew. Under the guidance and counsel of the Learned Ones, each of them became a powerful master at what they were taught.

Each night after dinner, Connie would collapse into the White Witch prince's arms as the two relaxed upon a bench in the palace park. With her rigorous schedule, it was the only time the two had to spend together alone.

Exhausted, she laid her head on Kana's chest and whimpered, "Everything hurts, even my brain!"

With his free hand, Kana began to slowly stroke the girl's hair as he replied, "If it makes you feel any better, your instructor commented on how impressed he was with your level of skill in hand-to-hand combat. He said you far surpass everyone else!"

"I should," she responded with a yawn, "I've been studying since I was a child." Yawning again, Connie continued, "Don't let me fall asleep. It's becoming embarrassing not remembering how I get into bed."

The prince smiled as he continued to gently run his fingers through her hair. He knew she was already asleep.

The two disappeared from the park bench and reappeared in Connie's room. Tenderly kissing her forehead, he carefully laid his beautiful angel upon her bed.

A female voice behind Kana quietly scolded him, "You are working her too hard!"

"I know," the White Witch prince whispered as he turned around and smiled, "but each night, I leave her in your capable hands, Mrs. Cane!"

Silvia smiled back at the compliment. With a shooing motion, she began waving the young man out of Connie's room so that she could finish putting the sleeping girl to bed.

Finally, much to everyone's joy, Kana decided to give them all a break. Along with Shilo, he assembled the entire class inside the small alcove in the Space of Doors known as Myshunar.

"Today," the prince informed them, "we are going to embark on a tour of the mystical worlds."

Everyone cheered as this brought about a new spark of enthusiasm from the whole group, including Mr. Wenstrom.

Connie smiled and affectionately squeezed Kana's hand. The thought of being able to spend a whole day with him sounded like heaven to her.

"Each door here in Myshunar," the White Witch explained, "leads to a world God set aside because of its magic, fantasy, mystery, or special beauty. As you have been told before, Satan has been permanently locked out of them all by God, thus, none of the worlds in Myshunar have been touched by any form of evil.

"The first one I'm going to show you is called Paravage. It is a jungle world of unadulterated savagery."

The group followed their mystical tour guide as he stepped into one of Myshunar's many doorways.

Ryon suddenly found himself seated in a flat-bottom river-boat. The wooden vessel was slowly floating down a river of clear, purple water. From where he sat, it appeared to be a quarter of a mile wide from one shore to the other. Although the wooden vessel was large enough to seat everyone comfortably without crowding each other, Ryon felt dwarfed by the magnitude of their surroundings.

Ancient trees several hundred feet tall soared upward along both shores, creating the illusion that the boat was floating down a wide canyon. Just the sheer immensity of the trees of the primal forest made each one of the earthlings feeling like miniature beings in the land of giants.

Ryon was amazed at the incredible variety of colorful vegetation underneath the dense jungle canopy. He noticed that the assortment of plant life was closely rivaled by the diverse number of wildlife species flying, crawling, slithering, meandering, or stalking through the dense jungle. Affectionately squeezing Shilo's hand, he grinned with pleasure while watching mammoth-sized reptiles wade along the shore of the purple water. Reaching up with their long necks, the giant creatures grazed upon the broad leaves of the tree's midsection. It was an amazing sight. He also observed birds of every size, shape, and color imaginable constantly flying in and out of the jungle canopy, their repetitive squawking an almost deafening racket.

"This is Paravage," Kana announced, waving his hand across the purple river bordered by green jungle beneath an orange sky.

"It is a world where a person who gets the thrill of challenging death from day to day can live in ecstasy. Lurking everywhere are strange and beautiful animals vehemently ready to tear you apart! This is not only on land, but also in the trees, the air, or the water."

The entire class could clearly hear the prince's enthusiasm for this world in his voice.

"Do people of any form live here?" Mr. Wenstrom asked while watching with concern as something very large rolled over just beneath the surface of the water and not too far away from the side of the boat.

"Yes," their White Witch guide answered, "there are the river people, an amphibious race ruled by the lovely Queen Santerra. They actually live at the bottom of this river, which is called the Great River. Then there is Du, the beautiful queen of the tree people. The tree people are part humanoid and part plant. They mate with trees and eat through photosynthesis. They are a very gentle race in this harsh world."

"There sure are a lot of lovely queens here!" Connie commented, looking the prince square in the eye.

"Yep, there sure are." He smiled right back at her.

In the orange sky above, red lizard-like birds began to circle high over the small group.

"What are those?" Mitch asked.

"They are mind-eaters," Shilo answered. "They gain their nourishment by mentally draining their victim's brain. Don't worry unless they start to dive. They have to be close to their victim to do any harm and can only feed on single thought patterns. If you fill your mind with chaotic thoughts, they will become confused, and it drives them away."

"You seem to know quite a bit about this place also," Ryon commented to the princess.

"What?" she replied back, "do you think I sit around and let the guys have all the fun?"

Ryon threw his hands up, indicating no further explanation was needed while everyone else unsuccessfully tried to suppress their amusement.

As the boat continued drifting down the river, the savage beauty of Paravage overwhelmed each member of the Mystic Arts Class. There was no question in anyone's mind that survival of the fittest was the only law in the strangely beautiful jungle world. The whole group stared wide-eyed when they witnessed a creature eating a smaller one while it itself was being devoured by an even larger one.

"We're not alone, are we?" Ryon finally asked, feeling like they were being watched.

"Very good!" Kana replied, impressed Ryon could sense that. "For quite some time now, a group of the tree people have been following us, just inside the jungle."

Suddenly, about five of the mind-eaters gathered up enough courage to attack, and everyone in the boat filled their minds with chaotic thoughts. The lizard-like birds let out a frustrating screech while soaring over the group's heads. Flying off into the trees, the creatures went searching elsewhere for an easier meal. Relief filled the mortals' faces until a piercing cry came from behind them. That feeling of relief suddenly transformed back into fear. What appeared to be a huge dragon flew down the valley created by the trees lining the river, straight toward the terrified travelers.

"Kana," Shilo emphasized with concern, "get us out of here!"

"Just wait," the White Witch prince calmly responded as the creature drew closer.

Once again, the beast gave an earsplitting cry, displaying several rows of needle-sharp teeth in its massive jaws.

"Kana!" Shilo hissed through clenched teeth.

"Just wait," he repeated, not taking his eyes off the massive creature.

Connie yelped in surprise when a serpent suddenly came erupting out of the water and seized onto the dragon's neck with razor-like fangs. Launching themselves up from the river, several more of the aquatic serpents latched onto both of the great beast's wings. Their sheer weight brought the flying creature plunging down into the purple water. In a wild frenzy, a whole school of the serpents tore the dragon to pieces in a maelstrom of bloody froth, with Connie and her friends watching in horror.

The White Witch prince used his powers to keep the boat upright in the wake created by the dragon crashing into the water. He was also making sure they were a safe distance from the carnage of the river serpents' wild feeding frenzy.

Turning to his friends with a triumphant smile, Kana concluded, "And *that* is the essence of what is Paravage!"

The only response the prince got was several pairs of eyes silently staring at him, as if he were a little touched in the head.

"Moving on then," Kana calmly continued while transporting them all back out into Myshunar.

On earth, Mádeohn ordered the first strike by the mighty army Satan had worked for years to establish there. He silently watched with satisfaction as the operation began to unfold across the entire planet before him. After several years of planning, deadly acts of terrorism launched at once all around the world. The sudden, savage attack created a wave of bloody deaths and catastrophic destruction on a scale never seen before in human history. The ensuing worldwide panic and chaos brought about just as much devastation as the suicide bombings.

Next, Satan's son began to launch carefully planned small wars in preselected locations all around the earth. He smiled as these small skirmishes strategically began to increase tensions between all the superpowers as those nations began to choose sides.

Then Mádeohn ordered the First Beast to strike. The beast's attack took the already reeling humans by complete surprise. Like a virus, the Electrical Beast seized control of all computer systems worldwide. Everything from the powerful satellites orbiting the earth to computers, even personal cell phones, suddenly came under the creature's control. With that, all money, transportation, and defense networks began to move at Mádeohn's command, in whatever way he saw fit.

The governments around the world were no longer in control of anything, including policing their own countries.

Out of utter desperation, the people of earth began to take their defense into their own hands. Lawlessness quickly spread everywhere. Crime rose to terrifying levels as more and more people were being won over to Satan's dark side. To add to the chaos, Mádeohn had the network of gray-robed priests scattered around the entire planet start a propaganda campaign, preaching of a coming apocalypse. Those who chose to follow this new rise in power, which was slowly taking control of the entire planet, were promised money, comfort, and power at the end of the war.

The son of Satan chuckled to himself at the ineffectiveness of the army started by the Mystic Arts Class. The feeble group was completely unprepared for the sudden attack, especially one on the massive scale that spanned across the entire earth. About the best they were capable of doing was to hastily set up havens of safety around the globe for those who chose to resist the spreading evil. The few small attacks they did manage to launch were a mere annoyance at the most.

Mádeohn smiled as his father's operation progressed successfully before him. Everything was going as planned.

Floating once again with his friends in Myshunar, Kana noticed the perturbed look on everyone's face.

"I'm sorry," he apologized and then explained, "the thrill of that world has always been special to me. Argon and I spent a lot of time playing there when we were younger. I will try to be more careful from now on."

The White Witch prince decided to give the group a break after their shaking experience. He floated over to a door where, once inside, the group appeared in the middle of a meadow surrounded by a beautiful orchard. Everywhere they looked, all different kinds of animals played together. After briefly being interrupted by the appearance of the newcomers, their frolicking quickly resumed.

"What is this beautiful place?" Connie asked, thoroughly enthralled by what she saw.

"The Garden of Eden," Kana answered.

"No way!" Rhonda exclaimed.

"You are the first of God's children to set foot here since Adam and Eve were expelled," Shilo said, smiling and watching her friends gaze in wonder at the beauty of this special world.

"Anyone hungry?" the prince asked as he strode over to one of the trees.

"Wait a minute!" Ryon exclaimed. "How do we know which fruit not to eat?"

Kana smiled as he picked a pear and bit into it.

"God removed the Tree of Forbidden Fruit from the garden ages ago," he answered. "Everything here is safe. Go ahead, enjoy yourselves."

They all began to relax and sample the orchard's many delightful delicacies.

After eating, Connie and her prince wandered off into the trees together. A wolf bound up to Kana with a stick in its mouth, growling playfully. Taking it, the White Witch prince threw the stick, and the dog immediately raced off after it. Picking up the toy, he brought it back to Kana, who took it again, and the whole process was repeated.

This went on several times as Connie watched, grinning until Kana threw the stick and, smiling with enjoyment, mentally held it up in the air out of the canine's reach. Barking, the wolf tried again and again to jump up and snatch it out of the air. Feeling sorry for the poor thing, Connie mentally grabbed the beast and lifted it up to the stick. The wolf grabbed its toy, and Connie gently let it back down.

She turned to Kana and grinned.

"You've been hanging around Shilo too long," he said as he turned to grab her.

Connie started giggling and took off running. She stopped after a short distance, turned, and watched Kana slowly walking toward her. She let him get almost to her and then took off running again. Kana allowed her to play her little game with him two more times before reaching out mentally and grabbing her before she could put up any mental defenses. Raising her a few feet off the ground, he walked over to stand below the girl.

"Hey! Put me down!" Connie cried. "You're not fair! Turn loose of me!"

The White Witch prince gently lowered her into his arms.

"I know," she mocked, "you were not trained to lose!"

Kana kissed her, and his magic shot through her body as he carefully lay with her on the ground. The two lovers rolled around on the soft lawn, kissing and caressing. Sitting up on top of her prince, Connie stared deep into his eyes as she began to unbutton her blouse.

Kana reached up and took her hand into his.

"There will be time for that later," he softly said.

Then the prince gently pulled her down to himself, losing himself in her eyes.

"Connie Tanner," he whispered, gently kissing the tip of her nose, "I love you." With his lips tenderly brushing one cheek and then the other, he continued revealing the emotions surging through his heart to the angel in his arms, "More than I knew I could love anyone."

As he softly kissed her forehead, Connie heard an odd sizzling noise before she could respond with her own deep feelings. Reaching up to where his lips had been, she felt something strange there. Then she saw a sparkle upon Kana's forehead, where a twinkling star suddenly appeared.

"What are they?" the earth girl asked.

"They are called Sign of Choice. It's the White Witch symbol of engagement. I can remove them if you don't wish to accept."

Momentarily stunned, Connie sat there with her mouth agape before crying out, "Yes!"

With her eyes misting over with joy, she began kissing him again and again.

"I love you," she whispered with tears streaming down her face.

"I love you too," Kana softly replied.

"It's so pretty!" Shilo exclaimed when she saw the Sign of Choice on Connie's forehead. Then she gave her new sister-in-law-to-be a big hug while explaining to the rest of the class, "It means he asked her to marry him!"

Everyone gathered around to congratulate the two. After a short while, Kana called for everyone's attention.

"It's time to go," he said.

Seeing sorrow spread through the group, he proclaimed, "Cheer up! I promise you, when your work is done, Eden will be reunited with earth once again!"

With that, they all departed paradise.

Returning back out to Myshunar, Kana took Connie's hand while leading her and everyone else into a black doorway.

"This is Nau," the prince informed the class as they disappeared inside.

The group faded into a universe that consisted of nothing but black light space speckled with stars as far as everyone could see. Clinging to Kana's arm, Connie noted that once again they floated in midair, just like out in the Space of Doors.

"This is the home of the Time Keeper and the Innocent Ones," their White Witch tour guide continued explaining to the group. "In fact, here comes one now."

Looking in the direction the prince indicated off in the distance, Connie noticed an orange spot that steadily approached where the class floated. As it got closer, the spot eventually began to take shape. To her amazement, the object slowly took the form of an orange dragon with worn, fragile, green-and-blue wings. She could see two people riding on the back of the strange creature, just above its delicate wings. Both of the riders were wearing Spartan-style clothing. The woman's dress was hemmed short to make riding easier and had a halter-style top. Amazed, Connie noticed the woman's dark-purple hair that moved around as if it were alive, while the man's was just orange and mangled. The female rider's eyes were sharp and alert, and his were glazed over and looked useless. It appeared to Connie that the skin of the two dragon riders glowed with a violet hue.

"State your business," the woman's voice boomed in her mind.

"I am Kana, prince of the White Witches. My friends and I wish to see the Time Keeper."

There was a long pause, and then the feminine voice came back, "Follow!"

As the group traveled behind the orange dragon through the black light space, Kana explained, "In this world, the women are telepathic. This is necessary to communicate with the men, who are born blind, deaf, and mute. Their basic role here is for assisting the women and reproduction. Here, the women rule."

Rhonda mischievously poked Mitch with her elbow and grinned at him from ear to ear. He just rolled his eyes back at her.

"The Innocent Ones guard the Palace of Time," the prince continued, "which houses the Time Keeper and the Hall of Time."

The group marveled in wonder as they approached a lone asteroid, upon which sat a magnificent palace made of emerald and gold. Their escort left them as they entered the palace's main doorway.

Still clinging to Kana's arm, Connie commented as they stood waiting in the foyer, "It feels good to be back on solid ground."

Two new women, plus their men, came to escort the group through the sparkling halls to a lavishly decorated room. At its center, upon several cushions and surrounded by men waiting on her, sat a stunningly beautiful woman. Seeing her new guests, she rose to greet them, brushing all the men aside.

"Kana, love, how nice to see you."

The two embraced, and to Connie's surprise, she kissed him—on the lips. And she was pretty sure he kissed back.

"Where have you kept yourself for so long? I have missed you!" the Time Keeper's sweet voice filled the entire room.

"He just asked me to marry him not more than an hour ago, and he's already kissing another woman!" Connie thought, glaring at the two as Kana went on with his introduction.

"I am fighting a war on earth. These people I have brought to meet you are the leaders of my army. Class, this is Kristarra, the Time Keeper. Kristarra, this is the Mystic Arts Class."

He then introduced each one of them to her in turn.

When he introduced Connie, Kristarra commented, "I see you two share the Sign of Choice. You are very lucky, pretty one."

"Thank you," Connie replied, staring affectionately into the prince's eyes. Still a little annoyed about the kiss, she decided to make sure both the woman and Kana had no doubt whom the White Witch was marrying. Reaching up and passionately kissing her fiancé, she took her time, making their host wait patiently with a smile of amusement on her face.

"I would like to show them the Hall of Time," Kana stated, completely oblivious to what was going on with Connie.

"For you, it is always open," Kristarra cooed. "You know where it is."

Taking their leave from the Time Keeper, Kana escorted the class through the emerald halls of the palace. On their way, he noticed Connie was unusually quiet and had him completely blocked out mentally. Completely perplexed by it, he let her alone to her own thoughts out of respect.

Reaching his destination at the end of the hall they were in, the prince dismissed that train of thought as he stopped in front of a huge vault door. Right next to it stood a smaller, oak door. Opening the vault, he turned his back to it and faced the class, explaining to everyone, "This is the Vault of Time. It houses the fabric of time."

Turning loose of her grip on Kana's arm, Connie curiously began examining the black substance covered with silver speckles filling the inside of the vault.

"What you are looking at here," the White Witch prince continued his explanation, "is similar to an unexposed role of film: the future with nothing printed on it!"

Turning, Kana found Connie about to press her finger on the fabric.

"Don't touch it!" he exclaimed, but it was too late. Startled by him shouting, her finger left a white smear where it contacted the fabric.

"Why not?" she asked, irritated that he had raised his voice.

"Because it destroys whatever occupies that particular space in the future," Kana replied in a lower tone, while pursing his lips, distraught.

Completely forgetting her irritation with the White Witch prince, Connie stared at the new smear on the black fabric, and all color drained from her face.

"What if someone was standing there?" she thought to herself in horror.

The prince walked over to the wooden door. Opening it, he motioned to everyone to follow while stepping inside. The interior was a hallway that appeared to extend forever. On one side ran a wall of glass where they were able to look into the vault from the outside. The first view the class saw on the far side of the glass was the scene of a forest.

"From here," the prince explained, "you can catch glimpses of the future. You see that part of the forest over there that is dead?"

Everyone looked at where Kana was indicating. The lush green of the trees abruptly stopped at one point, replaced by diseased, brown poles of dead timber.

"That is where you touched the fabric on the other side."

Whispering with dread, Connie asked, "Can you fix it?"

"No," Kana sighed. "It is in the future. I can't do anything about it."

With her mental blocks down and forgotten, he could tell that Connie was really upset about what she had done.

Putting an arm around the girl to comfort her, the prince added sympathetically, "We just need to be glad it is nothing worse."

He then slowly took them down the hallway, allowing them to see different parts of the future. On the other side of the glass wall, scenes of devastating wars and times of tranquil peace unfolded before the group of humans. They watched in wonder at the rise and then the downfall of powerful kingdoms. Each of them stood misty-eyed as they witnessed the beauty of a universe being born, growing to maturity, and then slowly withering back to dust. Standing in awe, the class even got a glimpse of the end of time.

WHITE WITCH WARRIOR

O nce again assembled in Myshunar, Ryon floated over to one of the doorways, asking, "What is in this gray door?"

"Don't go in there," the prince warned. "That is the doorway to purgatory, home of the Gray Witches."

"Tell us about the Gray Witches," Mr. Wenstrom suggested, always eager to learn something new.

"Purgatory is a special place God set aside for the souls not quite clean enough to get into Heaven but not bad enough to be sent to Hell. It is described in the *Tablets of Time* as Hell's twin sister. The only difference is that the souls in there," the White Witch pointed at the gray doorway, "know that eventually they will see the glory of Heaven.

"Not much is known about the Gray Witches themselves. They always move unseen in shadows. The only time any of them have actually come out into the open is during the First Age, when they, together with White Witches, kept Satan from capturing the soul of the warlock Karen."

"We need to go now!" Argon stated, suddenly appearing next to the White Witch prince.

"What's wrong?" Kana asked a little worried. He had never seen Argon look so seriously upset.

"Satan has attacked!" The unusual alarm in Argon's voice was unmistakable. "His armies have all openly advanced on the whole planet." Kana's best friend continued, "The First Beast has control of all computer systems, including every nuclear bomb! The entire world has plummeted into a state of anarchy! I have begun to mobilize our troops over to there, but I have no idea how much time we have left. You guys need to get there now! The people you left in charge are getting massacred!"

"It's time," the prince said firmly. "Let's go!"

Quietly hiding in the light high above the Mystic Arts Class, Na-amah and two dregs clung to one of the walls of the Space of Doors, patiently waiting. Each one of the beasts shielded themselves so completely that no one was able to detect their presence, even mystically.

The she beast touched her cheek and smiled, warmly reminiscing about what transpired between her and her mother after Satan's little family meeting.

"Go my child," Lilith lovingly caressed her daughter's cheek. "It is not over yet! You can still accomplish what you were trained to do. Now go!"

Tenderly kissing the young woman's beautiful face, Satan's wife ushered her child on her way.

Their targets came into view below while crossing out of Myshunar and moving toward the doorway to earth. The three hell spawn silently leaped from their perch in unison, stealthily dropping like missiles. The demons exploded through the unprepared group, hitting the White Witch prince, Mitch, and Rhonda with such force that it knocked the three unconscious. The abductors and their captives continued to descend into the darkness below, quickly leaving the group of dazed humans behind.

"Kana!" Connie cried out in panic, suddenly racing down after them.

"Connie, don't!" Argon shouted, diving down past her. He stopped the girl's decent as she ran into his arms.

"Argon! Do something! Help him!" Connie pleaded hysterically.

"Connie, sweetheart, listen to me!" he said while taking her by the shoulders and confidently looking into her eyes as Shilo joined them.

"He will be all right," Argon continued. "Kana and I have been to Hell several times in our schooling. He knows his way around down there. We have to get you guys to earth to gather your armies together. If he runs into trouble, I will know and lead a whole battalion of White Witch warriors to his aid. I promise!"

"How will you know?" Connie frantically asked.

"Yeah?" Shilo added doubtfully, "how can you be so sure?"

"Haven't you guessed by now, my pretty little princess?" Argon smiled at Shilo, thoroughly pleased with himself. "I am the new Valitarian!"

With that, Argon floated up to join the rest of the group, leaving the two girls alone.

"What is a Valitarian?" Connie asked, confused.

Unusually shocked into silence, Shilo watched Argon as he moved away. She certainly didn't see that one coming. He was right, that was something that should have been obvious to her by now. While continuously trying to ignore her brother's annoying best friend, even though all the other girls constantly threw themselves at him, that fact totally slipped past the princess.

Slowly, she turned back to Connie and explained, "It is the highest position in the White Witch palace guard, the king's guard. The Valitarian himself is the king's personal bodyguard. They are selected from all the other children his age when the king is a youth. The Valitarian is raised and taught in special classes. The two boy's friendship is cultivated from the beginning, and their minds are worked together so closely that they almost become one. It is the Valitarian who fights at and protects the king's back!"

Now she had him, and she would use the White Witch prince up until he broke and no longer existed! Then the master would be pleased, and she would earn her reward. She eagerly dreamed about him summoning her to his chamber and taking her to new heights of ecstasy beyond her wildest dreams.

Na-amah had the prince on an altar in the center of her chambers. Memories of the many victims she had raped on that altar, male and female, flooded back through her mind. Hours and hours of training overseen by her mother, preparing her for the task she was about to complete.

The excitement in the she demon grew as she slowly ran her hands across his chest, then up and down his thighs, feeling the powerful muscles the White Witch possessed. While thinking about all the others that had given her sexual pleasure on this altar, a smile broke out across her pretty face, knowing that none would be as sweet as this one.

Discarding the skimpy costume she wore, Na-amah spilled out the marvels of her femininity before the unconscious prince. She ran her hands up and down her round, bare rump, arching her back and giving out a low moan of pleasure. The she demon then crawled on top of the White Witch, pressing her bosom to his, and drank in the sweet, intoxicating sensation it brought to her. After a while, she slowly rose up and straddled him. Running her hands slowly up her thighs, Na-amah arched her back, closed her eyes, and began to massage her breasts, offering them to her unconscious victim. Every cell in her body ached for the erotic pleasure he would bring her. Putting her hands on his shoulders, she began rotating her hips, moaning as the fire of her need slowly built up inside of her.

Kana awoke with the she beast on top of him, consumed in the stench of her lust. With disgust, he reached up, grabbed the demon by the shoulder, and flung her from him. Na-amah flew across the room and crashed against the wall with such force that she landed in an unconscious heap on the floor. Sitting up on the altar, the prince mentally examined the area to locate his position in order to leave. He had to get to earth with Connie and the others. What he saw in his mental scan sent him rushing from the hell-spawned bitch's bedchamber.

The White Witch prince stepped out of one of Hell's labyrinths of dark corridor's into a huge cavern. The ceiling was several hundred feet high, and the floor consisted mainly of muddy sandbars surrounded by dark ponds of marsh water. On one sandbar, in the center of the room, he spotted Rhonda sitting with her knees pulled up to her chin and arms wrapped around her legs, petrified with fear. A rusty chain was locked around her ankle, and the other end was attached to some unknown anchor deep in the swamp's endless, murky waters.

"Kana! Behind you!" Rhonda cried when she saw him.

The prince turned just in time his to see a dreg leap off a ledge above the mouth of the hallway he had just stepped out of. The beast swooped down on outstretched wings straight at him. Reaching up with a powerful, white-gloved arm, the White Witch swatted the creature away. It went rolling across the swampy floor for a short distance before getting up and flying off, shrieking.

When Kana reached her, Rhonda stood and ran into the protection of the prince's outstretched arms. The girl stood there sobbing in her tattered clothes for a long time. As for what had happened to her since her abduction in the Space of Doors, she could only guess. All that Rhonda could imagine was the worst.

"What happened?" the prince asked.

"I don't know," came her muffled reply from his shoulder. "I was knocked unconscious when I was hit, and I woke up here, just like you found me, with this filthy chain around my ankle."

Kana let her go and stooped down to examine the chain while nonchalantly explaining, "You were brought here as a backup plan, in case the she demon failed to destroy me. You are bait for a trap."

A short burst of energy from the White Witch prince's fingers separated one of the links of the chain in a shower of sparks. Kana protected the girl's leg with his cloak. Now all that remained was the anklet the chain was hooked to.

The prince began to examine it when Rhonda jumped back, exclaiming, "Oh my God!"

Kana stood, prepared for anything. What he saw was horrifying.

"I was wondering when they would appear," he commented out loud.

"What are they? They look so grotesque."

"They were once humans," Kana answered.

The two watched in disgust as hundreds of gnarled and twisted forms painfully crawled out of the slimy water and slowly crept toward the two outsiders. They resembled humans in a way but were covered with mildew, moss, and other forms of rot and decay.

"Like everything Satan breathes his foul breath on," Kana continued explaining while carefully watching the creature's advancement, "they are now part of his plague of death. No use to him any longer, he tossed them here, out of his way."

Looking around, the prince also noticed an army of dregs flying toward them from the far end of the cavern.

Suddenly Kana felt something grab his ankle, and Rhonda screamed. Looking down, the prince saw a gnarled and rotting arm reaching out of the dark pond they stood next to, a slimy hand wrapped around his ankle. Staring up out of the murky water was the putrefied face of Mitch.

Reaching down into the stagnant pond with one hand, Kana grabbed the ulcerated face staring at them, dragging it, with the rest of its owner, out of the water. After tossing the body on the sandbar, it twisted around and slowly rose up to stand with its back to them. Kana noticed that as the thing that used to be Mitch stood, all the other swamp creatures stopped their advancement.

The White Witch prince had known from the beginning Mitch was one of Satan's spies. The youth's White Witch guarding angel frustratingly kept trying to save the young man, but to no avail. The dark one must have promised the boy he could rule in Hell for his help. All Kana could do was make sure Mitch was never privy to any real information he could pass on to the enemy. So now, as payment for his service to Satan, Mitch was the overlord of all the lost souls in this subterranean swamp.

Raising his arms and letting out a wail that sounded like a thousand people dying, Mitch turned around and faced his former human friends. Horrified by what she saw, Rhonda immediately fell to her hands and knees. Gagged by Mitch's repulsive form, her stomach heaved, and she threw up. Looking up once again at what used to be the man she loved, Rhonda's mind could not accept what she was seeing and shut down.

Standing next to the woman's unconscious form, Kana took a good look at the creature that once used to be her boyfriend. His face had no nose anymore. There were just two open holes with a milky liquid running out. Both his eye sockets were empty and half dried up. The worst thing of all was Mitch's chest. The spot where his heart should have been was now a gaping hole. Splinters from the busted rib cage jaggedly protruded out of the hole, and inside, the prince saw that all but a very small piece of his heart was missing. It looked to Kana as if Mitch's heart had been literally ripped out of his chest, leaving behind open veins and arteries oozing a green pus-like liquid. Mitch's entire body was covered with festering boils.

"Mitch!" Kana said firmly. The empty eye sockets turned toward him.

"Look!" The prince stepped aside so that the creature could see the still form lying on the ground. It took a step forward, and Kana stopped it.

"It's Rhonda, Mitch! Rhonda! You remember with that little piece of heart left to you! Remember Rhonda! You love Rhonda, Mitch! You don't want to hurt her. No one must hurt Rhonda.

No one! All those things out there you rule, they want to hurt Rhonda! You must keep them from hurting Rhonda! Only you can keep them from hurting Rhonda!"

Mitch looked around, hissing at all the other swamp creatures. They all cringed back at their leader's sudden outburst. Looking at the ceiling of the huge chamber, a beam of energy shot from Mitch's dried eye sockets, blasting a whole in the cavern roof right above the sandbar.

Kana fell to the ground next to Rhonda, protecting both of them from the debris falling from above with an energy field. When the rock was no longer raining down, he looked up at the newly created opening. Fiery lava from one of the streams of fire on Hell's surface began to ooze through the new crevice and drip down into the cavern.

Scooping the girl up in one arm, the White Witch prince used his skill with levitation and quickly leaped into the air. With a shield to protect them from the globs of lava dropping from above, he shot straight for the new hole in the ceiling.

Startled by Kana's sudden action, Mitch cried out in anger, letting out a new wail that shook the whole cave. The dregs began to attack the escaping humans, but Mitch destroyed every one that got close to them with a laser blast.

The White Witch prince didn't even bother to look back at the small battle that took place in the swampy cavern below. He just shot through the crevice to Hell's surface, with Rhonda's unconscious form in his arms, and out to freedom above in the Space of Doors.

Sitting astride Cloudrunner, Kana gravely surveyed the bleak vista on earth that unfolded before him.

After leaving Hell, the prince took Rhonda to Lysta'cu'mha and left her in the care of his mother. Extremely concerned after doing her own initial assessment, Queen Mirha took the young woman to the infirmary and personally monitored the care given to her there by White Witch healers.

Kana quickly headed for the stables to get Cloudrunner before leaving for earth. Stepping out of the palace, he walked straight into what appeared to be organized chaos. Across the courtyard, he spotted King Marcan supervising the flurry of activity. The prince stopped and admired his father commanding the mobilization of the White Witch army for battle on earth. Kana recalled Argon mentioning that there were advance troops already on the planet, setting up a base camp. When Marcan spotted his son across the busy courtyard, the king mentally instructed Kana, "Go! Your friends need you!"

Hastily following the Mystic Arts Class back to their home world, the prince sat appalled by the wasteland that now spread out around him in every direction. The once vibrant, lush world so full of life was now nothing more than an arid, barren desert—a dead world populated with despondent souls whose lives as they once knew them had been violently ravaged away by the forces of Hell.

As far as his eyes could see, flat, cracked earth resembling a dried-up lake bed covered the region for miles around the White Witch prince. The barren waste was randomly peppered here and there, with piles of boulders. Off in the hazy distance, abruptly towering up out of the desolation, Kana noticed a jagged mountain range with a dark canyon cutting through it. Over his head hung an overcast sky with ominous gray clouds threatening to storm at any minute.

Kana sat for a moment, silently watching people from all directions wander across the desolate plain, their feet kicking up dust as they shuffled toward the mountain range. Everyone appeared to be forlornly bound for the same destination: the canyon that split through the mountains.

A mental scan of the dismal area brought about two new revelations to the White Witch. Every group of wayward travelers was being escorted across the gaunt wasteland by one of Satan's gray-robed priests. Kana had no doubt each person was promised some sort of paradise at the end of their journey and was now being lead like sheep to slaughter.

The other fact the prince discovered was the White Witch army's camp location. That was just a few miles to the east of his current position.

All of a sudden, from the southern horizon, a massive ball of fire rose up beneath the gray clouds. The prince watched fascinated as it rolled across the overcast sky, disappearing again behind the mountains. Kana eventually found this to occur regularly every hour.

In his continuous effort to rinse out the layers of dust that caked his dry mouth, Trever took another swig of water. The gray-robed priest slowly led his flock of vagabonds across the now barren world, and everything was covered with the annoying dust. His boots, his robe, his hair, every inch of him was coated with the powder-fine dirt. The occult leader constantly dreamed about a nice, cool shower when they reached their destination. No, relaxing in a cool, crystal-clear pool; that would be it. Wait a minute, why not a cool shower first, to get rid of all the dirt, then relaxing in a pool of cool water? Yeah, that would be it. Then, a nice, thick, bloody steak with a bottle of red wine...

The priest was abruptly awakened from his reverie when Kana slowly rode out from behind one of the many piles of boulders scattered about the region, stopping Cloudrunner in front of the startled group of transients. Recognizing the White Witch, Trever immediately attacked, throwing a blast of energy at the prince. Kana's shield easily deflected the blast, and the priest redoubled his efforts, but to no avail.

Without taking his eyes off the gray-robed priest, Kana slowly dismounted Cloudrunner, patting the beast upon the neck. He carefully began to circle the priest.

Frustrated, Trever continued trying to break through the prince's force field, with no results.

As Kana positioned himself between the priest and the group of people he was leading, the prince expanded his own shield to protect them all from the endless volleys of energy being thrown at him. The White Witch warrior then threw a concentrated ball of energy of his own at the annoying priest. It not only shattered through the Trever's shield but also sent the occult leader flying backward, abruptly stopping when the unicorn's horn exploded out of his chest.

Wings fully extended, Cloudrunner snorted and stirred up a cloud of dust as he stomped one of his front hooves on the dry ground. Everyone standing there watched in quiet disbelief as the mythical creature shook his head until the corpse slid off the horn into a heap on the ground.

The dried, moisture-starved earth quickly soaked up the blood gushing from the gaping hole in Trever's impaled torso.

Ignoring the hushed murmurs of the crowd behind him for the moment, Kana stepped over to the priest, ripping a good chunk of the gray robe off the dead body. Using the rag, he began to clean the bloody gore off of Cloudrunner's horn and forehead. The voices behind him slowly died away. The prince did not hesitate for a moment with his task, even when the sound of a gun being cocked next to the back of his head broke the silence.

"Where is my daughter?" a voice behind the pistol demanded authoritatively.

Continuing to polish the unicorn's horn and without turning around, Kana calmly replied, "Sheriff Tanner, you just saw me deflect every energy blast that priest threw at me. Do you really think that you can hurt me with that puny weapon of yours?"

The White Witch prince then turned around, coldly meeting the frustrated stare of Connie's father.

"Please put the gun down before you get hurt," Kana asked flatly. "Your daughter would never forgive me if you were."

The sheriff hesitated a few moments longer before finally growling through clenched teeth, "I don't care who, what, or how powerful you think you are, if anything has happened to my little girl because of you, I will kill you!"

The White Witch prince's gaze never wavered as he calmly responded, "Sheriff, you will never get the chance to. I will *die* before I let any harm come to your daughter!"

Finding truth in the White Witch's eyes, Connie's father slowly holstered his gun.

"Where is she?" he insistently asked again.

"I'm on my way to go find her," the prince stated, "but first, I need to know what happened here."

"What do you mean what happened here?" the sheriff snapped sarcastically. "Look around you! The whole world has gone to hell!"

"No," Kana calmly replied back, "Hell has come to earth. I'm here to put a stop to that. But first, I need to know what transpired here over the last several months. Can you please just picture what has happened in your mind? I will be able to see it."

"I don't want you in my mind!" Connie's father snarled, automatically reaching for his weapon out of habit.

"Please, Sheriff Tanner," Kana tried to smile reassuringly, "the sooner you show me, the sooner I can go find Connie."

Slowly relaxing his grip on his gun again, the sheriff finally nodded his head in acceptance. Closing his eyes, he went over in his mind all that had transpired over the last few months as the world slowly destroyed itself.

With increasing concern, he, along with everyone else, watched as the amount of terrorism around the world grew. Suicide bombings were a daily occurrence worldwide. No nation, no matter how large or powerful, was immune to the attacks that killed thousands. Several different wars broke out all around the planet. Nations began to side with other nations, adding their own military power, thus, increasing the amount of death and destruction globally.

The sheriff's hands were full at home, constantly trying to keep everyone in the sleepy little college town from going into a panic. His law-enforcement force was stretched thin when he had to deploy officers inside various retail outlets around town just to maintain some form of order in them. Residents began to overreact to the events going on around the world and started hoarding everything they could get their hands on at the stores.

"The problem is only going to get worse," one worried store owner told him. "The same thing is happening everywhere. I don't know when or if I'm going to be able to get any new stock to replace what's gone now. This might be it if things don't change!"

Then the unthinkable happened.

During morning classes, three kids walked onto various parts of the college campus, simultaneously detonating hidden suicide bomb vests each wore. The blast rocked the entire town, bringing it to a standstill.

Sheriff Tanner raced up to where the fire department had already set up a triage area, just on the outskirts of the blast zone. Getting out of his vehicle, Tanner stared in disbelief at the devastation spread out before him. The whole school was leveled to the ground. He could see nearby homes and businesses also destroyed. Beyond that ring of devastation, windows in cars, homes, and buildings were shattered for blocks in every direction.

Dust and smoke from several fires inside the blast area floated through the air. The townspeople who had already arrived were helping the injured slowly move toward the temporary medical staging area. The sheriff's own men, who arrived before him, were also assisting. Beyond that, several acres of what use to be a bustling, college campus surrounded by homes and businesses were now nothing but a smoldering pile of rubble.

"Sheriff?"

Looking down, one of his men was staring at him questioningly. Bringing himself out of his initial state of shock, Tanner's instincts took charge as he began issuing orders.

"Keep these people moving the best you can over to the med area. You two over there," he summoned a couple more, "you, get with the police chief and cordon off the whole blast-affected area. Evacuate everyone inside it, and don't let anyone back in. We need to keep anyone else from getting hurt and minimize looting as much as possible.

"You," he turned his attention to the second officer, "take a few men, and cordon off that parking lot over there that still looks in pretty good shape. We're going to need it for the bodies."

Looking back out over the demolished campus, he added, almost whispering to himself, "There are going to be a lot of bodies!"

The fire chief walked up to him, asking as he too gazed over the devastation before them, "Are you ready?"

"No," Tanner replied, and the two headed into the blast zone to make their initial assessment.

Pushing forward to perform their grisly task, the sheriff activated the shoulder microphone on his radio, calling, "Tanner to dispatch."

"Dispatch, go ahead, sheriff," the radio responded.

"Get a hold of the mayor, and have him call the governor. We're going to need the National Guard down here, ASAP!"

"Right away," dispatch acknowledged. "How bad is it, sir?"

Tanner snapped! "Goddamn it, they're gone!" he shouted into the radio, almost choking on his own grief. "A whole school of kids, *and they are all gone!*"

He had no idea how many bodies he numbly pulled out of the wreckage before someone forced him to quit and get some rest. What sleep he did get was filled with gruesome nightmares of carrying bloody, twisted corpses of kids out of the rubble that used to be a college. The death toll was in the hundreds.

As horrid as that was, nothing had prepared Sheriff Tanner for what earth experienced next: the First Beast.

The Electrical Beast silently wormed its way into the World Wide Web, the one thing that, in one way or another, linked the entire planet together. The beast completely took control of all the computers, communications, transportation, defense, and nuclear systems in the world. Everyone watched as the beast played with the planet for a few weeks, manipulating things in whatever way amused it.

Then, the hell spawn creature did the unthinkable. Horrified, Sheriff Tanner helplessly watched, along with the rest of the world, as the First Beast launched every nuclear weapon on the planet.

There was nothing anyone could do to stop it. A massive windstorm was created by the nuclear holocaust, running south to north in the Western Hemisphere and north to south in the Eastern. Hurricane gusts of wind in excess of two hundred miles per hour brought even more destruction to the already decimated planet. The devastating winds did one good thing, though, it destroyed the First Beast.

All electrical power, including the First Beast, along with the radioactive fallout from the bombs, was sucked up into the nuclear storm, storing it inside itself. This huge mass of energy then condensed into the great ball of fire now orbiting the dead world just outside of man's reach.

Thus was the birth of the Second Beast.

The sheriff discovered that people were paying the gray-robed priest to lead them to the supposedly last city left in the world with electrical power. The rumors he heard said that it was to be the birthplace of the new world to come. This new paradise, he was informed, existed on the other side of the mountains, just north of where they all stood right now.

That was where the sheriff had hoped to find his daughter.

The prince got all of this in just a few seconds.

"Thank you," Kana said appreciatively.

There were tears streaming down Sheriff Tanner's face. With a distant look of despair, the sheriff whispered, "Why?"

"Why what?" Kana inquired sympathetically.

"If everything Connie told me is true, and Satan wants to conquer earth, why set off the bombs and kill everybody?"

"You're still alive," the prince pointed out. Nodding to the group of people silently watching the two, he continued, "They are still alive."

"How are we supposed to survive? Everything is dead or destroyed!"

"Humankind will survive," the White Witch stated, emphasizing with conviction, "because people like you will show them how to survive."

Then, looking at the crowd of lost souls standing silently behind Connie's father, the prince continued, "We have an encampment set up just a few miles off to the east of here. If you would lead these people to it, you will all find refuge there."

Throwing the gore-soaked rag down onto the corpse of the dead priest at their feet, Kana went on, "Stay clear of these things on your way there. They are evil! I vow to you, I will bring your daughter to the camp safely or die trying!"

With that, the White Witch prince leaped back up onto Cloudrunner. Spinning the beast around in a cloud of dust kicked up by the unicorn's hooves, he quickly headed for the canyon that cut through the mountains.

"Argon!" He reached out mentally, "where are all of you?"

"Kana! You made it!" The reply came to him, "I don't know where the rest of the class is right now. We all got separated when we arrived here. Where are you?"

"I'm on what looks like a dried-up lake bed on the south side of a mountain range, heading for a canyon that everybody here is traveling to. What happened? Is Connie all right?"

Argon explained, "The she beast from Hell that is infatuated with you, she captured Connie and I. I'm pretty sure we are the bait in a trap for you."

"Yeah," the prince replied, "I'm getting a lot of that lately. Connie is with you?"

"No," the White Witch prince's Valitarian replied, "at this moment, I am encased in a force field I can't get out of. Talking to you mentally is the only mystical power that can go beyond it—to lure you here, I assume. I can see Connie from here, though. For the moment, she is all right. The she demon has a bunch of her thugs trying to attack her, but the girl is holding her own for right now. I don't know how long she is going to last, though. There are several of them, and I can't do anything to help. You had better hurry!"

"Hang on, buddy, I'm honing in on the direction your thoughts are coming from. On my way!"

When Argon said the she demon's minions were attacking Connie, his heart skipped a beat at the fear of her being harmed... or worse. That last thought brought a large lump up in his throat that almost gagged him. Pushing that thought aside, Kana willed himself to calm down and not panic. He would not be able to rescue her if he wasn't able to think straight. As his heart stopped racing with fear, the prince prodded Cloudrunner to pick up the pace. He could not let anything happen to Connie.

The ball of fire once again rolled across the sky. All the people traveling toward the mountains watched the colorful figure on a mythical beast streak across the dead lake bed at an impossible speed, leaving a plume of dust in their wake. They just shook their heads in wonder, as it seemed like nothing in the world was real anymore.

Immediately after the Second Beast disappeared behind the mountain range, there was a large explosion that brought everyone, including the prince, to a standstill. Fire filled the sky on the backside of the rocky range, turning them into a rugged silhouette.

"What was that?" Argon asked.

"The Second Beast is dead," the prince replied gravely. "That means the doorway is just about complete!"

Kana soberly stared at the graveyard of burnt trees starkly rising up before him. What had once been a beautiful green forest flourishing with an abundance of life was now nothing more than a desolate waste of disfigured, blackened tree trunks. Gnarled and twisted limbs branched out of the mighty shafts of dark timber, giving each tree the horrified look of dying in great pain by fire. It made the White Witch sick with disgust to see this once beautiful planet turned into a desolate wasteland.

Upon approaching the dead forest, the prince stopped and instructed Cloudrunner to retreat to the White Witch war camp. He then continued on foot, completely shielded so that no one could see him physically or mystically. Mentally scanning the interior, Kana found the forest infested with Satan's army. Connie and Argon were on the other side of that hell swarm, at the foot of one of the mountains. According to Argon, Connie was about to collapse from fatigue, constantly fending off assaults as the she beast's minions relentlessly sported with her.

The thought of any harm coming to that girl once again spurred Kana forward. With a cold sense of urgency, he boldly strode into the forest, completely shielded from any form of detection. Like a shadow, the White Witch stealthily maneuvered through the blackened underbrush without a sound, avoiding any contact with the enemy army patrol all around him.

Upon reaching the far side, the prince remained hidden from both physical and mystical detection while he quickly assessed the situation that spread out before him.

At the base of one of the mountains, the dead trees abruptly ended, giving way to bare dirt. Kana took note that the entire open area was completely covered by a massive overhang of rock protruding out of the foot of the mountain. Several fires scattered across the cavern floor lit up this natural amphitheater. In the center, he saw Connie, obviously on the verge of toppling over with exhaustion. Deformed shadows created by the dozens of Hell's denizens dancing about the area and sadistically playing with their female earth victim danced on the back wall. The prince watched for just a moment with pride as Connie valiantly fought off the vile hell spawn relentlessly attacking her with both her mystical and martial arts training.

Then Kana's blood slowly turned to ice as he continued to observe his love undergoing such merciless torture.

Wrapping up his quick assessment of the situation before him, Kana could see the she demon farther back in the cavern, watching the abuse being inflicted upon Connie. Argon was on display, trapped spread eagle in a force field mounted partway up the back wall of the cavern, right behind her.

The White Witch prince quickly formed a brutal attack strategy in an instant. Seething with the need for vengeance, he was going to make sure the hell spawn before him paid dearly for what they were doing to Connie. Mentally relaying what he was about to do to Argon so that his friend could prepare for what was coming, the prince hastily began the work of setting up his plan.

Na-amah impatiently paced back and forth near the back wall of the cave, watching the White Witch prince's bitch being endlessly tormented before her. The she demon gave her minions specific instructions that the earth girl was not to be permanently harmed. Just the thought of making the prince's little whore her personal slave here on earth brought a smile of satisfaction to Na-amah's lips.

Now all she needed was the prince. Where was he?

The she beast was positive the other White Witch was in communication with him. Glancing up to Argon suspended on the wall behind her with the same type of force field her father had imprisoned Mádeohn with, Na-amah smiled to herself once again. This one was quite a catch. He was very pretty. When her task was complete with the White Witch prince, she would enjoy making this one her personal sex toy.

"Lilith will be extremely proud of what her daughter accomplished with these two victims," Na-amah thought to herself and smiled.

The sudden feel of the White Witch prince's connection to the fabric of the universe brought the she demon's attention back to the present. She mentally searched for the source of the connection while simultaneously alerting the army of demons around her that their target had arrived. Everyone stopped what they were doing and watched the tree line for movement.

Connie dropped to her hands and knees, exhausted, taking advantage of the reprieve from attacks to catch her breath. She too desperately searched the tree line. Kana had to be here, thank God. It was the only reason she could think of that would bring the demons' harassment to a halt.

Na-amah became frustrated that she could not locate the White Witch prince. She was tired of waiting. Where was he?

None of them had long to wait to find out.

Kana exploded out of the dead forest, cutting a swath through the enemy army so fast it almost looked like he was flying. Bolt after bolt of energy flew from the White Witch's hands, destroying any demon that stood in his way. Any counterattack the evil force threw at him, the prince easily deflected with his shield. The void created by the wake of dead bodies behind the White Witch prince didn't take long to fill in. Kana mentally observed more and more of the evil force flowing out of the dark trees and into the cavern as he continued to cut his way to Connie's side.

One of the foul beasts grabbed Connie by the arm and violently began to jerk the girl to her feet. Using her upward momentum, she swung her free hand around and smashed it as hard as she could into the creature's groin. Continuing to rise to her feet on her own,

Connie brought her knee up and slammed it into the beast's face as it was doubled over with pain from the groin attack. The demon flipped backward and landed in an unconscious heap at her feet.

Suddenly she could feel the comfort of Kana's protective presence next to her. Back to back, the two stood ready to battle any attack thrown at them.

No further attack came. The agitated creatures just stood their ground, shuffling about while quietly staring at the two trapped in their midst.

Kana mentally watched the demon army continue to flow into the cavern from the dead forest while also staying alert for any sudden advancement from the beasts surrounding them. The more of the evil force that gathered into the cavern, the better his plan would work.

The crowd of beasts at the back of the cave parted, and the two had a clear view of the she demon, with Argon suspended upon the back wall behind her.

Na-amah slowly sauntered forward, smiling triumphantly while looking the White Witch prince in the eye and silently challenging him to try something.

"I hope you have an escape plan," Connie stated behind the prince.

Kana looked up at Argon, and with a slight nod brought his gaze back down to the she beast standing victoriously before him.

He coldly smiled back at her, daring the demon from Hell to make the next move.

Na-amah chuckled, amused by the prince's arrogance.

"In the end," she thought, "his overconfidence will be his undoing."

Slowly lifting her hands up from her side, the she beast erected a force field around the two lovers, like the one she had the other White Witch encased in. Now she had the prince and his bitch trapped.

Na-amah watched curiously as the force field formed around the two with no resistance from the White Witch prince. He just stood there with a smug smile of satisfaction plastered across his handsome face.

When the force field completed forming, Na-amah learned of her fatal mistake.

Before Kana had emerged from the dead forest, he had mentally gone into the mountain above the cavern and searched for cracks and crevasses in the rock. Entering them with his mind, he flexed his mental muscles, causing what supported the rock to give way and rest upon his mental presence there. The second the she demon's force field surrounded the two, that support was cut off, and with the sound of thunder, the ceiling of the cavern came crashing down on everyone inside it.

TRETERRAZ

Connie buried her face in the White Witch prince's chest as the side of the mountain came crashing down upon them. With her eyes closed, the overwhelming roar of stones cascading down above the two, and the ground violently shaking beneath their feet, seemed to go on forever. When the rock slide finally did subside, the ensuing silence was broken by the prince asking, "Are you all right?"

It felt so good to finally be back in his protective embrace. Connie cherished the feeling for a moment longer before cautiously opening one eye. Peering around, she noticed him standing there with a ball of light in his hand, illuminating their new little rock prison. The White Witch's own force field protected the two from the tons of dirt and stone surrounding them.

Completely exhausted from battling for her life the past few hours, Connie sighed, "Yeah," in reply. Feebly raising a fist and dropping it on his chest, she wearily added, "Some rescue this is, we're buried alive! I hope you have a better plan for getting out of this one!"

Kana smiled.

The small stone room collapsed as soon as the two disappeared from their little prison.

They reappeared at the edge of the dead trees, next to Argon.

The White Witch Valitarian just shook his head in disbelief at his best friend.

"Do you have to be so dramatic? Couldn't you have just come in with a couple hundred troops?"

"I didn't know how much time you had left to live!" the prince defended his actions.

"Me? I was perfectly safe until you decided to start rearranging the planet!" Argon retorted while scanning the area to make sure there were no enemy stragglers the prince missed with the side of the mountain.

"I have an idea!" he contained ranting. "Next time, just destroy the whole planet! Satan loses, boom! Problem solved!"

Kana could tell his friend was angry with himself for having to be rescued. He needed to get over that, forcing the point by emphatically replying, *"You're welcome!"*

Without stopping his mind sweeps, Argon reluctantly admitted his appreciation, silently nodding thanks.

"How many troops do we have here?" Kana tried changing the subject.

Taking a deep breath, attempting to release his anger, Argon calmly answered while exhaling, "Not sure, it depends on how many got through before the doorway sealed completely closed. I was seriously beginning to wonder if you were going to make it."

Unable to help himself by including that last little sting, Argon turned, looking over the prince's shoulder, inquiring, "Is she all right?"

Wandering off alone a short distance from the two men, Connie stood silently staring at the new pile of rock.

Walking over and gently putting his arm around the girl, Kana asked, concerned, "What's the matter?"

"That bitch from Hell isn't under there, is she?"

Seeing the rage smoldering behind her eyes, Kana sighed, responding, "I don't think so."

After a short period of silence to digest the confirmation of her suspicion, Connie's eyes softened. Changing her train of thought, she leaned against her prince for support, hopefully asking, "Are Rhonda and Mitch all right?"

"Rhonda is safe in Lysta'cu'mha. Mitch we lost to Hell before I ever stepped on earth," the prince replied compassionately.

"Oh my God! No!" Connie exclaimed in shock. Tears began to well up in her eyes as she moaned, "Poor Rhonda!"

Sympathetically, the White Witch prince tried to comfort the woman he loved with a hug. It literally tore his heart apart every time he saw her in pain. He knew she was about ready to collapse with exhaustion but stubbornly refused to.

After a short time of just standing there quietly together, he reached out with his mind, asking, "Ryon, where are you?"

"Kana! You're all right!" Ryon replied excitedly. "I'm at a lookout point at the northern mouth of a canyon."

Kana told him to picture it in his mind. Argon nodded his readiness, and the prince used that image to transport the three of them to Ryon's side.

"Oh my gosh!" Argon exclaimed as soon as he materialized upon the lookout point at Ryon's side.

"What is it?" Connie asked, awestruck by what lay out before them.

"It is called Treterraz, the Third Beast!" Kana said coldly.

Below, at the foot the mountain, spread a vast forest as far as the four of them could see. The solid green carpet was a refreshing change from the drab gray of the dying planet on the other side of the mountain range. The prince's eyes followed a road emerging from the canyon, piercing into the trees for about a quarter mile, and abruptly ending at the foot of a gigantic iron gate. The gate itself was mounted to a massive stone wall surrounding a huge city in the middle of the forest.

Neon lights, the first the White Witch had seen since returning to the dead planet, invited man to come back to a world he once knew. A world with electricity, transportation, communication, and luxuries as small as running hot water and as large as money-filled empires—a familiar, man-made world.

Ryon established his camp just outside the northern mouth of the canyon running through the mountain range. Connie leaned against Kana for support as the four slowly made their way down from the observation point to the encampment below.

Greeting them at the edge of the outpost, Shilo gave her sister-in-law-to-be a big hug, proclaiming, "We were so worried when you two were taken!"

"Thank you," Connie gratefully returned the embrace.

"What happened?" Shilo inquired with concern.

Connie mentally showed the princess everything that happened to her and Argon, from the time of their capture in the canyon through to Kana's rescue. The whole process only took a few seconds. When it was complete, Shilo turned to Argon, smacking him in the chest with the back of her hand.

The sudden attack took him completely by surprise, and the White Witch warrior yelped as if the blow actually caused him great pain.

"What was that for?" Argon growled.

"For getting captured, Mr. I'm-the-new-Valitarian!" Shilo mocked.

"Did you ever stop to think, Your Highness," Argon shot back annoyed, "that I might have sacrificed myself to keep the rest of you from getting captured also, so you could go on to do what you came here to do?"

Everyone waited silently as the princess just stood there shocked. Her brother's annoying, best friend put himself in harm's way to protect her? The concept was so foreign to Shilo she was having a hard time wrapping her mind around it.

"Oh!" she finally stammered, embarrassed, "in that case, thank you!"

Argon grunted his acceptance of the princess's sort-of apology. Turning to Kana, he rolled his eyes in disbelief.

The prince smiled back in amusement, knowing full well Argon just made all that up and mentally replied, "Nice save!"

"Whatever it takes with your sister," Argon mentally responded back.

Shilo suspiciously watched the two. She could tell they were communicating secretly between each other about her. They always did that, and it infuriated her.

"Well, on that note," Ryon piped in, seeing a new confrontation brewing in the princess's eyes, "let's get something to eat while we rest a bit and talk."

Putting his arm around Shilo, the two led their friends to a ring of tents at the center of the camp. A huge crowd formed around the group of leaders as everyone tried to get a glimpse of the White Witch warrior prince. Finally Ryon had to give orders for everyone to disperse so they could have a little bit of peace and hear each other without shouting over the noise of the crowd.

Kana was very impressed by the security and order Ryon already had set up throughout the camp in the short time since his arrival. Ryon's training in the White Witch World showed everywhere.

"Connie!"

Turning at the sound of the familiar voice, Connie smiled, "Rylee, I'm so happy to see you safe."

Rylee, the young girl Ryon had saved from being sacrificed before the Mystic Arts Class left earth for their training in Lysta'cu'mha, fought her way through the retreating crowd. Bouncing with excitement, she raced up to Connie.

The two embraced, and Rylee's smile turned to concern once she got a good look at the woman who had changed her life.

"Oh my God!" the young girl exclaimed, "You look like you're about to collapse!"

"I am," Connie replied.

"Here, lean on me." Rylee instructed. "Your chairs have been set up right over here by this fire."

Once everyone was seated, Ryon asked Rylee to get them something to drink and then bring food.

"Right away!" Rylee bound off to do as she was asked.

After resting a bit and quenching their thirst, the prince began to gather information while they awaited their food.

"What do we know of the city?" he asked.

"Not much yet," Ryon answered. "Neither it, nor we, have been here very long."

"Did you see how it came about?"

"Boy, did we!" Ryon replied and then went on to answer Kana's question.

"Besides the fact that the whole world was destroyed, the first thing we discovered after arriving was people traveling to this place. They all were seeking what was supposed to be last of modern civilization in existence. So the group of us followed everyone, hoping that most of the army we had begun to train would naturally have traveled here also. A great number of them had already gathered at this spot, establishing this camp. You already know we were ambushed in the canyon. The she beast took Argon and Connie, leaving the rest of us. Once we recovered from the shock of the sudden attack, without knowing what else to do, we continued on. Like everyone else emerging from the canyon, I expected to see a large, thriving metropolis. All that we found was a half-dead forest and the lifeless ruins of what used to be a huge city.

"That was short-lived, though. The ball of fire that was circling the earth came crashing down on the ruins with a huge, blinding explosion."

Throwing his hands up in the air to emphasize what he was describing, Ryon went on, "When we were all able to see again, the fortress out there now had replaced the dead city. We tried to stop people from entering its walls, and some we've won to our side, but for the most part, the comfort of modern society inside there is too inviting."

Everyone sat in silence for a while, absorbing what Ryon had just described. The remainder of the Mystic Arts Class joined the circle around the fire as Rylee brought their food. Everyone solemnly ate as Kana explained what had happened to him in Hell. He told them about Rhonda's safety, and how, regrettably, Mitch had been lost to them from the beginning.

Then, after taking a deep breath to prepare himself for what he had to tell them next, Kana relayed Sheriff Tanner's story and what happened at the college campus. They all had friends there, and he knew they had a right to know.

When the White Witch finished, the crackling of the fire was the only sound for several minutes as the entire class sat there stunned by the horrific tale. He could see the pain in all of their eyes.

Ryon was the exception. The pain was there, but not the shock.

"You already knew, didn't you?" the prince asked.

"I was informed by our leaders here, shortly before you contacted me," Ryon answered quietly. Staring into the fire, he continued as if relating a dream.

"I went up to the lookout point to think." Pausing a moment, he sighed and then continued, raising his eyes up to meet those of everyone else in the circle, "To think of how I was going to tell the rest of you."

Looking at the White Witch prince, Ryon willed his voice to remain calm in spite of the anger and pain that started to overwhelm him at the moment. "Our rebel force started there. They must have figured that's where we were based!"

It was as much a question as it was a statement.

"That would be my guess," Kana replied sympathetically.

"Your Highness," Rylee interrupted the prince as politely as she could.

Turning his attention to the young girl, she quietly pointed to his side. Everyone looked to where she was indicating and found Connie sitting in her chair, with her half-eaten plate of food lying in her lap, sound asleep.

Smiling, Kana turned questioningly to Shilo, who nodded her understanding.

"Rylee?" the princess asked, "would you please prepare the cot in my tent and let me know when it is ready?"

"Right away, Your Highness!" the young girl replied, eager to please.

Turning to race off and do what she had been asked, Ryon stopped her, instructing, "Rylee, inform the princess mentally."

"Absolutely." She smiled and sprinted off.

Kana looked at Ryon, and he answered the prince's silent inquiry, "Learning issue, she needs the practice."

The White Witch prince chuckled.

"We will get tents prepared for you," Ryon said as he stood and stretched the cramps out of his legs.

"There shall be no rest tonight," Kana replied, also standing. "We have much to do. It is not safe to camp this close to the evil one."

Suddenly a guard came bursting into the circle of tents, racing wildly into the middle of the group.

"Your Highness," he said bowing to Kana, "a fog surrounds the camp."

"What!" Ryon exclaimed.

Kana raise a hand to quiet everyone down.

"Ryon, get everyone packed and ready to move. My White Witch army has a base camp out on the plain on the other side of the canyon. Select a few to stay and keep this camp operational. We are just going to observe for a while. That task will be run out of this camp. The rest of us will move to, and remain at, the main camp out there."

"What about the canyon?" Ryon asked concerned. "We have been ambushed in there once. It will be the perfect place to wipe out a column of people the size of the one we'll have."

"My friend here will take care of that," Kana said, turning to Argon. "I want the canyon secured. I also want the best spies you have that got through before the door was closed in the city. We need to know what goes on in there. They will base themselves here at this camp. I also want the entire perimeter of the city watched. Be careful, they will have troops patrolling the forest also."

"What door closed?" Ryon inquired, confused.

Turning to his ward, the White Witch prince explained gravely, "The gray clouds that surround the earth are a power field created by Satan and was completed when the Second Beast died. It keeps all outside this universe from getting in, and any inside from going out. We are literally on our own here now."

Although three hours of sleep wasn't nearly enough, Connie did feel much better when they began their trek.

It was a solemn procession as the small army moved quietly through the canyon. The mist that surrounded the camp now stretched from one end of the natural corridor to the other, making the trip seem that much more ominous.

"What's causing this fog?" Connie asked, worried, as she walked with Shilo. Being attacked and captured the last time she was in this canyon was very fresh in her mind. It was not something she wanted to go through again.

Shilo nodded toward her brother at the head of the marching column, Ryon and Rylee at his side.

"It is something he learned a long time ago," she explained. "It is a blanket of protection. Whoever enters it winds up lost and confused, aimlessly wandering in circles and never finding Kana. Believe me, nothing can get through it, I have tried several times before."

The vision in her mind of the princess wandering aimlessly in a fog, angrily trying to find her brother, brought a smile and some comfort to Connie. Watching the three leading the march ahead of them, she could tell Ryon was still trying to teach Rylee how to create a shield. This was something Connie remembered Rylee had not mastered yet before they left earth. The young girl hung on every word he uttered.

"You do realize, don't you, she is totally infatuated with Ryon?" Connie asked with a smirk on her face.

"How can you miss it?" Shilo's voice had an edge of bitterness, watching Rylee look at Ryon with her big puppy eyes.

"Look at him," Connie added with a look of amusement, "he's totally oblivious to it."

"That," the princess replied as a matter-of-fact, "is her one, saving grace!"

The column of weary travelers didn't reach the White Witch war camp until midmorning the next day. With tears streaming uncontrollably down her face from sheer exhaustion, Connie collapsed into her father's embrace the moment she saw him. Without a word, Sheriff Tanner nodded his thanks to Kana and began to lead his little girl away.

"We have a tent over here to ourselves," he informed his daughter. "Seems the father of the fiancée of the White Witch prince gets certain privileges."

"I," Connie choked out between sobs, "need...uh...uh...to...te-tell...uh...you about...uh...uh...that!"

"Shush," the sheriff whispered, kissing his daughter upon the top of the head. "You can tell me everything you need to later."

Rylee began to follow the two but was stopped short by Ryon grabbing the back of her collar.

"I don't think so," he said. "I know you want to help, but you're as tired as everyone else. We're going to find out where they will have all of us quartered. Get some sleep, and then see what we can do to help afterward."

Crestfallen, Rylee looked at him.

"Stop pouting," he instructed, annoyed.

Aromas from several different cooking fires in the area assaulted Kana's nostrils as he stepped out of his tent. Dust from the dead lake bed drifted up into the overcast sky as people moved about, intent upon their personal tasks at hand. The White Witch prince was completely engulfed by the busy noise of the fully awake camp.

"All is going well," Kana contently thought to himself.

Connie and Argon emerged out of the tent to join the prince. He had just finished having a very enjoyable breakfast with the two of them and now eagerly looked forward to his daily survey of the White Witch army camp. In the two weeks since his arrival, the new settlement had grown into a small metropolis of its own. First, there was the main base camp where he and the rest of the warriors lived. All military personnel who were not stationed at the secondary camp near Treterraz either trained or was being trained inside the new war encampment. Argon constantly rotated his soldiers between the two camps, that way those so close to the fortress of evil stayed fresh and alert. At the main camp, White Witch warriors continued to instruct and develop Ryon's army.

His army and the earth students were not the only thing the prince had to concern himself with. Argon pretty much had all of that under control. Outside the main encampment, several little tent villages grew daily, housing people persuaded not to enter the city of sin. Water and food to feed the thousands was one of Kana's most pressing concerns. White Witch knowledge helped dig several water wells and produce acres of crops on the desolate planet, at a very astonishing speed.

Morale was another thing the prince had to think of. Waking up every day to a gray, dead world was enough to depress anyone. On a daily basis, Kana made it a point to personally tour around the ever expanding refugee camp. It appeared to the White Witch prince that his very presence lifted everyone's spirits. He too really enjoyed getting out among the people. Everywhere he went, young and old flocked to see him.

A huge tent had been erected near the main war camp for large gatherings. On Saturday afternoons, Kana held a public council meeting inside that structure. All the information gathered during the week from Argon's network of White Witch spies inside the city of sin was reported to the prince at that time.

Everyone stood silently inside the huge tent on the first Saturday as a messenger from the spy camp recreated holographic images showing what went on inside Treterraz. Just as Kana suspected, the entire perimeter of the city was patrolled on foot and in the air by evil troops. The outer edges of the city were slummy and run-down. The prince noted that the closer you got to the city's center, streets, buildings, and people became cleaner and more modern-looking. Sleek, tall, glass skyscrapers towered up above streets devoid of automobiles. Public transportation was provided by both above and belowground light-rail trains. All roads inside the metropolis led to a central park, like spokes of a wheel.

With disgust, they all witnessed every kind of evil and corruption imaginable as it went on inside the great stone walls. Rape, drugs, prostitution, murder, and any other form of immorality were the daily routine, propelled by greed for power and money. The corrupt city government ignored all, unless it interfered with their agenda, then it was punished by torture or death.

The messenger reported that the gray-robed cult priests held almost all of the municipality's administrative positions. They even policed the streets, imposingly patrolling from atop of massive, dark, demon horses. Kana watched as one of the equine beasts from Hell, clad in black battle armor, waded through throngs of people while carelessly trampling anyone that did not get out of its way.

Bile rose up into the throats of many in the tent, repulsed by what they saw of Treterraz, but it was the last image presented that turned out to be the ultimate shocker to the Mystic Arts Class.

Shilo could plainly see the pain in Ryon's eyes as he watched the holographic image of his oldest friend addressing the citizens of Treterraz at a huge gathering in the city's central park. Mádeohn was clearly in charge of the city of sin. It was later learned that Satan's son held this gathering every Friday at midnight.

As Kana made ready for his daily tour, Rylee brought Cloudrunner to the prince. The first time the young teen laid eyes on the unicorn, she became enamored with the mystical creature, relentlessly begging Kana to allow her to learn how take care of him. So the prince struck a bargain with the girl.

"You put more effort into your mystical instructions with Ryon and continue to progress to his liking, and you can learn to take care of Cloudrunner."

Without even taking a breath, Rylee eagerly agreed to the proposition. According to Ryon, the arrangement was working out quite well. The girl's progress with her learning had greatly improved. Now, if anyone wanted to find her, all they had to do was look in the unicorn's stable. That was where she spent all of her free time. Fortunately for her, Cloudrunner had taken a liking to the young, female human.

Mounting the unicorn, Kana was ready to get underway. Shilo joined Connie, and the two walked together while chatting. Seeing the two becoming such good friends really pleased the prince. Kana knew Ryon unfortunately had guard duty at the small camp outside Treterraz, so he would not be able to join rest of his friends with their tour. A small White Witch guard unit appeared surrounding Cloudrunner, and the little procession began.

Like always, everywhere he went, people flocked to see the White Witch prince. He waved and spoke to as many as he could, even recognizing quite a few of them upon sight. Stopping frequently, Kana took personal interest in what different individuals were doing to contribute to the successful operation of each of the tent villages. He continually emphasized everywhere he went that the skills each person possessed were vital to the survival of everyone.

When they reached the fourth village of their tour, a gunshot rang out above the crowd. Kana painfully felt the bullet graze his shoulder as Cloudrunner leaped into the air, his massive wings driving people to the ground in a cloud of dust. The prince unsuccessfully tried to maintain his seat, rolling off the unicorn's back and landing with a jarring thud on the ground. Although stunned by the fall, Kana's warrior instincts kicked in, and he raised a shield around himself for protection.

Argon immediately scanned the area for the shooter as soon as he was satisfied the prince had his shield in place. Locating the assassin retreating through the crowd, he sent a couple of guards to retrieve him. Turning around to check on the prince again, Argon spotted a second one with a crossbow aimed at Kana's back. The Valitarian's link with the White Witch prince's mind told him Kana was still trying to clear cobwebs out of his head while slowly rising to his knees. A quick burst of energy from Argon's hand exploded into the crossbowman's chest, eliminating that threat but not before he released the bolt in the crossbow. It bounced off Kana's shield and shot straight into the air over the gathered crowd. Argon mentally grabbed the projectile and safely brought it down into his own hand before it had the chance to harm anyone else.

After quickly scanning the crowd again to make sure there were no more accomplices, the White Witch Valitarian mentally reached out to Shilo and communicated what he needed her do. The princess understood, rapidly grabbing Connie and Rylee while Argon finished helping Kana to his feet. Together, the five of them were transported away from the area, directly back to the prince's tent.

Kana lowered the goblet of wine and took a deep breath.

"There were just two?" he asked.

"As far as I can tell," Argon answered.

"I'm insulted! What about Cloudrunner?" the prince asked.

A healer was examining what turned out to be just a scratch on Kana's shoulder.

"He is back at his stable," Argon replied, slowly pacing the floor. "He was taken back by the guard when they brought the first assassin in. Since I don't see Rylee anywhere, I would assume she is with him."

"I take it," Kana commented as he initiated the healing process on the small wound, "that we are not the only ones with spies in the enemy's house."

"Apparently not," Argon replied.

As his wound slowly disappeared, the White Witch prince noticed the look of concern on Connie's face, and he smiled reassuringly at her.

It was later learned from their first prisoner that he was just a diversion for the second assassin to sneak in and actually complete the job. Because of this, much to Kana's disliking and for his own protection, the frequency of the prince's personal tours were cut down.

Sitting astride Cloudrunner at Ryon's observation point, Kana looked out over the green carpet of pine forest that covered the valley below. The Third Beast, the city of sin, Treterraz, was the only thing to break that sea of green.

"How long until they complete it?" the prince asked.

"At this rate, two or three weeks," Argon responded, standing at the side of the unicorn. "It will, of course, have entry ports for the patrol copters, but otherwise it will completely seal the top of the city."

The two observed in silence as a dome steadily began to take shape over the large metropolis at a miraculous pace.

"Atmospheric control," Kana finally stated. "Mádeohn knows what a lure sunshine inside the city will be while we sit in this perpetual, gray overcast!"

"Yep," Argon agreed.

Suddenly, from below the White Witches and up over the trees, one of the deadly patrol copters burst, with its guns blasting.

Kana casually watched the craft soar over their heads, bullets disintegrating in a shower of sparks as they hit his force field. The chopper circled and returned, hovering in front of the two about thirty yards away. Reaching out mentally, the prince grabbed the propeller blades, stopping them dead while causing the rest of the aircraft to go into a spin. Releasing the machine, it plummeted to the forest floor, leaving behind a pile of twisted metal.

Argon walked over to the rim of the ledge they were standing upon and glanced down at the wreckage below. Turning to the prince, he nonchalantly commented, "You shouldn't leave messes like that in the forest."

The two then disappeared, returning to the main base camp.

"All rise!"

Prince Kana entered the crowded council tent and took his seat, followed by Argon, Connie, Ryon, and Shilo. The first order of business on the agenda was for him to arbitrate disputes that could not be settled by the lesser police system—a system he had delegated to Connie's father to develop and head in order to monitor the great number of people which now populated the large area outside of the White Witch war camp. It took about an hour for the prince to hear and rule on all of the week's new cases.

Kana then listened to reports from the different departments in charge of the various functions necessary to maintain the tent city, such as food, water, and health care, to name a few. This took him another hour.

The White Witch prince developed a greater appreciation for his father, who performed these same mundane duties in Lysta'cu'mha, since before he was born.

Finally, turning to Argon, he asked, "And what do we hear from inside the walls of Treterraz?"

Argon rose and motioned to someone in the crowd. He then stood before Kana. To his side came a cloaked and hooded figure. Slowly pushing back the hood, a luscious mane of golden hair fell free about her shoulders. She then presented herself to the prince with a bow of her head.

Argon smiled with satisfaction at Kana, and Shilo rolled her eyes at Connie, who smiled back in amusement.

"This is Natual," Argon said proudly. "She is the leader of my spy force. What she has to report she felt was of such importance that it should be delivered to you in person."

Kana nodded acknowledgment to Natual, and the female spy began to convey her report.

"What I have to relay to you, Your Highness, is extremely alarming! Last night at midnight, Mádeohn held his usual Friday-night worship services in the central park. As always, by Mádeohn's law, everyone in the city was there."

An image of Mádeohn appeared before Kana, and he watched as Satan's son went through his now familiar ritual of sacrificing people to his evil father. All the victims had been convicted of crimes against the city government as announced before their execution. This time, though, when it was all over and he had the crowd drunk with lust for blood, he made his big announcement.

"Next week, my children," Mádeohn's voice boomed throughout the huge tent, "you will advance in your journey to my father's paradise. Next Friday, when we are gathered here again together, we will sacrifice a child!"

That announcement shocked the crowd in the tent into an immediate and intense silence.

Mouth agape, Connie's gaze shot to where Rylee stood. As appalled by Mádeohn's words as she was, she was more concerned about how her young friend would react, knowing the girl was the only one present who had already lived through that kind of ordeal.

Rylee stood with her hand over her mouth, trying to stifle a scream. Tears welled up in her eyes as the horrible memories of the sacrifice she herself almost went through surfaced from the depths of her mind, where she had them carefully buried.

Connie immediately jumped up from her seat and ran over to console the upset girl.

Shilo could see the disbelief in Ryon's eyes as he stared at the image of his best friend before him. She reached out sympathetically and put her hand in his. He took it and unconsciously began to squeeze it painfully. She bit her lip and compassionately endured the pain in silence.

Questions by the dozens began to race through the tent, followed by cries of rage.

"We must attack now!"

Kana calmly gazed across the angry throng, silently contemplating their pleas for action. Making his discussion on how to proceed in his mind, he raised his hand, silently waiting for the roar of the crowd to die down.

Standing with disgust, the prince brushed his arm through Mádeohn's image, dissipating it from view while sternly dictating to Natual, "Young lady, make sure Argon has your full report!"

Immediately switching focus to his Valitarian, communicating mentally so that no one else could hear, Kana gravely commanded, "Order the mind sweeps! Find all of Mádeohn's people, and lock them down! We hold a council of war in my tent tomorrow evening. This is not happening, and I don't want that son of a bitch to know we're coming!"

The White Witch warrior prince then vanished from the council tent.

PHYCU

In the dead of night, the forest surrounding Treterraz was pitch black. Sitting silently upon Cloudrunner in the darkness, Kana's mind remained unquestionably resolved on the action he was committing everyone to. The black ribbon of the road leading up to the massive iron gates of the city ran almost unseen to his left from inside the trees. At ground level, this was their only entrance through the great, gray walls surrounding the city of sin.

Gathered in solemn silence within the dark cover of trees on either side of the road stood the main body of the White Witch warrior's army. White Witches and God's children stood side by side, ready to do battle. The long hours of training were over. A single thought burned through everyone's mind, binding them all together: outrage at the thought of sacrificing an innocent child. Anger smoldered in the hearts of each and every warrior standing there from the very idea of such an ugly, pagan act. A long time had been spent in preparing for this battle.

"Ryon's people are not ready," Argon voiced his concern to Kana at the Council of War in the prince's tent.

"They are going to have to be," the White Witch prince replied calmly, unwavering in his decision. "We are attacking, and hopefully, he won't know we're coming!"

Zaia's words echoed in Kana's ears: "There is a time when preparation must end and action begin!"

Argon's mind sweeps proved to be very affective. White Witches strategically positioned throughout makeshift camps in the middle of the night mentally swept the unprotected minds of the sleeping humans. Several dozen of Mádeohn's spies scattered throughout the encampments were discovered and immediately immobilized—hopefully before they could raise any kind of alarm, at least that was the plan.

"You did what?"

The look of horror on Connie's face the next day was heartbreaking to the prince. Gazing in disbelief across the tent covering the prone prisoners comfortably lying comatose on the ground, Connie angrily continued her rant.

"This is completely unethical! First you invade everyone's privacy by raping their minds, then you trap these people in an induced coma. Have you lost all your morals?"

"I told you before, we only do that when needed for battle," Kana calmly tried explaining. "These are Mádeohn's people. You tell me who you think is the bigger monster. Him, for wanting to murder an innocent child, or me for preventing his spies from warning him we are coming to save that child?"

Waiting in the dark forest, the prince could feel the comforting presence of Connie sitting behind him, lost in her own thoughts. Cloudrunner impatiently shifted beneath the two, and Kana mentally soothed the beast, telling him he would be free soon. In order to not raise suspicion, the white unicorn was outfitted with battle armor similar to that of the demon horses that the gray-robed priests rode to patrol the streets of Treterraz. Cloudrunner's wings were hid under a light chain-mail blanket designed to break away when the beast needed to discard it in order to fly. The unicorn was also fitted with an ornate headpiece that very convincingly made his horn appear to be a vicious weapon protruding out of the forehead section of the face shield. To complete the disguise, Kana draped one of the gray robes the evil priests wore over his own battle armor.

So that their presence couldn't be detected, the entire army stood stone-still with their shields built up to the maximum. One of Treterraz's patrol copters passed by with its searchlights flooding the area before the iron gates. When it was gone, Kana mentally nodded to Argon, who stood at his post next to Cloudrunner. The Valitarian sent out a mental signal, and a small group of White Witch warriors rushed up to the gates, blasting them open. Right on their heels, a second group raced in behind the first and seized the gate guards, taking control of the entryway before an alarm could be sounded. Once inside, the entire army split up into three groups. Ryon, Shilo, and Rylee, broke off with a third of the army and went to the right, following the outer edge of the city along the wall. Another third moved to the left, using the same procedure. Kana, Argon, and Connie, with the remainder of the army, marched straight down the main road leading through the huge metropolis toward the central park.

Observing the city of sin for the first time from inside, Kana took a good look around as he rode through the twisted iron gates. He smiled with humor at the stars and a full moon visible in the artificial night sky above. The outer edge of the city was trashy. Garbage filled the streets lined with rundown buildings. Even the people were dirty. Bums, drunks, junkies, and homeless occupied the outskirts of the town.

A mass migration of Treterraz's citizens was underway, as everyone marched toward the central park. It was almost time for Mádeohn's weekly midnight address. The White Witch army blended right in with the crowd. The White Witch prince observed neon lights that burned brightly the deeper into the city they progressed, lighting the streets into artificial daylight. This was an extreme contrast to the unending gray of the overcast world outside. The buildings, streets, and the crowd became progressively cleaner, Kana noticed, the nearer to the city's center he rode, but their activities all remained the same.

Whores and pushers lined the streets, taking advantage of the large crowds. Public sex and drugs were pushed, promoted, and practiced. Murders, robberies, and rapes took place everywhere, with no one paying any attention to the blatant acts of violence.

The prince felt Connie's chin in the middle of his back as she stared at his long brown hair, trying not to look at the atrocities taking place everywhere around them. He could sense the disgust emanating from her mind.

As they passed a gray-robed priest mounted on one of the demon horses without incident, Kana breathed a mental sigh of relief that Cloudrunner's disguise had held up.

"So far, so good!" he commented over his shoulder to Connie.

Suddenly, Argon heard the scream of a familiar voice that brought him to a dead standstill. Kana reined in Cloudrunner next to his friend. Looking down an alley, the prince's Valitarian saw three men on top of a woman, raping her. Two were holding her down by the arms while one of the gray-robed priests was mounted between her legs. She screamed again, and the one using her slapped the woman into unconsciousness.

"Natual!" Argon shouted, vehemently plunging into the alley. Two quick energy bursts from his hands sent the accomplices holding the White Witch spy down flying to the back of the alley, dead. When he reached the dark priest, Argon grabbed him by the nape of the neck and violently jerked the rapist off the girl, flinging him into the wall of one of the buildings lining the alley. The back of the scumbag's skull was crushed into a bloody pulp by the impact. Argon then angrily picked him up and smashed the bastard's face in with his fist. Disappointed that the priest was dead and couldn't feel any more pain, the White Witch shook the corpse violently and threw it to the ground.

Turning to Natual, Argon covered the girl the best he could while crying out loud, "I need a healer! Now!"

A healer and four guards raced down the alley. Argon stood back, waiting anxiously as the man of medicine carefully tended the girl. When he was done, the healer instructed the four guards to take her to the hospital at the main camp. Each took a place around the young woman, one at her head, one at her feet, and one to each side. Then Natual's unconscious form floated up off the ground between them. The five then disappeared, transporting her back to the main camp.

Turning to Argon, the healer stated compassionately, "There is no irreparable physical damage. She will be all right."

Kana slowly rode up to Argon's side.

Connie sat quietly behind the prince, appalled at what she had just witnessed. With her hand still over her mouth in shock, she looked down at the pain covering Kana's best friend's face, and it tore at her heart. The true consequences of what was about to happen had become real. Seeing someone she knew brutally attacked and injured slammed home the reality of what she and her friends were marching toward, and the battle hadn't even started yet. The same thing could happen to any one of a number of people she knew who were now inside the city. Some of them may not make it through the battle alive.

Connie's stomach did a flip at that last realization.

Reaching down to his friend's shoulder, Kana softly said, "Come, we have work to do."

Argon's eyes fiercely shot up to the prince's.

"You're damn right we do!" the Valitarian said between clenched teeth. He then stormed out of the alley and into the crowd.

The rest of the march through Treterraz went without any further incident. Like water flowing from small streams into a main river, people steadily marched out of side streets and onto the primary thoroughfare.

"How are all these people going to fit into the park?" Connie asked the White Witch prince.

The well-lit canyon of glass office buildings lining the street abruptly gave way to several hundred acres of well-manicured lawn. Gushing out of the roadway onto the sea of green grass, the crowd continued traveling toward the far side of the enormous park.

"I guess now we know the answer to that," Kana replied over his shoulder while following the flow of the crowd.

The two of them observed the inhabitants of Treterraz pouring into the grassy area by the hundreds. They could also see several smoldering urns mounted on pillars of stone scattered throughout the huge park. Each was burning what the prince knew to be a drug. To keep them from being affected by it, the White Witch healers had prepared a resistant to the narcotic and gave it to the whole White Witch army. All the citizens of the sin city were intoxicated with the inhalant.

From Cloudrunner's back, Kana was able to see the crowd's destination. Towering up on the opposite side of the park from where he entered, luring the citizens of Treterraz unto it, stood a huge, glass-faced building. Upon nearing the structure, he noticed a massive stage erected inside a curved courtyard formed by the large building's horizontal, crescent shape. What really dominated the prince's attention, along with everyone else's in the park, was the side of the building itself. Each glass panel made up a section of a gigantic video screen, which was currently projecting the image of a metal rock band performing on the stage below.

The three sections of the White Witch army emerged from the city and into the park from their respective directions, slowly encircling the crowd.

After meeting up with Ryon and Shilo, Kana began weaving the unicorn through the throng toward the stage. Several hooded dark priests also wandered through the crowd, some mounted on the huge demon horses. The prince watched silently as every so often, one would harass some poor soul into fearful submission or haul them away to an unknown fate.

Stopping several feet away from the stage, the White Witch prince could see a wall of dregs protecting the huge platform from encroachment. Watching as one drunk soul tried charging through the beastly wall, he witnessed the barrier of bloodthirsty demons immediately begin ripping the idiot to shreds.

Once again, Kana could sense Connie's strong feelings of revulsion as she quickly turned away from the same grisly scene.

After observing the park for about half an hour, the prince could detect the tone of the music begin to change. Along with everyone else, he brought his attention back to the band. From his position on the back of Cloudrunner, Kana had an unobstructed view of everything that took place.

With Connie peering curiously over his shoulder, the two watched as the video screens on the face of the building went black and a single green laser light shot up into the air from the stage. All around them, the citizens of Treterraz began to scream as the midnight show began. The laser light fanned out right and left, then slowly lowered itself horizontal over the top of the crowd. The light illuminated the smoke smoldering up from the burning urns, creating a ceiling of green haze over the heads of the people.

Startled, Connie suddenly jumped in her seat behind Kana as several of the deadly patrol choppers emerged out from behind both sides of the glass building. Hovering in a single row, one hung above the other, from stage level to the top of the tower. The brilliant spotlight on each machine randomly swung back and forth across the crowd, whipping it into an even greater frenzy. Approaching the dramatic climax of the song, a wave of explosions began to erupt on the stage in time with the music.

Watching in fascination through the green haze, Kana was entertained as much as the rest of the crowd.

Then, in unison, the patrol copters' spotlights froze in one position, and the entire stage lit up with one gigantic, pyrotechnic eruption. The music ended abruptly, except for the keyboardist holding a single, haunting chord. With another explosion on stage and a crash of drums, the copters' spotlights fanned out, pointing directly away from the glass building. Once again there was the sound of the keyboard holding the same dark chord.

With one last thunder of drums, Mádeohn's white eyes suddenly popped open on the face of the building above the stage, staring down at the crowd below.

The son of Satan's voice boomed throughout the park, "Welcome, my children!"

All around the White Witch prince, the crowd exploded, chanting over and over, "Mádeohn! Mádeohn!"

Connie's grip around his waist tightened at the sight of Mádeohn's smoldering eyes glaring out from the face of the glass structure. The band on stage began to pound out music again as the patrol copters resumed sweeping the wild throng with the spotlights. Mádeohn's gaze rose up from the crowd to the artificial night sky above. Following suit, the spotlights on the copters converged together upon one spot, high above the building.

Through squinted eyes, Kana could barely make out a red dot in the center of the circle of lights. After watching the dot for a while, the White Witch prince realized that it was getting larger, descending rapidly toward the park.

Mádeohn's eyes then slowly faded from the gigantic video screen, replaced by the image of the red dot in the sky. As it drew closer, it slowly became apparent that the object was on fire and falling fast. It wasn't long before the prince and the crowd could clearly see what was plummeting toward the park, and a new round of cheering erupted. The image of Mádeohn balancing on a platform of flame filled the video screen. As if riding on a lift made of fire, Satan's son plunged past the top of the glass building, exploding down onto the stage in a dramatic display of power. Leaping up from his crouched landing position, Mádeohn emerged out of the blinding tempest of the eruption to the wild roar of the crowd.

Circling the stage once, he then raised his arms and brought the throng below to silence.

"My children!" the prince of Hell's voice boomed. "Tonight you will take your next step on your journey to my father's kingdom!"

With a new explosion of lights and fire, the band started to play again. Connie and Kana watched as eight beautiful women slowly ascended up onto center stage, riding up on a platform from below. The women were bare breasted, and from their hips hung a shear skirt trimmed in gold. They surrounded an altar in the center of the lift.

Realizing that upon the altar sat a little eleven-year-old girl, the White Witch prince could feel Connie tensely catch her breath behind him. It was obvious from the way the little one was staring into space, body weaving back and forth, that she was heavily drugged.

Once again Connie's grip around Kana tightened as the two continued to watch silently.

"Tonight," Mádeohn shouted, "this little one will give her life so that YOU may be closer to paradise!"

Connie's chin dug painfully into the prince's shoulder while watching the women carefully lay their young victim down on the altar, then spreading out in a half circle behind it. The little one was so lethargic from the drugs that all she did was stare at the artificial stars above. Visions of Rylee lying on an altar in a basement kept flashing through Connie's mind. Glancing down, she could see Rylee's cloaked figure standing next to Ryon. Hauntingly peering out from beneath dark cloak's hood, the young woman's half covered face was white as a ghost. Connie could only imagine that the same horrific memories where flooding through the young girl's mind also!

The band's music blasting throughout the park only fed the bloodthirsty passion of the crowd. Standing above the little girl, arms raised in the air, a long, curved knife appeared in Mádeohn's hands. Connie turned away sick, unable to watch what was about to take place as the demon prince made ready to drive the weapon into his victim's heart.

White-knuckled and unable to take anymore, Connie shouted over the music into Kana's ear, "Do something!"

"Enough!" came a cry from the crowd, and a burst of energy blasted the sacrificial knife from Mádeohn's hands. Bewilderment swept through the people in the park, and once again the music stopped. Both the dregs and the gray-robed priests came to immediate attention.

"Who dares?" Anger pierced Mádeohn's voice as he glared out to the crowd below, trying to locate the source of the sudden attack.

"I dare!" came the reply, and Ryon materialized on the stage. The two just stared at each other for a few moments.

Suddenly a smile broke out on Mádeohn's face.

"Ryon, my old friend!"

Ryon sneered, "My old friend would not be standing here about to commit such a grotesque crime as murdering a child!"

Mádeohn's face clouded over again. Not taking his eyes off Ryon, he shouted into the crowd.

"Kana! I know you are out there; show yourself!"

Reaching up and pulling his hood back, Kana coldly stared up at Mádeohn on the stage. Helping Connie down to the ground where Shilo and Rylee stood, he never took his eyes away from Satan's son. Slowly moving the unicorn a short distance away from his friends, the White Witch prince discarded the gray robe. The spotlight on each of the helicopters hovering next to the glass building all converged on the prince. Nudging his mount, Cloudrunner spread his wings, shaking off the cumbersome, chain-mail blanket, and those who stood near shrank back from the powerful beast. Still wearing the fearsome-looking head armor, the white unicorn took to the air, driving people to the ground with the force of his mighty wings. As if transfixed in the spotlights, he flew over the crowd and gently glided to a landing on the platform opposite of Ryon, with Mádeohn between the two.

"Well, here we are, the prince of dark, and the prince of light!" Mádeohn spoke, turning to face the White Witch.

He continued, "Once you spared me from battle when you first exposed me to the Mystic Arts Class. I now return the favor.

You, and what army you have with you, may leave in peace, never to return to my city again."

Kana slowly moved Cloudrunner forward until he stood next to the opposite side of the altar from Mádeohn, its young victim still staring blankly upward. He gently waved his hand over the little girl, and she disappeared.

Shock swept the crowd.

"Damn you!" Mádeohn shouted, attacking the White Witch prince, but Kana was ready for him. His shield deflected the energy blast Satan's son threw. Jerking Cloudrunner's reins, the unicorn rose into the air on outstretched wings, the beast's front hooves kicking out at Mádeohn.

"Kill them!" the prince of Hell shouted, dodging the attack from above and throwing a burst of energy at Ryon's shield with such force it blew him completely off the stage.

The first thing the White Witch army did when the battle began was to take out the deadly patrol copters before they could fire upon Kana and Cloudrunner. A swift volley of energy blasts from below and the machines exploded in midair and then came crashing down in balls of flame. People scattered everywhere to avoid the falling debris. The crowd went into a panic as dregs and the gray-robed priests began to attack people. The eight women and the band members all ran off to the safety of the sides of the stage. Soon, the entire park became one huge battlefield.

Kana had transported the child off the altar, over to Connie and Shilo's feet, and the two of them began to look after her. When the fighting broke out, Shilo ordered a small guard of White Witch warriors to surround and secure the area around them and then called for a healer to come and administer to the little girl. Connie anxiously watched as the healer who came to Natual's aid in the alley stepped through the guard and began to examine the little one. He gave her some of the drug resistant, and it wasn't long before her mind was clear and swiftly filled with fear.

"She will be all right," the healer stated to the two women and then left to go attend to other casualties.

Kana swooped down a second time, attacking Mádeohn and blasting him to the back of the stage. The demon prince crashed up against a tower of electrical equipment, which exploded upon his impact, knocking him unconscious. Collapsing, the tower buried Satan's son under the pile of equipment.

At that moment, a powerfully built, jet-black creature suddenly appeared upon the massive video screen. Eyes of white fire stared down at the mass of people and dregs fighting below.

"I am tired of this foolish child's play!" Satan's voice boomed out, bringing the entire battle to a halt.

One massive, black wing erupted out of the side of the building in a shower of sparks and glass shards, stretching out to where Kana and Cloudrunner hovered above the stage. The attack was so sudden and swift that it caught the prince off guard, and Satan swatted the two in midair. The unicorn tumbled several times above everyone's head before he was able to catch himself from falling with outstretched wings. Kana, on the other hand, fell off the beast's back and crashed to the ground in an unconscious heap.

"Most powerful White Witch, indeed! Pathetic! He is nothing compared to me!"

With an earsplitting, wrenching noise, the rest of the demon king began to emerge out of the giant video screen. Glass exploded, and sparks flew as the devil slowly took real form, stepping out onto the stage from the side of the building. When the transformation was finished, Satan had retained the huge size he was upon the video screens and stood towering over everyone.

Like a swarm of insects, denizens of Hell erupted out of the jagged hole in the building their master had just created and began to attack whatever human they encountered.

When Satan entered earth's universe, he broke his own spell. The power field he had in place around the planet to keep any outside help from entering was now gone. The moment the field came down, Marcan and the rest of the White Witch army swiftly moved in, immediately engaging in a counterattack.

"Your dreams to own this world end today, Satan!" the White Witch king stated after blasting the demon king to his knees.

With a wicked laugh, Satan looked up to where Marcan was hovering in the air above him, the king's own personal Valitarian at his back.

Through a sneer of needle-sharp fangs, the demon king asked, "Do you really think a mere mortal such as yourself has the power to defeat an archangel!"

"I may be mortal," the White Witch king responded, "but, unlike you, a fallen angel, I *will* spend eternity in Heaven's light!"

Angered, Satan rose up to his full height again and immediately engaged in mind-to-mind combat with Marcan. The two stood stone-still, gruesomely glaring at each other as the mental battle went on between them.

Kana slowly awoke. Shaking the pain from his head, he rose up from where he was lying in Connie's arms. She had run to where he fell in sheer panic. Seeing the concern in her eyes, he smiled at her reassuringly and stated, "I'm good," and then turned to see what was happening in the battle. Suddenly seeing his father hovering in midair, engaged in a mental battle with Satan, the young prince cried out before he realized what he had done. Upon hearing his son's voice, the White Witch king lost concentration for a fraction of a second. That was long enough for Satan to move in and mentally overpower and then crush Marcan's mind.

Kana watched in dumbfounded silence as his father's body began to fall. It seemed to take an eternity for the limp form to crash down to the ground several feet away. Landing in a sprawled heap, the White Witch king's lifeless eyes were looking over at his son, as if pleading for help.

Somewhere, in the muted background, Kana thought he heard Shilo screaming.

Marcan's Valitarian went berserk with the death of his best friend, attacking Satan with a flurry of energy blasts that the demon king's shield deflected. The intense bombardment of the enraged assault was so brutally powerful, though, it did knock

Satan back a couple of steps toward the gaping crevice in the side of the building. A dark cloud of dregs quickly began to swarm up from the park to defend their evil master from the savage attack. White Witch warriors swiftly rose up also, engaging the horde of demons and turning the air into a gory battle storm above the bloody combat below.

Once surrounded by the swarm of dregs, Marcan's Valitarian had to switch from offensive to defensive maneuvers to ward off the beasts' attacks. Lifeless demons began to rain down from the sky from his deadly rampage. Consumed by his rage, the White Witch did not notice the bony tip of Satan's black wing until it exploded out of his chest. Looking down in shock at the blood-covered appendage protruding from his ribs, the life slowly faded from the White Witch's eyes.

With a flick of his leathery limb, the demon king flung the corpse through the air, callously taking out both White Witch and dreg alike with the dead body. He then turned his attention to the battle below and smiled. So far, all was going well. As more and more of his vile pets surged out of the dark crevice, he knew it wouldn't be long before the White Witch army was overwhelmed by sheer numbers. The eons of careful preparation were finally paying off. Victory would be his before dawn.

Looking down at the lifeless form of his father, the White Witch prince began to quiver with fury. "No! No!" softly escaped from his lips over and over again. For the first time in his life, the prince knew true anger. It boiled red inside of him; it twisted and churned until his insides felt like knots. Then it exploded.

Raising his arms and voice to the sky, he cried out, "NOOOO!"

Everyone shrank back in fear as a mystical doorway cracked open in the domed ceiling above Kana. Two white beams of energy from Heaven began flowing down through the opening and into the prince's outstretched arms. Everyone silently watched in awe at this new display of power by the White Witch.

Even Argon stood frozen in shock. He had no idea what was happening.

As suddenly as it had begun, the shower of energy from Heaven ceased. In its wake, Kana stood armed with the Sword of God in his right hand and the Shield of God in his left. Their weight felt good to the White Witch warrior, who was glowing and sizzling with energy from Heaven.

"Surround him!" Satan's voice suddenly boomed, recognizing the holy weapons.

All of the demon's followers standing near jumped into action, forming a circle of hate around the prince. Slowly, the circle began to collapse in, and then they attacked. Whenever one of the vermin got within reach of the sword, Kana killed it. Flourishing the sword with trained precision, everything it contacted it destroyed. To the White Witch warrior's astonishment, the sword cleaved through bone like it was passing through thin air. Dead bodies and severed limbs began to pile up around him. Soon the attacker's advancement stopped.

"Destroy him!" Satan cried out again.

Once more, the evil force pressed in upon the White Witch prince, and once again, the sword brought death and destruction to them. None could get beyond its deadly kiss. Like a swarm of cockroaches, more and more of Satan's foul army crawled out of the dark crevice behind the demon king and pressed in upon the prince.

They just kept coming. No matter how many he destroyed, more would take their place. Kana kept slaughtering in the heat of his anger. He kept right on killing.

To get her out of the ring of danger collapsing in on him, Kana swiftly transported Connie and his father to where Shilo had collapsed while trying to run to her father's fallen body. Unable to breathe from the pain in her heart, her legs gave out, and all she was able to do was lie there, hysterically crying. The White Witch princess could not believe he was gone. Tenderly holding his still form to her bosom when it suddenly appeared next to her, Shilo shook uncontrollably with grief. Not knowing what else to do, Connie put a caring arm around her friend in an effort to console the princess.

"Princess! Look out!"

Both Connie and Shilo turned at the sound of the familiar voice. Through a fog of tears, Shilo saw a dreg approaching from behind their position, arm raised and firing a blast of energy at her. In surreal slow motion, she watched Rylee leaping through the air to intercept the blast, the triangles of her shield forming around her. Not completely locked into place, a good portion of the blast made it through Rylee's shield, fatally striking her. The young woman's charred body rolled limply to a stop next to the princess, eyes staring vacantly upward.

"Rylee!" Connie screamed, scrambling to examine the girl. Feeling for a pulse and not finding one, Connie carefully closed Rylee's eyes, resting her own forehead upon the young girl's still chest.

Shilo could tell by the way Connie started shaking with grief that the annoying little one had just sacrificed her own life to save hers.

"Why?"

The princess didn't even like the irritating young girl constantly following Ryon around like a love-starved pet. With her heart already drowning in grief from witnessing her father's murder, to have someone she couldn't stand give her own life to save hers was just too much.

Something inside Shilo snapped.

Looking up, the White Witch princess saw the sneering dreg still approaching with several of its ugly friends closing in from every direction. Slowly laying her father gently upon the ground, she stood, coolly marching toward the creature that had just killed Rylee.

"Shilo! NO!" Connie shouted, jumping up to stop her.

With a fling of her hand, Shilo pinned Connie back onto the ground where the bodies of their two loved ones lay. Stopping, she slowly began turning in a circle, patiently watching as the group of monsters from Hell eagerly surrounded her. Hungry for easy blood, the beasts began collapsing in on the woman.

The princess of the White Witches rewarded the vile group of hell spawn with a deadly taste of her wrath. Flaunting an evil grin of her own, Shilo closed her eyes while crossing her arms in front of her chest. Flinging them outstretched to each side, a lethal wave of energy erupted from her body in every direction, sweeping through the ring of dregs. Every one of the ugly beasts began disintegrating into a pile of ash, with no chance of defending itself.

Still smiling viciously, Shilo opened her eyes to see Connie's tear-stained face staring back at her in shock. Wiping her hand across her running nose, Connie watched the princess calmly return to where her father lay. She had no idea Shilo was capable of such destructive power. Silently staring down at Rylee's still body for a moment, her stomach began churning. The sound of weapons clashing against weapons or crunching through bone and the screams of those wounded or killed continuously assaulted her ears. Her nose was so saturated with the smell of blood, burned flesh from energy blasts, and death that she knew she would never be able to get rid of the awful stench. Looking up, Connie numbly watched the two armies literally tearing each other apart all around her. Briefly turning her attention to Kana, she focused for a moment on the prince, who was completely surrounded by demons hell-bent on killing him. Once again, looking down at Rylee, Connie thought for a moment about the father-in-law she now would never get to know.

Taking a deep breath and closing her eyes, Connie plugged into the fabric of the universe, thinking to herself, "I wish I could do this with my eyes open like Kana can!"

"Give it time," she could hear his voice. "It will come to you."

The battle took on a whole new perspective with her mystical vision. She could see Shilo's personal guards surrounding them again, raising a shield to protect the princess and the king. Focusing on the bloody war raging outside their little safe haven, Connie could mystically see everyone else also currently connected to the fabric of the universe, thanks to the advanced training she received in Lysta'cu'mha. Transfixed, she knelt there watching the vicious mystical battle between the White Witch army and the never ending tide of demons erupting up out of the black crevice. The idea of two alien races at war over the fate of her world seemed so surreal.

The young woman was tired of doing nothing but watching as the hell spawn slaughtered others around her. Finally resolving on what she needed to do, Connie opened her eyes while raising a force field around herself and standing up. Walking over to two of the princess's guards, she stopped in front of the force field erected between them, calmly demanding, "Let me through!"

Stepping out of the protected area, Connie could sense the two guards immediately closing the opening behind her.

Reaching out mentally, she shouted, "Ryon, gather the rest of the class and bring them to me!"

"What's wrong?" Ryon's voice came back to her, concerned. "Is Shilo OK?"

"A White Witch guard unit is surrounding her for protection as we speak. Listen! The *Tablets of Time* state that an army of youth from earth will help Kana drive Satan from earth forever."

Turning to glare at the demon king towering over the battle-swept park, Connie continued with venom in her voice, "We're going to send every last one of these evil bastards back to Hell!"

"What do you have in mind?" Ryon asked, appearing next to her.

Connie's cold eyes met his while replying, "We're going to do what Kana taught us!"

Natual's unconscious form lying in a dark alley burned hot in Argon's mind. He wrought havoc and destruction to Mádeohn's dark army everywhere he went. An intricate dance that combined blasts of energy with swordplay, left a bloody trail of severed limbs and grisly corpses in Argon's wake. One of the demon horses came charging toward him, and the White Witch warrior callously blasted the galloping legs right off the beast. Spinning to his left as the creature collapsed screaming in pain next to him, Argon decapitated the beast's helpless rider with his sword. He then severed the head of the demon horse with a beam of energy from his free hand as he followed through with his spin. Lightly landing on his feet, Argon coldly moved on to find his next victim.

None stood against the venom of the White Witch soldier's wrath.

Thankfully, Kana's little display of power brought the Valitarian back to his senses, and he transported himself across the park to his assigned position.

Kana suddenly felt Argon at his back where he was supposed to be. At least that would relieve the pressure of attack from that direction as the demons from Hell continually pressed in on the two White Witch warriors.

Once Connie and Ryon had the rest of the Mystic Arts Class gathered, Ryon instructed the group to form in a wedge pattern, with him at the tip. Together as a unit, Ryon led the charge, piercing into the mayhem surrounding their two White Witch leaders, just like an arrow through flesh. As soon as he broke through to the center, Ryon mentally instructed everyone to surround Kana and Argon. Joining their minds together, the class constructed a force field similar to the one they had created months ago upon the barren hill with the lone tree outside of their town on earth. Once in place, the force field held the evil horde back, leaving the prince and his Valitarian standing alone in the middle of their comrades.

Suddenly, the relentless press of the deadly enemy was gone. Covered with layers of bloody gore, chest heaving while desperately fighting for air, and with the Weapons of God brilliantly blazing in each hand, Kana stood wavering with exhaustion. Slowly turning, he saw Connie smiling triumphantly at him. With a return grin of pride, he nodded his thanks back. Looking through the grid of the force field, he could see the mob from Hell swarming in every direction, wild with the lust of wanting to tear him apart.

Kana stumbled and sloshed on top of the bloody pile of body parts and dead creatures kissed by his sword. He continued surveying his surroundings until his eyes came to rest upon the black figure of Satan towering above everyone.

The vision of his father crumbling to the ground, lifeless eyes pleading at his son, boiled up like bile in Kana's mind. The painful scene repeated over and over behind the veil of smoldering anger in his eyes. That fury rose with each replay of the vision. Once more, the battle noise going on around the White Witch prince became muted with the new flare-up of his rage. Finally, his anger exploded again.

Letting out a terrible battle cry, Kana put the Lord's Shield in front of him and leaped into the air, hell-bent on executing his wrath. Bursting through the larger shield created by his friends, the prince flew like a roaring ball of fire, rocketing straight at the dark one.

Satan swiftly raised a shield of his own for protection. The king of Hell was not about to let this lowly human destroy eons of work and spoil the victory he was on the verge of achieving.

The look of hatred in the demon king's eyes swiftly turned to shock as the White Witch shattered through Satan's shield upon impact, as though it wasn't even there.

Smashing the lord of Hell square in the chest with the Holy Shield and a great explosion, Kana hurtled both of them back into the huge, dark crevice in the side of the glass building. With a curse of frustration, Satan spread his wings wide, desperately catching the jagged edges of the opening he had ripped in the building. With a metal crushing grip of his claws, the demon stopped the two adversaries' descent into the black hole.

The abrupt, bone-jarring halt caught Kana off guard. Rolling forward with his momentum, he quickly recovered before he fell off the demon's large torso and swiftly transitioned into a new mode of attack.

Spread eagle in an almost prostrate position over the dark drop, Satan looked down his chest to the White Witch prince charging up his body. With renewed anger and determination, two beams of deadly energy shot out of the white fire in the demon king's eyes, blasting the puny being advancing up his chest.

Kana quickly blocked the energy blast with the Shield of God, but the attack stopped his advancement. The blood and gore that covered his boots made getting a firm foot hold on the beast's chest impossible. Frustrated, the prince slowly began to slide backward toward Satan's belly. Intolerable heat from the dark one's blast flowed around his shield. Out of desperation to stop his backward momentum, Kana quickly switched his grip on the Sword of God, and with a grin of satisfaction, buried it up to its hilt in the demon's abdomen.

Satan roared as pain from the Holy Sword burned throughout his body. The bloodcurdling scream brought the entire battle in the park to a halt. Instinctively releasing his grip on the building while folding his wings protectively around his body, the demon king trapped the White Witch prince where he was, and the two suddenly disappeared down the dark crevice.

Connie was shocked speechless after witnessing the dark beast's leathery wings enveloping her prince. Involuntarily covering her mouth as the two swiftly vanished into the black hole, she had to force air into her lungs, crying out in panic, "Kana!"

Once more, Argon had to physically restrain her from following the prince down into Hell.

Both armies stood momentarily transfixed as they listened to Satan's cry of pain fade down the abyss.

"Damn it, Argon!" Connie screamed, struggling to free herself from the White Witch's powerful grasp. "Let go of me! *Let me go!*"

Patiently trying to calm down the woman fiercely struggling in his arms, Argon put his lips near her ear so she could hear over the battle noise.

"Connie, I know you have no fear of joining him in battle, but you are not skilled enough to go down there. All you would do is get yourself killed, and he would never forgive me for that!"

Argon only hesitated briefly before charging Ryon with protecting Connie. The Valitarian then sent out a mental order for a battalion of the White Witch army to mobilize by the stage. He was taking them down into the abyss after the prince.

Firmly in Ryon's embrace, Connie gave up struggling to get free. Watching in horror, the black hole in the side of the building lit up again and again, reflecting flashes of energy from the epic battle going on below. After a few minutes, the chasm in the side of the glass building suddenly became cold and dark.

With cold fear seizing her heart, Connie slowly slumped down out of Ryon's grasp to the blood-soaked park lawn. He had to be all right.

As Argon and his forces converged on the destroyed tower, a wall of dregs protecting the crevice confronted them. Without hesitation, Argon slammed his White Witch forces into the evil barricade and began to cut a bloody swath through the vile horde.

Everyone in the park suddenly stopped, ducking in unison as a red ball of fire came belching out of the chasm with the sound of a volcano erupting. Immediately following the ball of flame, a cloud of black smoke began churning up out of the dark crevice.

Suspiciously watching the dark cloud completely engulf the twisted structure of the glass building, the sound of wind howling through a tunnel slowly became audible to Argon. The horrific nose grew in intensity until he and everyone in the park had to cover their ears in an effort to mute it. A dreg standing next to the White Witch warrior abruptly put his clawed hands to the side of his head, screaming with excruciating agony. Argon watched as all of Satan's dark army joined in the shrill wailing, amplifying the already deafening shriek coming from the dark cloud.

One by one, the denizens of Hell began to rip through the air and disappear into the dark cloud. Soon the air above the park was filled with the helplessly flailing creatures being sucked up by an invisible force into the churning black mass.

Ryon quickly pulled Connie down to the ground and put a shield up to protect them from the forlorn creatures soaring past. Mentally shouting, he ordered the rest of the class, "Re-erect your force field!"

Within a few seconds, safely inside the dome of their shield, the small group stood mystified at the sight of Satan's forsaken horde of followers disappearing into the black cloud. The mass extraction did not quit until they were all gone. All except the son of Satan.

The demon-infested, black cloud was suddenly sucked back down into the dark crevice. Perplexed, Argon, the White Witch army, and the remainder of God's children stood there bewildered in the residual silence.

EPILOGUE

Mádeohn awoke in full possession of his own mind. It felt awesome to no longer be under his father's control, although every muscle in his body cried out in pain. A portion of the speaker tower he had slammed into lay partially on top of him. Grimacing with the effort, the son of Satan shoved the piece of electrical equipment away and slowly stood up. He looked around at what was left of the stage and the now destroyed city that used to be the Third Beast.

The sound of the speaker being moved attracted Argon's attention. He, and all who remained in the park, now watched Satan's son in silence, waiting to see what he would do.

Turning to Ryon, Mádeohn looked his best friend in the eye and mentally spoke to him, "Thanks for stopping me from the horrendous thing I was about to do."

Ryon nodded his acknowledgment. He could tell that the friend he grew up with had returned, and he mentally asked back, "What now?"

Looking into the huge crack in the building behind the stage, Mádeohn peered down the dark fissure. It tore his heart apart, but he knew that after everything he had done to help destroy his friend's world, he could no longer be with them. Turning once again to face the Mystical Arts Class, Ryon's own heart sank as he saw the answer in his friend's eyes. With a smile and a nod of farewell, the prince of Hell disappeared into the black rift.

Completely drained emotionally by the loss of those close to him, Ryon walked over to where Shilo sat with Marcan and Rylee's bodies. Plopping down next to the princess and staring at Rylee's still form, tears began to well up in his eyes as he put an arm around Shilo.

"I think she had a crush on me," he stated, wiping the back of his hand across his cheek.

Shilo laid her head upon her lover's shoulder and broke down in a new wave of grief while sarcastically replying, "You think?"

"Argon, what happened? Where is he?" Connie pleaded in fear as the White Witch rejoined the group.

Argon looked at her, still half-stunned by what he had seen.

"You just saw the Mighty Power of God! That was the Lord's Sword and Shield Kana received, straight from the hand of God. Nothing can stand against them. I don't know where he is right now, but he is all right. I can sense that," the Valitarian answered with a reassuring smile as he put a comforting hand on her shoulder.

Then the ground began to move, driving everyone standing to their knees. In fear, everybody in the park watched helplessly as a blinding fountain of fiery, white light exploded from the dark crevice. The roaring sound it made was deafening.

Ryon suddenly felt a strange sensation, as if there had been a shift in reality.

Slowly, the fountain began to shrink until finally, all that remained of it was a bright dome of light. The twisted structure of the huge glass tower was gone.

Argon stood again, once he was able to, and helped Connie to her feet. Looking into the dome was impossible. The light it emitted was just too bright. Looking at its outer edges was all anyone was capable of doing, and Argon suddenly saw movement there.

With the whole park watching, the object became clearer.

It was a person, a very angelic-looking person. He too was hard to look at, for the light not only came from the dome but also from his body. As he drew closer, Argon was able to finally make out whom the beautiful creature was, the Shield and Sword of God burning brightly in his hands.

Connie's heart jumped up into her throat as she cried out, "Kana!"

The weapons of the Lord disappeared, as if they were absorbed into the prince's body, and she ran joyfully to his arms. She hugged him with all her might, and he smiled down at her and gently kissed her forehead. Arms wrapped around each other, the two continued over to where the rest of their friends waited.

With his arm still around Shilo, Ryon looked about and noticed that none of Treterraz could be seen anymore. The fountain of light must have destroyed the roof over the city, and all the remaining buildings also. A very beautiful garden replaced it all, and in the center of the clearing they were in stood the glowing dome of light. The real sun was climbing in the eastern sky, and it was the most awesome sight he had seen in a long time.

"Satan has been driven from this world and will no longer be allowed on earth! That's God's new covenant to His children," Kana announced as he approached, Connie clinging to his arm with both hands.

"Just as He left His bow of colors for Noah as a reminder to never destroy the world again by water," the prince continued, "He leaves this dome of light, called Phycu, as a symbol and reminder of what happened here today and His new promise. The dome is also an open doorway that all may freely pass through between earth and Lysta'cu'mha."

Turning loose of Connie, Kana stepped over to where Ryon and Shilo sat, Marcan lying peacefully next to his daughter. Grief swept through the prince as he bent over the dead king and whispered, "It is complete, Father."

Kana stood up with Marcan in his arms and faced his earth friends. They were all looking at him, their leader, waiting for him to tell them what would happen next. Taking a deep breath, he pushed his own pain down inside and continued to do what he needed to do.

"Ryon," he spoke with authority, "look around you. Eden has been returned to its original home."

"That must have been the strange sensation I felt a few minutes ago," Ryon concluded while gazing across the beautiful park surrounding them.

"Although life has been brought back to this dead world," the White Witch prince continued, "people here need guidance in rebuilding their lives. You will provide that leadership. It is what you have been trained to do since we first met. Together with Shilo, rule wisely, and seek council from Lysta'cu'mha whenever you need it. Both of you rejoice in your love for each other and be happy here. Your people will be looking to both of you for hope."

Looking around from face to face, Ryon could see fear of the unknown future in everyone's eyes. He also saw the spark of new hope slowly igniting as Kana spoke. He nodded that he understood the White Witch prince.

Standing next to Kana, Connie reached out and gently reclaimed her grasp on his arm with both hands. Tenderly resting the side of her head on the prince's shoulder, she looked down at Rylee's peaceful form lying at their feet. Once again, grief seized her heart.

Tears began welling up in Connie's eyes as she recalled her own past experiences with the beautiful, live, vibrant young lady.

Sensing his beloved's mental pain, Kana glanced down at Rylee's still body. Seeing her like this seemed odd to him. Usually the hyper young girl was up bouncing around, trying to find something to do for somebody. Sighing with his own sorrow, a new thought occurred to him. Cloudrunner would be looking for his new friend at feeding time.

"Ryon," the prince said, "have your people gather up their fallen comrades."

Gazing out across the surrounding park, the White Witch went on, "We will lay them to rest here and build them a memorial befitting heroes. Each paid the ultimate sacrifice to keep their world free from Hell's oppression, and they deserve that honor!"

Trying to hide the emotions of pride and grief currently surging throughout his whole being, Ryon slowly stood up, gently helping Shilo to her feet. Holding the princess close, he swallowed hard, nodding once again that he understood.

As he was speaking to Ryon, Kana felt Connie's fingernails dig into his arm. Burying her face in his shoulder, she began sobbing uncontrollably while listening to his words.

Bending over and tenderly kissing the top of her head, Kana whispered, "Eden is a very beautiful place to live; you will like it."

Trying hard to regain control of herself, Connie looked up into her prince's eyes. With one hand—she was not about to let go of him—she attempted to wipe away the tears streaming down her face. Touching the star on his forehead and then the one on hers, she gulped down a new sob while trying to smile. Then, looking down at the lifeless form in his arms and realizing the pain both he and Shilo must be feeling right at the moment, a new flood of tears overwhelmed her. She knew it would tear her apart if it had been her father. Through the tears, Connie replied with her heart, "If you will have me, I choose to go with you!"

Then she added with half a grin between sobs, "Not every girl gets a chance to be queen."

Kana smiled and looked up to Argon.

"Go tell the council the task is complete and to make preparations to receive their king, a great warrior of God who died for the Lord. Tell them," he paused for a moment. Then, looking at Connie with a smile, he finished, "Prince Kana and his fiancée return!"

Nodding, the White Witch Valitarian turned and sent out a mental order to the White Witch warriors standing nearby: "Tend to the wounded, and carefully gather up the dead so they may be given the honor they also deserve!"

He then disappeared through the doorway of the white dome.

Once again attempting to wipe the tears from her eyes, Connie put her free arm around the little girl Kana had saved from being sacrificed, trying to reassure the little one. Wearing one of the White Witch guard's cloaks, fear and confusion were written all over the little girl's face. Together, by Kana's side, they joined the solemn procession entering the new doorway between worlds: Phycu.

This marked the dawn of the Third Age.

DICTIONARY

Aanahel: Archangel, first general in Lucifer's rebel army.

Alcove: Nickname for Myshunar.

Angelic Institute of Learning: Learning institution in Heaven, located in Zebul.

Angels: First beings created by God in the beginning to live in Heaven with Him. They are spiritual creatures, not human, although they can appear human when they want to.

Araboth: Seventh realm of Heaven, home to God's Crystal Palace and His throne room.

Archangels: Angels that are warriors in God's army.

Arein: (ā-rēn) Emerald about the size of a man's fist with the soul of the warlock Karen trapped inside it.

Argon: (r-gone) Kana's best friend since childhood. He is Kana's Valitarian.

Azrael: Lucifer's second in command during his rebellion in Heaven. Archangel and angel of death.

Black Witches: Once angels in Heaven, they were Satan's followers, and, thus, sentenced to Hell with him.

Buer: Instructor of philosophy, logic, and ethics at the Angelic Institute of Learning.

Cane, Sylvia: Mádeohn's mother.

Caran: (k-ran) World where dark power congregated during the First Age. It also housed the emerald Arein.

Cherubim: God's record keepers and guardians of harmony and wisdom.

City of Heaven: A vast metropolis located in the realm of Machanon, where most angels not seraphim, cherubim, or archangels, call home.

Cloudrunner: Name of the unicorn that Kana rides.

Connie: Earth girl who became Kana's girlfriend.

The Counsel: A group of White Witches made up of different state offices whose main job is to advise the king in making governing decisions.

Cyphis: (sī-fĭs) Elder adviser under the White Witch high priest.

Devil: Also known as Lucifer and Satan. Ruler of Hell, leader of the first rebellion against God in Heaven.

Dreg: (drĕg) Satan's first attempt at creating life. They make up the main labor force of Satan's army.

Du: (dew) Queen of the tree people on Paravage.

Eden: Garden upon earth where God put his children when He first created them.

Electrical Beast: The First Beast Satan sent to earth to take over the world's entire electrical network.

Fabric of Time: Housed in a vault in the Palace of Time, it is like an unexposed role of film—the future with nothing printed on it.

Fabric of the Universe: Similar to radio waves, the one thing that connects everything in the universe together in one way or another.

Falgon: (foul-gone) A wild creature found on Lysta'cu'mha that resembles a bird and a dragon.

First Age: All events from the time God created the universes until the creation of his children.

First Beast: First of the three beasts Satan released upon earth before Phycu. It is made of electricity.

FOTUS: (foe-tŭs) Fabric of the Universe Specialist: Studies the movements in the fabric of the universe to predict possible outcomes and reverse studies them when needing to know how or why something came about.

Gabriel: Archangel who governs the realm of Shamayim.

Gadreel: Headmaster of the Angelic Institute of Learning.

Gate to Heaven: A golden gate at the edge of Heaven, separating it from the VOID, or later, the Space of Doors.

God: The supreme being, creator of everything. God's home is Heaven.

God's Children: The people of earth.

God's Sword and Shield: A sword and shield made of pure energy. Belonging to God, He permits Kana to use them. Nothing can stand against the two holy weapons.

Great River: One of the main features of Paravage. The river is several miles across in some places and empties into the sea.

Gray Wind: The name of the unicorn Argon rides.

Gray Witches: Originally followers of Satan during the war in Heaven. During Vietorist I, they asked God for forgiveness, and He granted it. He made them the keepers of death and gave them a home outside of Heaven called purgatory, promising them a place in Heaven again after Judgment Day.

Guardian Angels: Another name for White Witches.

Hall of Time: Located in Nau in the Palace of Time. It is a hallway running parallel to the Vault of Time. Walking down the hall, you can look into the vault through a glass wall and observe events of the future.

Heaven: The kingdom and home of God. It is located at the far end of the VOID.

Hell: Satan's kingdom. Located at the point in the VOID farthest from Heaven.

Hell Spawn: Name given to anything that lives in Hell.

Judgment Day: The day physical time ends. All universes between Heaven and Hell are destroyed, and judgment of all souls takes place. Good souls go to Heaven; bad souls are sentenced to Hell.

Kana: Prince of the White Witches at the end of the Second Age and beginning of the Third Age. He was trained from birth to be the most powerful White Witch ever.

Karen: (kă-rēn) Powerful warlock who lived during the First Age on the world of Caran. Karen's soul was trapped in an emerald by Satan. When Karen dies, White Witches and Gray Witches fight Satan together for the warlock's soul.

Karn: (kărn) White Witch chess game.

King of The White Witches: Ruler of the White Witch World, Lysta'cu'mha. Marcan is king of White Witches, followed by Kana. The White Witch king is able to talk directly to God.

Kon: General in army of dregs during the coming of Phycu.

Kristarra: (chris-star-ah) Name of the Time Keeper. She is immortal and can move back and forth through time.

Kytern: (kī-turn) A domestic flying creature commonly found throughout the universes and is normally used by warriors.

Learned Ones: Name given to the group of White Witches who devote their lives to study and teaching.

Lilith: Female angel, Lucifer's wife, seducer.

Lucifer: Satan's original name when he was still an angel in Heaven.

Lysta'cu'mha: (law´stă kū´ măw) Name of White Witch home world.

Machanon: Fourth realm of Heaven, home of the city of Heaven.

Mádeohn: (mă-dē-ŏn) Half son of Satan and a mortal woman, Mrs. Cane. Mádeohn is Ryon's best friend.

Marcan: Father of Kana and Shilo. King of the White Witches. Husband to Mirha.

Master Otton: Head of all the Learned Ones. He sits on the counsel.

Mathey: Sixth realm of Heaven, home to all seraphim, cherubim, and archangels.

Michael: Archangel who governs the realm of Machanon.

Mind-Eater: A flying lizard-type creature on Paravage that feeds on a single mind wave of a victim, eating all the energy from the victim's mind and killing it.

Mirha: Queen of the White Witches, Marcan's wife, Kana and Shilo's mother.

Mitch: One of the Mystic Arts Class, Rhonda's boyfriend.

Myshunar: (my-shoe-nar) An alcove in the Space of Doors. A special section of the universes God set aside for His mystic worlds, where Satan is barred from. Home of Lysta'cu'mha, Purgatory, Nau, and Eden.

Mystic Arts Class: Class dealing with the study of ancient religions and the occult.

Mystical Warfare: Battling with universal powers instead of conventional weapons.

Na-amah: (nā-awh-mă) Daughter of Satan and Lilith. She was raised and trained in Hell by her mother for one thing: sex.

Natual: (naw-too-l) Female commander of White Witch army spy network. Very close friend of Argon.

Nau: (nā-ū) Universe filled with only stars, black space, and asteroids and located in Myshunar. It is the home of the Time Keeper, the Innocent Ones, the Palace of Time, Hall of Time, and the fabric of time.

Null Corridor: A corridor that connects a universe to the Space of Doors. It is all white and doesn't appear to have any walls, floor, or ceiling, but one can sense that they are there.

Palace of Time: An emerald palace that sits on an asteroid in Nau. It is the home of the Time Keeper and the Innocent Ones. It also houses the Hall of Time.

Paravage: (pair-ă-vāge) A savage, jungle world in Myshunar that Kana and Argon used as a playground in their youth. Home of the tree people, and the river people.

Phycu: (sī-koo) The word has two meanings, depending on how it is used:

1. Name of the dome of light left behind by Kana when he drove Satan from earth.

2. The period of time immediately following when Kana drove Satan from earth.

Power Storm: *See* "Second Beast."

Prince of the White Witches: *See* "Kana."

Purgatory: Home of the Gray Witches, located in Myshunar. Said to be Hell's twin sister. It is where souls go that are not quite good enough for Heaven and not bad enough for Hell. Souls in purgatory eventually do get to Heaven.

Queen of the White Witches: *See* "Mirha."

Raphael: Archangel who governs the realm of Raquia.

Raquia: Second realm of Heaven, an expanse of dry desert constantly pelted with lightning storms.

River People: A tribe of people who live on Paravage in an underwater city at the bottom of the Great River. They are amphibian but spend most of their time underwater. Their queen is Santerra.

Rhonda: Mitch's girlfriend.

Ryon: Human that Kana is guardian angel to. Mádeohn's best friend. Shilo's boyfriend and eventually husband.

Sagun: First realm of Heaven; it features rivers and lakes of fire and becomes the kingdom of Hell.

Santerra: Queen of the river people on Paravage.

Satan: Another name for the devil, meaning father of Lies. *See* "Devil" and "Lucifer."

Second Age: Period of time taking place between the creation of God's children and Phycu.

Second Beast: The second beast Satan sends to earth to destroy it. The Second Beast kills the First Beast by sucking all the electrical energy on earth inside itself, including the Electrical Beast. It takes the form of a huge ball of fire that orbits the earth.

Seraphim: Members of the angelic choir that sings praises to God.

Seraphiel: Second in leadership of the seraphim until Lucifer's fall, at which point he takes over leadership.

Seren: (sir-ēn) A dreg.

Shamayim: Third realm of Heaven with lush, tropical gardens, and deep-blue seas bordered by beaches of white sand; it becomes Lysta'cu'mha.

Shilo: Princess of the White Witches. Kana's sister. Eventually marries Ryon.

Shycoma: (shī-cō-mă) A palace on Lysta'cu'mha where the king of the White Witches and his family lives.

Sign of Choice: A star-shaped symbol worn by White Witches to show their engagement for marriage.

Space of Doors: The area between Heaven and Hell where all the doorways into the universes are.

Sunoma: (sun-ō-mă) Meaning "holy place," it is a room in Shycoma where the *Tablets of Time* are kept.

Tablets of Time: A book of prophecies written by White Witch high priest Zephrom, in the First Age.

The Golden City: *See* "City of Heaven."

The Teeth: Mountain range in Sagun on the border of Raquia.

Third Age: Period of time between Phycu and Judgment Day.

Third Beast: *See* "Treterraz."

Time Keeper: *See* "Kristarra."

Tree People: A tribe of women who live on Paravage that are part human and part plant.

Treterraz: (tray-tear-az) Third beast Satan puts upon earth just before Phycu. It destroys the Second Beast and becomes the only city on earth with electrical power.

Trever: An occult leader on earth.

Unicorn: Horse with wings and a horn on its forehead. Sometimes used instead of Kyterns as a riding animal.

Universal Door: Doorway at each end of a null corridor.

Universal Power: The power to use the mind to tap into and use the fabric of the universe.

Valitarian: (val-ĭ-tear-e-an) Highest position in the White Witch guard. The king's personal bodyguard. Fights at and protects the king's back.

Vietorist I: (ve-tor-ist) Trial in Heaven during First Age, when Satan and his followers are sentenced to Hell.

VOID: Before time began, all that existed outside of Heaven was the VOID.

Wenstrom: Instructor of the Mystic Arts Class.

White Witches: Originally angels in Heaven. During Lucifer's rebellion, instead of choosing one side or the other, they stayed neutral. During Vietorist I, God sentenced them to mortal bodies and gave them a home outside of Heaven. He appointed them to guard his children when He created them. They will earn their place as angels in Heaven again after the final war with Hell.

White Witch World: *See* "Lysta'cu'mha."

Zachiel: Archangel who governs the realm of Zebul.

Zebul: Fifth realm of Heaven, home of the Angelic Institute of Learning.

Zaia: (zā-ī-ă) White Witch high priest during Kana's time.

Zephrom: (zĕf-raw-m) White Witch high priest who lived early in the First Age. Primary author of the *Tablets of Time*.

Anthony Ray Olheiser is an author and avid fantasy reader living in the Phoenix, Arizona area. His love of the genre began after reading *The Hobbit*, followed by the three *Lord of the Rings* novels, and he's never looked back.

Inspired by the whole new universes created by his favorite authors, Anthony set out to create his own. *Kana's Quest* is his introduction to the White Witch World universe, and he is currently working on the second novel of the series.